A selection of the magnificent reviews for the
Fairyland books (so far)

The Girl Who Circumnavigated Fairyland in a Ship of Her Own Making

'A glorious balancing act between modernism and the Victorian fairy tale, done with heart and wisdom.' Neil Gaiman

'A mad, toothsome romp of a fairy tale full of oddments, whimsy, and joy.' Holly Black, author of *Zombies vs. Unicorns* and *The Spiderwick Chronicles*

'Pure escapism.' *Bliss*

'Get swept away by this charming book.' *Vogue*

'An *Alice in Wonderland* for the twenty-first century … So effortless, so vivid, so funny. Every page has a phrase or observation to savour and her characters are wondrous creations.' *Sunday Telegraph*

'A charming modern fairytale … with a knowing twinkle in its eye.' *Telegraph*

'A whole esoteric world of whimsy – Alice meets the Wizard of Oz meets the Persephone story with a whiff of Narnia.' *Independent on Sunday*

'Bundles of imagination and wry wit … This is a sophisticated world of forfeits, paradoxes and tricks.' *Financial Times*

The Girl Who Fell Beneath Fairyland
and Led the Revels There

'One of the strongest fantasy novels for young readers I've had the pleasure of getting lost in ... Shot through with menace and heroism, you never know what's coming next ... Masterful.'
Cory Doctorow, BoingBoing.net

'The strength of this fable for all ages lies in its droll tone and witty moralising. It is also stuffed with extraordinary and indomitable female characters.' *Financial Times*

'Familiar and original storytelling ... The rich prose oozes exotic, imaginative imagery ... Heartless September sprouts a heart during this remarkable, awesome journey.' *Kirkus* (Starred Review)

'A stellar sequel ... Valente's inviting, lush, and densely detailed world is evocative of well-travelled lands such as Neverland and Oz, but, at the same time, is uniquely its own. This is sure to draw new fans.'
Booklist (Starred Review)

'Valente fills her Fairyland with magical wonder.'
School Library Journal

'Valente is an enchantress of words ... Reading her book is like embarking on the most lavish, extravagant feast, where each course surpasses the last, but each magnificent mouthful delights with its rich, exotic and unexpected flavours. Her inventiveness is awe-inspiring and her style quirky and original ... I would recommend them to anyone wanting to read something deliciously different.'
Press Association

'*The Girl who Fell Beneath Fairyland* does not disappoint. Beautifully written.' Book Angel Booktopia

'Delightful, original, funny and scary.' *Bookbag.co.uk*

THE GIRL WHO FELL BENEATH FAIRYLAND and led the revels there

CATHERYNNE M. VALENTE

corsair

CORSAIR

First published in the US by Feiwel and Friends,
an imprint of Macmillan, 2012

This paperback edition published in the UK by Corsair, 2014

3 5 7 9 10 8 6 4 2

Copyright © Catherynne M. Valente 2012

The moral right of the author has been asserted.

A CIP catalogue record for this book
is available from the British Library.

ISBN 978-1-4721-0810-4

Printed and bound in Great Britain by CPI Group (UK) Ltd, Croydon CR0 4YY

Papers used by Corsair are from well-managed forests
and other responsible sources

MIX
Paper from
responsible sources
FSC® C104740

Corsair
An imprint of
Little, Brown Book Group
Carmelite House
50 Victoria Embankment
London EC4Y 0DZ

An Hachette UK Company
www.hachette.co.uk

www.littlebrown.co.uk

*For everyone who has taken a chance on a girl
with a funny name and her flying Library.*

Let the Revel begin.

Dramatis Personae

SEPTEMBER

HER MOTHER

HER FATHER

TAIGA, a Hreinn

NEEP, a Hreinn

CHARLIE CRUNCHCRAB, a Fairy King

SLANT, a Sibyl

A-THROUGH-L, a Wyverary

HALLOWEEN, Queen of Fairyland-Below

THE VICEREINE OF COFFEE

THE DUKE OF TEATIME

Their Children: DARJEELING

KONA

MATCHA

PEABERRY

THE LITTLEST EARL

SATURDAY, a Marid

WIT, a Crow

STUDY, his Sister, also a Crow

GLASSWORT GROOF, a Goblin

THE WATCHFUL DRESS, a Useful Tool

AUBERGINE, a Night-Dodo

BERTRAM, a Weeping Eel

GLEAM, a Paper Lantern

THE ALLEYMAN, a Lutin

AVOGADRA, a Monaciello

GNEISS, a Järlhopp

THE ONION-MAN

THE OAT KNIGHT, a Glashtyn

BELINDA CABBAGE, a Fairy Physickist

MAUD, a Shadow

IAGO, the Panther of Rough Storms

LEFT, a Minotaur

PRINCE MYRRH, a Boy

NOD, a Dream-Eating Tapir

THE SILVER WIND, a Following Wind

THE BLACK WIND, a Fierce Wind

THE RED WIND, a War Wind

THE GREEN WIND, a Harsh Air

CYMBELINE, the Tiger of Wild Flurries

BANQUO, the Lynx of Gentle Showers

IMOGEN, the Leopard of Little Breezes

CHAPTER I

Exeunt in a Rowboat, Pursued by Crows

In Which a Girl Named September Keeps a Secret, Has a Difficult Time at School, Turns Thirteen, and Is Finally Nearly Run over by a Rowboat, Thereby Finding Her Way into Fairyland

Once upon a time, a girl named September had a secret. Now, secrets are delicate things. They can fill you up with sweetness and leave you like a cat who has found a particularly fat sparrow to eat and did not get clawed or bitten even once while she was about it. But they can also get stuck inside you, and very slowly boil up your bones for their bitter soup. Then the secret has you, not the other way around. So we may be very glad that September had the better of her secret, and carried it with her like a pair of rich gloves which, when she was cold, she could take out and slip on to remember the warmth of days gone by.

September's secret was this: She had been to Fairyland.

This has happened to other children in the history of the world. There are many books about it, and for ever so long little boys and girls have been reading them and making wooden swords and paper centaurs and waiting for their turn. But for September, the waiting had ended last spring. She had fought a wicked queen and saved a whole country from her cruelty. She had made friends who, in addition to being funny and brave and clever, were a Wyvern, a Marid, and a talking lamp.

The only trouble was, precious few books about swashbuckling folk have much to say on the subject of how to behave when one gets home. September had changed profoundly from a girl who desperately wanted such things to be real to one who knew they were real. Such a change is less like getting a new haircut than getting a new head.

It did not particularly improve her school life.

Where once September seemed merely and quietly odd, staring out the window during Mathematics lectures and reading big colorful books under her desk during Civics, now the other children sensed something wild and foreign about her. The girls in her grade could not have said what it was about September that so enraged them. If you sat them down and asked them about it, the best they could have managed might have been, "She's just not like us."

And so they did not invite her to birthday parties; they did not ask about her summer vacation. They did steal her books and tell lies about her to their teachers. "September cheats on her algebra," they revealed in strictest confidence. "September reads ugly old books during physical exercise." "September goes behind the chemistry building with boys." They snickered behind her back in tones that sent up prickly hedges all around their tight huddles of lace dresses and ribboned curls. They stood on the inside of those hedges, the whispers said, and September would always stand on the outside.

Against all this, September held her secret. When she felt awful and lonely and cold, she would take it out and blow upon it like an ember, until it glowed again and filled her up: A-Through-L, her Wyverary, snuffling at Saturday's blue cheek until he laughed, and the Green Wind stamping his emerald snowshoes in the wheat. All of them waiting for her to come back, which she would—soon, so terribly soon, any moment now. She felt very much like her Aunt Margaret, who had never seemed quite the same after coming home from her travels. She would tell long stories about Paris and silk trousers and red accordions and bulldogs and no one understood her particularly. But they listened politely until she trailed off, looking out the window as if she might see the river Seine flowing by instead of acre after acre of wheat and corn. September felt she understood her Aunt now, and resolved to be specially attentive toward her when she visited again.

Every evening, September carried on. She washed the same pink-and-yellow teacups that she had always washed, minded the same small and increasingly anxious dog she had always minded, and listened to the tall walnut-wood radio for bulletins about the war, about her father. The radio loomed so tall and huge in their parlor that it seemed to her like a terrible door, ready to open at any moment and let bad news in. As the sun set on the long yellow prairie each day, she kept a keen eye out for a flash of green on the horizon, a spotted pelt flashing through the grass, a certain laugh, a certain purr. But autumn dealt its days like a pack of golden cards, and no one came.

Her mother had Sundays off from the airplane factory, and so September fell in love with Sundays. They would sit together comfortably by the fire and read while the dog worried their shoelaces, or her mother would slide under Mr. Albert's miserable old Model A and bang at it until September could turn the key and hear it grumble into life once more. Not so long ago her mother read out loud to her from some book or other concerning fairies or soldiers or pioneers, but now they read companionably, each to their own novels or newspapers, quite as September remembered her mother doing with her father, before the war. Sundays were the best days, when the sunlight seemed to last forever, and September would bloom under her mother's big, frank smile. On Sundays, she didn't hurt. She didn't miss a place she could never explain to a grown-up person. She didn't wish her small dinner with its meager ration of tinned beef were a fey feast of candy and roasted hearts and purple melons full of rainwater wine.

On Sundays, she almost didn't think about Fairyland at all.

Sometimes she considered telling her mother about everything that had happened. Sometimes she burned to do it. But something older and wiser within her said, *Some things are for hiding and for keeping.* She feared that if she said it out loud it would all vanish, it would never have been, it would blow away like dandelion cotton. What if none of it had been real? What if she had dreamed it, or worse, had lost her mind like her father's cousin in Iowa City? Any of these were too awful to consider, but she could not help considering all the same.

Whenever she thought those dark thoughts, that she might just be a silly girl who had read too many books, that she might be mad, September glanced behind her and shuddered. For she had proof that it had all really happened. She had lost her shadow there, on a distant river, near a distant city. She had lost something big and true, and could not get it back. And if anyone should notice that she cast no shadow before or behind, September would have to tell. But while her secret remained secret, she felt she could bear it all—the girls at school, her mother's long shifts, her father's absence. She could even bear the looming radio crackling away like an endless fire.

Nearly a year had passed since September had come home from Fairyland. Being quite a practical child, she had become very interested in mythology since her exploits on the other side of the world, studying up on the ways of fairies and old gods and hereditary monarchs and other magical folk. From her research, she reasoned that a year was just about right. One big, full turn of the sun. Surely the Green Wind would be sailing back over the sky for her any day, laughing and leaping and alliterating his way back into her world. And since the Marquess had been defeated and the locks of

Fairyland undone, this time September would have no awful feats to perform, no harsh tests of her courage, only delight and fun and blackberry trifles.

But the Green Wind did not come.

As the end of spring neared, she began to worry in earnest. Time ran differently in Fairyland—what if she turned eighty before a year passed there? What if the Green Wind came and found an old lady complaining of gout? Well, of course September would go with him anyway—she would not hesitate if she were eighteen or eighty! But old women faced certain dangers in Fairyland, such as breaking a hip while riding a wild velocipede, or having everyone do what you say just because you had wrinkles. That last would not be *so* bad—perhaps September could be a fabulous withered old witch and learn to cackle. She could get quite good at that. But it was so long to wait! Even the small and gloomy-faced dog had begun to stare pointedly at her, as if to say, *Shouldn't you be getting along now?*

And worse, what if the Green Wind had forgotten her? Or found another girl quite as capable as September at defeating wickedness and saying clever things? What if everyone in Fairyland had simply dropped a curtsy for the favor and gone about their business, giving no more thought to their little human friend? What if no one ever came for her again?

CHAPTER I

September turned thirteen. She did not even bother inviting anyone to a party. Instead, her mother gave her a stack of ration cards tied with a velvety brown ribbon. She had saved them up for months. Butter, sugar, salt, flour! And at the store, Mrs. Bowman gave them a little packet of cocoa powder to crown it all. September and her mother made a cake together in their kitchen, the small and frantic dog leaping to lick at the wooden spoon. The treat had so little chocolate that it came out the color of dust, but to September it tasted wonderful. Afterward, they went to a film about spies. September got a whole bag of popcorn to herself, and toffees as well. She felt dizzy with the lavishness of it all! It was almost as good as a Sunday, especially since she'd gotten three new books wrapped specially in green paper, one of them in French, sent all the way from a village liberated by her father. (We may be certain September's father had help in liberating the village, but as far as she was concerned he had done it single-handed. Possibly at the point of a golden sword, atop a glorious black horse. Sometimes September found it very difficult to think of her father's war without thinking of her own.) Of course she could not read it, but he had written in the cover, "I will see you soon, my girl." And that made it the greatest book ever written. It had illustrations, too, of a girl not older than September sitting on the moon and reaching out to catch stars in her hands, or standing on a high lunar mountain conversing with a strange red hat with two long feathers sticking out of it that floated right next to her as pert as you please. September pored over it all the way to the theatre, trying to say the strange-sounding words, trying to tell what the story was meant to be.

They demolished the dust-colored birthday cake and September's mother put the kettle on. The dog set upon a powerfully satisfactory marrow bone. September took her new books up and went out into the fields to watch the dusk come down and think. She heard the radio crackling and talking as she let herself out the back door, the pop and spit of static following her like a gray shadow.

September lay down in the long May grass. She looked up through the golden-green stalks of grain. The sky glowed deep blue and rose, and a little yellow star came on like a lightbulb in the warm evening. *That's Venus,* September thought. *She was the goddess of love. It's nice that love comes on first thing in the evening, and goes out last in the morning. Love keeps the light on all night. Whoever thought to call it Venus ought to get full marks.*

We may forgive our girl for ignoring the sound at first. For once, she had not been looking for strange sounds or signs. For once, she had not been thinking about Fairyland at all, but about a girl talking to a red hat and what that could possibly mean, and how wonderful it was that her father had got a whole village liberated. Anyway, rustling is quite a common noise when fields of wheat and wild grass are involved. She heard it, and a little breeze ruffled the pages of her birthday books, but she did not look up until the rowboat flew at ripping speed over her head on the tips of the wheat-stalks as if they were waves.

September leapt up and saw two figures in a little black boat, oars spinning furiously, bouncing swiftly over the fields. One had a broad hat on, slick and dark like a fisherman's. The other trailed a long silver hand out over the furry heads of dry grain. The arm sparkled metallic, shining, a woman's slim wrist gleaming metal, her hand tipped with iron fingernails. September could not see their faces—the man's back hunched huge and wide, obscuring the silver lady, save her arm.

"Wait!" September cried, running after the boat as fast as she could go. She knew Fairylandish happenings when she saw them, and she could see them bouncing away from her right that very moment. "Wait, I'm here!"

"Better look out for the Alleyman," called the man in the black slicker, looking back over his shoulder. Shadows hid his face, but his voice seemed familiar, a kind of broken, unruly rasping September could almost place. "The Alleyman comes with his rag cart and bone truck, and he's got all our names on a list."

The silver lady cupped the wind with her shining hand. "I was cutting barbed wire before you were cutting your milk teeth, old man. Don't try to impress me with your slang and your free verse and your winning ways."

"Please wait!" September called after them. Her lungs clenched tight and thick. "I can't keep up!"

But they only rowed faster, over the tips of the fields, and the night had its face on right and proper now. *Oh, I'll never catch them!* September thought frantically, and her heart squeezed. For though, as we have said, all children are heartless, this is not precisely true of teenagers. Teenage hearts are raw and new, fast and fierce, and they do not know their own strength. Neither do they know reason or restraint, and if you want to know the truth, a goodly number of grown-up hearts never learn it. And so we may say now, as we could not before, that September's heart squeezed, for it had begun to grow in her like a flower in the dark. We may also take a moment to feel a little sorry for her, for having a heart leads to the peculiar griefs of the grown.

September, then, her raw, unripe heart squeezing with panic, ran harder. She had waited so long, and now they were getting away. She was too small, too slow. How could she bear it, how could she ever bear it if she missed her chance? Her breath came too tight and too fast and tears started at the corners of her eyes, only to be whipped away as she ran on, stamping down old corn and the occasional blue flower.

"I'm here!" she squeaked. "It's me! Don't go!"

The silver lady glittered in the distance. September tried so hard to see them, to catch them, to run faster, just a little faster. Let us lean in close and nip at her heels, let us whisper in her ear: Come now, you can do more, you can catch them, girl, you can stretch out your arms just a little further!

And she did clamber faster, she did stretch further, she did move through the grass and did not see the low, mossy wall cutting suddenly through the field until she had tripped and tumbled over it. September landed facedown in a field of grass so white it seemed as though snow had just fallen, except that the lawn was cool and smelled marvelously sweet, quite like a lemon ice.

Her book lay forgotten on the suddenly empty grass of our world. A sudden wind, smelling ever so faintly of every green thing, of mint and rosemary and fresh hay, turned the pages faster and faster, as if in a hurry to find out the end.

September's mother stepped out of the house, looking for her daughter, her eyes puffy with tears. But there was no girl in the wheat anymore, only three brand-new books, a bit of toffee still in its wax wrapper, and a pair of crows winging off, cawing after a rowboat that had already vanished ahead of them.

Behind her, the walnut radio snapped and spit.

CHAPTER II

SHADOWS IN THE FOREST

In Which September Discovers a Forest of Glass, Applies Extremely Practical Skills to It, Encounters a Rather Unfriendly Reindeer, and Finds that Something Has Gone Terribly Awry in Fairyland

*S*eptember looked up from the pale grass. She stood shakily, rubbing her bruised shins. The border between our world and Fairyland had not been kind to her this time, a girl alone, with no green-suited protector to push her through all the checkpoints with no damage done. September wiped her nose and looked about to see where she had got herself.

A forest rose up around her. Bright afternoon sunshine shone through it, turning every branch to flame and gold and sparkling purple prisms—for every tall tree was made of twisted, wavering, wild, and lumpy glass. Glass roots humped up and dove down into the snowy earth; glass leaves moved and jingled against one another like tiny sleigh bells. Bright pink birds darted in to snap at the glass berries with their round green beaks. They trilled triumph with deep alto voices that sounded like nothing so much as *Gotitgotitgotit* and *Strangegirl!Strangegirl!* What a desolate and cold and beautiful place those birds lived in! Tangled white underbrush flowed up around gnarled and fiery oaks. Glass dew shivered from leaves and glass moss crushed delicately beneath her feet. In clutches here and there, tiny silver-blue glass flowers peeked up from inside rings of red-gold glass mushrooms.

September laughed. *I'm back, oh, I'm back!* She whirled around with her arms out and then clasped them to her mouth—her laughter echoed strangely in the glass wood. It wasn't an ugly sound. Actually, she rather liked it, like talking into a seashell. *Oh, I'm here! I'm really here and it is the best of birthday presents!*

"Hullo, Fairyland!" she cried. Her echo splashed out through the air like bright paint.

Strangegirl! Strangegirl! answered the pink-and-green birds. *Gotitgotitgotit!*

September laughed again. She reached up to a low branch

where one of the birds was watching her with curious glassy eyes. It reached out an iridescent claw to her.

"Hullo, Bird!" she said happily. "I have come back and everything is just as strange and marvelous as I remembered! If the girls at school could see this place, it would shut them right up, I don't mind telling you. Can you talk? Can you tell me everything that's happened since I've been gone? Is everything lovely now? Have the Fairies come back? Are there country dances every night and a pot of cocoa on every table? If you can't talk, that's all right, but if you can, you ought to! Talking is frightful fun, when you're cheerful. And I am cheerful! Oh, I am, Bird. Ever so cheerful." September laughed a third time. After so long keeping to herself and tending her secret quietly, all these words just bubbled up out of her her like cool golden champagne.

But the laugh caught in her throat. Perhaps no one else could have seen it so quickly, or been so chilled by the sight, having lived with such a thing herself for so long.

The bird had no shadow.

It cocked its head at her, and if it could talk it decided not to. It sprang off to hunt a glass worm or three. September looked at the frosty meadows, at the hillsides, at the mushrooms and flowers. Her stomach turned over and hid under her ribs.

Nothing had a shadow. Not the trees, not the grass, not

the pretty green chests of the other birds still watching her, wondering what was the matter.

A glass leaf fell and drifted slowly to earth, casting no dark shape beneath it.

The low little wall September had tripped over ran as far as she could peer in both directions. Pale bluish moss stuck out of every crack in its dark face like unruly hair. The deep black glass stones shone. Veins of white crystal shot through them. The forest of reflections showered her with doubled and tripled light, little rainbows and long shafts of bloody orange. September shut her eyes several times and opened them again, just to be sure, just to be certain she was back in Fairyland, that she wasn't simply knocked silly by her fall. And then one last time, to be sure that the shadows really were gone. A loud sigh teakettled out of her. Her cheeks glowed as pink as the birds above and the leaves on the little glass-maples.

And yet even with a sense of wrongness spreading out all through the shadowless forest, September could not help still feeling full and warm and joyful. She could not help running her mind over a wonderful thought, over and over, like a smooth, shiny stone: *I am here, I am home, no one forgot me, and I am not eighty yet.*

September spun about suddenly, looking for A-Through-L and Saturday and Gleam and the Green Wind. Surely, they had got word she was coming and would meet her! With a grand picnic and news and old jokes. But she found herself quite alone, save for the rosy-colored birds staring curiously at the loud thing suddenly taking up space in their forest, and a couple of long yellow clouds hanging in the sky.

"Well," September explained sheepishly to the birds, "I suppose that would be asking rather a lot, to have it all arranged like a tea party for me, with all my friends here and waiting!" A big male bird whistled, shaking his splendid tail feathers. "I expect I'm in some exciting outer province of Fairyland and will have to find my way on my lonesome. The train doesn't drop you at your house, see! You must sometimes get a lift from someone kindly!" A smaller bird with a splash of black on her chest looked dubious.

September recalled that Pandemonium, the capital of Fairyland, did not rest in any one place. It moved about quite a bit in order to satisfy the needs of anyone looking for it. She had only to behave as a heroine would behave, to look stalwart and true, to brandish something bravely, and surely she would find herself back in those wonderful tubs kept by the soap golem Lye, making herself clean and ready to enter the great city. A-through-L would be living in Pandemonium, September guessed, working happily for his grandfather, the Municipal Library of Fairyland. Saturday would be visiting his grandmother, the ocean, every summer, and otherwise busy growing up, just as she had been. She felt no worry at all on that account. They would be together soon. They would discover what had happened to the shadows of the forest, and they would solve it all up in time for dinner the way her mother solved the endless sniffles and coughs of Mr. Albert's car.

September set off with a straight back, her birthday dress wrinkling in the breeze. It was her mother's dress, really, taken in and mercilessly hemmed until it fit her, a pretty shade of red that you could almost call orange, and September did. She fairly glowed in the pale glass forest, a little flame walking through the white grass and translucent trunks. Without shadows, light seemed able to reach everywhere. The brightness of the forest floor forced September to squint. But as the sun sank like a scarlet weight in the sky, the wood grew cold and the trees lost their spectacular colors. All around her the world went blue and silver as the stars came out and the moon came up and on and on she walked—very stalwart, very brave, but very much without encountering Pandemonium.

The soap golem loved the Marquess, though, September thought. *And the Marquess is gone. I saw her fall into a deep sleep; I saw the Panther of Rough Storms carry her off. Perhaps there are no tubs to wash your courage in any longer. Perhaps there is no Lye. Perhaps Pandemonium stays in one place now. Who knows what has happened in Fairyland since I have been studying algebra and spending Sundays by the fire?*

September looked about for the pink birds, of whom she felt very fond since they were her only company, but they had gone to their nests. She strained to hear owls but none hooted to fill the silent evening. Milky moonlight spilled through the glass oaks and glass elms and glass pines.

"I suppose I shall have to spend the night," September sighed, and shivered, for her birthday dress was a springtime thing and not meant for sleeping on the cold ground. But she was older now than she had been when first she landed on the shore of Fairyland, and squared herself to the night without complaint. She hunted out a nice patch of even grass surrounded by a gentle fence of glass birches, protected on three sides, and resolved to make it her bed. September gathered several little glass sticks and piled them together, scraping away most of the lemony-smelling grass beneath them. Blue-black earth showed, and she smelled fresh, rich dirt. She stripped off glass bark and lay the curling peels against her sticks to make a little glass pyramid. She wedged dry grass into her kindling and judged it a passable job—if only she had matchsticks. September had read of cowboys and other interesting folk using two stones to make fire, though she remained doubtful that she had all the information necessary on that score. Nevertheless, she hunted out two good, smooth, dark stones, not glass but honest rock, and gave them a mighty whack, one against the other. It made a frightful sound that echoed all through the wood, like a bone bursting. September tried again, and again got nothing but a loud crack that vibrated in her hands. On the third strike, she missed and mashed one of her fingers. She sucked it painfully. It did not help to consider that the trouble of making fire was a constant one in human history. This was not a human place— could she not find a bush that grew nice fat pipes or matchbook flowers, or better yet, a sort of enchanter who might wave her hand and produce a crackling blaze with a pot of stew over it for good measure?

Nursing her finger still, September looked out through the thin mist and saw a glow off in the night, in the space between the trees. It flared red and orange.

Fire, yes, and not far!

"Is anyone there?" called September. Her voice sounded thin in the glassy wood.

After a long while, an answer came. "Someone, maybe."

"I see you've something red and orange and flamey, and if you'd be so kind, I could use a bit of it to keep warm and cook my supper, if I should find anything to eat here."

"You a hunter, then?" said the voice, and the voice was

full of fear and hope and wanting and hating in a way September had never heard before.

"No, no!" she said quickly. "Well, I killed a fish once. So perhaps I'm a fisherman, though you wouldn't call someone who only ever made bread once a baker! I only thought maybe I could make a mushy soup out of any glass potatoes or glass beans I might happen upon, if I was very lucky. I'd planned to use a big leaf as a cup for cooking. It's glass, see, so it mightn't burn, if I was careful." September felt proud of her inventiveness—several things had gone missing from her plan, namely potatoes or beans or apples, but the plan itself held solid in her head. The fire was paramount; the fire would show the forest her mettle.

The red flamey glow came closer and closer until September could see that it was really just a tiny speck of a little coal inside a pipe with a very big bowl. The pipe belonged to a young girl, who clamped it between her teeth. The girl had white hair, white as the grass. The moonlight turned it silvery blue. Her eyes showed dark and quite big. Her clothes were all soft pale fur and glass-bark, her belt a chain of rough violet stones. The girl's big dark eyes showed deep worry.

And in the folds of her pale hair, two short, soft antlers branched up, and two long, soft, black ears stuck out, rather like a deer's, their insides gleaming clean and lavender in the night. The girl looked September over unhurriedly, her soft face taking on a wary, haunted cant. She sucked deeply on her pipe. It glowed red, orange, red again.

"Name's Taiga," she said finally, clenching her pipe in her teeth and extending a hand. She wore a flaxen glove with the fingers cut off. "Neveryoumind that mess." The strange girl nodded at the lonely pieces of September's camp. "Come with me to the hill and we'll feed you up."

September must have looked stricken, for Taiga hastened to add, "Oh, it would have been a good fire, girl, no mistaking it. Top craftsmanship. But you won't find eatables this far in, and there's always hunters everywhere, just looking for . . . well, looking to shoot themselves a wife, if you'll pardon my cursing."

September knew a number of curse words, most of which she heard the girls at school saying in the bathrooms, in hushed voices, as if the words could make things happen just by being spoken, as if they were fairy words, and had to be handled just so. She had not heard the deer-girl use any of them.

"Cursing? Do you mean *hunter*?" It was her best guess, for Taiga had grimaced when she used it, as though the word hurt her to say.

"Nope," said Taiga, kicking the dirt with one boot. "I mean *wife*."

CHAPTER III

THE REINDEER OF MOONKIN HILL

In Which September Considers the Problem of Marriage, Learns How to Travel to the Moon, Eats Fairy Food (Again), Listens to the Radio, and Resolves to Mend Fairyland as Best She Can

*S*eptember hugged her elbows. She and Taiga had been walking for some time without speaking. The stars had trudged down toward dawn in their sparkling train. She wanted to talk—the talk boiled inside her like a pot left on just forever with no one minding it. She wanted to ask how things in Fairyland had gone since she'd left. She wanted to ask where she was relative to the Autumn Provinces or the Lonely Gaol—north, south? A hundred miles? A thousand? She even wanted to throw her arms around the deer-girl, who was so obviously magical, so clearly Fairylike, and laugh and cry out, *Do you know who I am? I'm the girl who saved Fairyland!*

September blushed in the dark. That seemed suddenly a rather rotten thing to say, and she took it back without ever having uttered the thing. Taiga kept on as the land got hillier and the glass trees began to get friends of solid, honest wood, black and white. She said nothing, but she said nothing in a particularly pointed and solemn and deliberate way that made September say nothing, too.

Finally, the grass humped up into a great hillock, looking quite like an elephant had been buried there—and not the runt of its litter, either. Big, glossy fruits ran all over the hill, their vines trailing after them. September could not tell what color they might be in the daytime—for now they glowed a shimmery, snowy blue.

"Go on, have one," Taiga said, and for the first time she smiled a little. September knew that smile. It was the smile a farmer wears when the crop is good and she knows it, so good it'll take all the ribbons at the county fair, but manners say she's got to look humble in front of company. "Best moonkins east of Asphodel, and don't let anyone tell you different.

They'll be gone in the morning, so eat up while they've got a ripening on."

September crawled partway up the hill and found a small one, small enough that no one might call her greedy. She cradled it in her skirt and started back down—but Taiga took a running start and darted past her, straight to the top. She sprang into the air with a great bounding leap, flipped over, and dove right down into the earth.

"Oh!" September cried.

There was nothing for it—she followed Taiga up the hill, making her way between giant, shining moonkins. Glassy vines tangled everywhere, tripping up her feet. When she finally reached the crest, September saw where the deer-girl had gone. Someone had cut a hole in the top of the hill, a ragged, dark hole in the dirt, with bits of root and stone showing through, and grass flowing in after. September judged it big enough for a girl, though not for a man.

Much as she would have liked to somersault and dive like a lovely gymnast, headfirst into the deeps, September did not know how to flip like that. She wanted to, longed to feel her body turn in the air that way. Her new, headless heart said, *No trouble! We can do it!* But her sensible old legs would not obey. Instead, she put her pale fruit into the pocket of her dress, got down on her stomach, and wriggled in backward. Her bare legs dangled into whatever empty space the hill contained. September squeezed her eyes shut, holding her breath, clutching the grass until the last moment—and popped through with a slightly moist sucking noise.

She fell about two feet.

September opened her eyes, first one, then the other. She was standing on a tall bookcase, and just below it stood a smaller one, and then a smaller one again, and another, and another, a neat little curving staircase of books down from the cathedral ceiling of the moonkin hill. Down below, several girls and boys like Taiga paused in their work to look up at the newcomer. Some of them wove lichen fronds into great blankets. Some of them boiled a creamy stew full of moonkin vines that smelled strange but not unpleasant, like peppermint and good thick potatoes. Some had on glasses and worried away at accountants' books, some refilled the oil in pretty little lamps, some relaxed, blowing smoke from their pipes. The coziness of the scene quite overpowered September, whose feet and fingers still tingled with numb coldness. Here and there peeked everything that made a house feel alive, paintings on the walls and rugs on the floor and a sideboard with china and an overstuffed chair that didn't match anything else. Everyone had very delicate, very bare feet.

"I daresay doors are more efficient." September laughed as

she made her way down. "They aren't hard to make, either. Not much more than a hinge and a knob."

Taiga held up a hand to help September off of the last shelf.

"Hunters can use doors. This way we're safe."

"You keep talking about hunters! We didn't see one on the way here and really, I can't believe someone would hunt a girl! I don't think girls make very good roasts or coats."

"They don't want to kill us," Taiga said darkly. "They want to marry us. We're Hreinn."

September bit her lip. Back home, she had gotten used to knowing things no one else knew. It was a nice feeling. Almost as good as having a secret. Now she was back in the country of never knowing anything.

Taiga sighed. She took off her boots and her gloves and her coat and folded them neatly onto the mismatched chair. She took a deep breath, then tugged on her deer-ears. Her whole body rolled up like a shade suddenly drawn—and then standing before September was not a girl but a smallish reindeer with black fur and white spots on her forehead, a big, wet nose, and big, fuzzy, heavy antlers. She was somewhat shorter than September expected a reindeer would be, big enough to look her in the eye, but not to make her feel afraid. Yet Taiga was not cuddly or sweet like a Christmas reindeer in a magazine—rather, muscles moved under her skin, and everything in her lean, graceful shape said speed and strength and a feral kind of thrill in biting things. Taiga turned her head and caught her ear in her teeth, yanking on it savagely, and her sleek reindeer-self rolled down into a dark puddle. The girl with white hair and black ears stood before September again.

And then, slowly, Taiga pulled the puddle into her arms. It was black and furry. She held it lovingly.

"This is my skin, you see," Taiga whispered. "When we're human, we have this little bit of reindeer left over. Not just deer, you know. Deer are gossips and prank-pullers and awful thieves. Reindeer. *Hreinn*. Reindeer aren't from around here, you know. We come from the heavens—the moon is our motherland."

"But no one can live on the moon!" said September. "It's too cold and there's no air. I'm in the astronomy club, and Miss Gilbert was very specific about that."

"Then I'm sorry for your moon—what a poor, sad planet! We will set a place for her at dinner, out of respect. Our moon is rich and alive. Rice fields and moonkin meadows as far as you can see. And Hreinn like moss spores, so many and scattered so far. And hunters. All kinds—Fairies, Satyrs, Bluehearts, Ice Goblins. Once the moon was generous enough for all of us. In our reindeer-bodies, we ran and hid from pelt traders and hungry bowmen. That was fine. That's how the moon plays her hand—she's a tough, wild matron. We eat and they eat. Grow fleet and clever went our lullabies. Escape the hunter's pot today, set your own table tomorrow. But once the huntsmen saw us change, they knew our secret, and they wanted more than stew. They stole our skins and hid them away, and when a body has your skin, you have to stay and cook and clean and make fawns for them until they get old and die. And sometimes then you still can't find your skin, and you have to burn the cottage down to catch it floating out of the ash. They chased us all the way down the highway to Fairyland, down from the heavens and into the forest, and here we hide from them, even still."

"You're cooking and cleaning now," September said shyly. A Hreinn boy looked up from kneading dough, his pointed ears covered in flour. She thought of the selkies she'd read about one afternoon when she was meant to be learning about diameters and circumferences: beautiful seals with their spotted pelts, turning into women and living away from the sea. She thought of a highway to the moon, lit with pearly streetlamps. It was so wonderful and terrible her hands trembled a little.

"We're cooking for *us* to eat. Cleaning for *us* to enjoy the shine on the floor," Taiga snapped. "It's different. When you make a house good and strong because it's your house, a place you made, a place you're proud of, it's not at all the same as making it glow for someone who ordered you to do it. A hunter wants to eat a reindeer, just the same as always. But here in the Hill we're safe. We grow the moonkins and they feed us; we love the forest and it loves us in its rough way—glass shines and cuts and you can't ask it to do one and not the other. We mind our own, and we only go to Asphodel when we need new books to read. Or when a stranger tromps around so loudly someone has to go out and see who's making the racket."

September smiled ruefully. "I suppose that's my racket. I've only just arrived in Fairyland, and it's hard to make the trip quietly." She hurried to correct herself, lest they think she was a naive nobody. "I mean to say, I've been before, all the way to Pandemonium and even further. But I had to go away, and now I'm back and I don't want to trouble you, I can clean my own floors quite well even if I complain about it. Though I think I would complain even if it were my own dear little house and not my mother and father's, because on the whole I would always rather read and think than get out the wood polish, which smells something awful. I honestly and truly only want to know where I am—I'm not a hunter, I don't want to get married for a long while yet. And anyway where I come from if a fellow wants to marry a girl, he's polite about it, and they court, and there's asking and not capturing."

Taiga scratched her cheek. "Do you mean to say no one pursues and no one is pursued? That a doe can marry anyone she likes and no one will leap on her in the night to make the choice for her? That if you wanted you could live by yourself all your life and no one would look askance?"

September chewed the inside of her lip. She thought of Miss Gilbert, who taught French and ran the astronomy club, and how there had been quite the scandal when she and Mr. Henderson, the math teacher, meant to run off together. The Hendersons had good money and good things, big houses and big cars, and he only taught math because he liked to do sums. Mr. Henderson's family had forbidden the whole business. They'd found a girl all the way from St. Louis with lovely red hair for him and told the pair of them to get on with the marrying. Miss Gilbert had been heartbroken, but no one argued with the Hendersons, and that was when the astronomy club had gotten started. The Hendersons were hunters, and no mistaking, they'd snuffed out that St. Louis belle with a quickness. Then September thought of poor Mrs. Bailey, who had never married anyone or had any babies but lived in a gray little house with Mrs. Newitz, who hadn't married either, and they made jam and spun yarn and raised chickens, which September considered rather nice. But everyone clucked and felt sorry for them and called it a waste. And Mr. Graves who had chased Mrs. Graves all over town singing her love songs and buying her the silliest things: purple daisies and honeycomb and even a bloodhound puppy until she took his ring and said yes, which certainly seemed like a kind of hunting.

But still, September could not quite make the sums come out right. It was the same, but not the same at all. Because she also thought of her mother and father, how they had met in the library on account of them both loving to read plays rather than watch them. "You can put on the most lavish productions in your head for free," her mother said. Perhaps, if hunting had occurred, they had hunted each other through the stacks of books, sending warning shots of Shakespeare over one another's heads.

"I think," she said slowly, adding and subtracting spouses in her head, "that in my world, folk agree to a kind of hunting *season,* when it comes to marrying. Some agree to be hunted and some agree to be hunters. And some don't agree to be anything at all, and that's terribly hard, but they end up knowing a lot about Dog Stars and equinoxes and how to get all the seeds out of rose hips for jelly. It's mysterious to me how it's worked out who is which, but I expect I shall understand someday. And I am *positively* sure that I shall not be the hunted, when the time comes," September added softly. "Anyway, I'd never hunt *you*—I wouldn't even have taken a bite of your crop if you hadn't invited me. I just want to know where I am and how far it is to Pandemonium from here, and how long it's been since I left! If I were to ask about the Marquess, would you know who I meant?"

Taiga whistled softly. Since the reindeer-maid had shown her skin and not been immediately whisked off to a chapel, several of the Hreinn had deemed September safe. They rolled up into reindeer and now lay about, showing their soft sides and beautiful antlers. "That was a bad bit of business," Taiga said, rubbing her head.

"Yes, but . . . ancient history or current events?" September pressed.

"Well, last I heard she was up in the Springtime Parish. I expect she'll stay there a good while. Neep and I"—she gestured to the flour-speckled boy—"we went to the pictures in town once and saw a reel about it. She was just lying there in her tourmaline coffin with her black cat standing guard and petals falling everywhere, fast asleep, not a day older than when she abdicated."

"She didn't *abdicate*," September said indignantly. She

couldn't help it. That wasn't how it had gone. Abdication was a friendly sort of thing, where a person said they didn't want to rule anything anymore so suds to this and thank you kindly. "I defeated her. You won't believe me, but I did. She put herself to sleep to escape me sending her back where she came from. I'm September. I'm . . . I'm the girl who saved Fairyland."

Taiga looked her up and down. So did Neep. Their faces said, *Go on, tell us another. You can't even turn into a reindeer. What good are you?*

"Well, I guess it was a few years ago now, to answer your question," Taiga said finally. "King Crunchcrab made a holiday. I think it's in July."

"King Crunchcrab? *Charlie* Crunchcrab?" September shrieked with delight at the name of the ferryman who had once, not very long ago, steered the boat that brought her into Pandemonium.

"He doesn't like us calling him that, really," Neep hushed her. "When he gets on the radio he tells us, 'Ain't a Marquis and ain't a King, and can't somebody get these frippering dresses out of my closet, hang you all.' Still, he's a good sort, even if he grumbles about having to wear the tiara. Folk thought a Fairy should move into the Briary, after everything. He was the only one they could catch."

September sank into a coffee-colored sofa. She folded her hands and braced herself to hear what she suspected would follow, but hoped would not. "And the shadows, Taiga? What about the shadows?"

Taiga looked away. She went to the soup and stirred vigorously, scraping bits of savory crust from the pan and letting them float to the top. She filled a bowl and thrust it at September. "That won't hear out on an empty stomach. Eat, and crack your moonkin, too, before the sun comes up. They're night beasts. They wilt."

For a moment, September did not want to. She was overcome by the memory of fearing Fairy food, trying to avoid it and starve bravely, as she had done before when the Green Wind said one bite would keep her here forever. It was instinct, like jerking your hand away from fire. But, of course, the damage had long been done, and how glad she was of it! So September did eat, and the stew tasted just as it smelled, of peppermint and good potatoes, and something more besides, sweet and light, like marshmallows, but much more wholesome. It should have tasted foul, for who ever heard of mixing such things? But instead it filled September up and rooted her heart right to the earth where it could stand strong. This flavor was even better: like a pumpkin but a very soft and wistful sort of pumpkin who had become good friends with fresh green apples and cold winter pears.

Finally Taiga took her bowl and clicked her tongue and said, "Come to the hearth, girl. You'll see I wasn't keeping things from you. I only wanted you to eat first, so you'd have your strength."

All the Hreinn drew together, some in reindeer-form and some in human, at the far edge of the long hill-hall. A great canvas-covered thing waited there, but no fire or bricks or embers. Neep pulled back the cloth—and a radio shone out from the wall. It looked nothing like the walnut radio back home. This one was made of blackwood branches and glass boughs, some of them still flowering, showing fiery glass blossoms, as though the sun somehow still shone through them. The knobs were hard green mushrooms and the grille was a thatch of carrot fronds. Taiga leaned forward and turned the mushrooms until a crackle filled the air, and the Hreinn drew close to hear.

"This has been the Evening Report of the Fairyland News Bureau," came a pleasant male voice, young and kind. "Brought to you by the Associated Pressed Fairy Service and Belinda Cabbage's Hard-Wear Shoppe, bringing you all the latest in Mad Scientific Equipment. We here at the Bureau extend our deepest sympathies to the citizens of Pandemonium and especially to Our Charlie, who lost their shadows today, making it six counties and a constablewick this week. If you could see me, loyal listeners, you'd see my cap against my chest and a tear in my eye. We repeat our entreaty to the good people of Fairyland-Below, and beg them to cease hostilities immediately. In other news, rations have been halved, and new tickets may be collected at municipal stations. Deep regrets from King C on that score, but now is not the time to fear, but to band together and muddle through as best we can. Keep calm and carry on, good friends. Even shadowless we shall persevere. Good night, and good health."

A tinny tune picked up, something with oboes and a banjo and a gentle drum. Taiga turned the radio off.

"It's meant to tune itself to you, to find the station that has the tune or the news you want to hear. Cabbage-made, and that's the best there is." Taiga patted September's knee. "It's Fairyland-Below, everyone knows it. Shadows just seep into the ground and disappear. They're stealing our shadows, and who knows why? To eat? To murder? To marry? To hang on their walls like deer heads? Fairyland-Below is full of devils and dragons, and between them all they've about half a cup of nice and sweet."

September stood up. She brushed a stray moonkin seed from her birthday dress. She looked once upward, and her heart wanted her friends Ell, the Wyverary, and Saturday, the Marid, with her so badly she thought it might leap out of her chest and go after them, all on its own. But her heart stayed where it was, and she turned her face back toward Taiga, who would not be her friend after all, not now, when she had so far yet to go. "Tell me how to get into Fairyland–Below," September said quietly, with the hardness of a much older girl.

"Why would you go there?" Neep said suddenly, his voice high and nervous. "It's *dreadful*. It's dark and there's no law at all and the Dodos just run riot down there, like rats. And . . ." he lowered his voice to a squeak, "the Alleyman lives there." The other Hreinn shuddered.

September squared her shoulders. "I am going to get your shadows back, all of you, and Our Charlie, too. And even mine. Because it's my fault, you see. I did it. And you must always clean up your own messes, even when your messes look just like you and curtsy very viciously when what they mean is, *I am going to make trouble forever and ever.*"

And so September explained to them about how she had lost her shadow, how she had given it up to save a Pooka child and let the Glashtyn cut it off her with a terrible bony knife. How the shadow had stood up just like a girl and whirled around in a very disconcerting way. She told Taiga and Neep and the others how the Glashtyn had said they would take her shadow and love her and put her at the head of all their parades, and then all of them dove down to the kingdom under the river, which was surely Fairyland-Below. Though she could not quite work it out, September felt sure that her shadow and everyone's shadows were all part of the same broken thing, and broken things were to be fixed, whatever the cost, especially if you had been the one to break it in the first place. But September did not tell them any more about her deeds than she had to. When it came down to it, even if hearing that she was good with a Fairy wrench might have made them more sure of her, she could not do it. It was nothing to brag about, when she had left Fairyland so upset in the doing of it. She begged them again to tell her how to get down to that other Fairyland; she would risk the hunters that ran so rampant in the forest.

"But September, it's not like there's a trapdoor and down you go," insisted Taiga. "You have to see the Sibyl. And why do that, why go see that awful old lady when you could stay here with us and eat moonkins and read books and play sad songs on the root-bellows and be safe?" The reindeer-girl looked around at her herd and all of them nodded, some with long furry faces, some with thin, worried human ones.

"But you must see I can't do that," September said. "What would my Wyvern think of my playing songs while Fairyland was hurting? Or Calpurnia Farthing the Fairy Rider or Mr. Map or Saturday? What would I think of myself, at the end of it all?"

Taiga nodded sadly, as if to say, *Arguing with humans only leads to tears.* She went to one of the bookshelves and drew out a large blue volume from the top shelf. She stood on her tiptoes.

"We've been saving it," she explained. "But where you're going you'll need it more."

And she opened the midnight covers. Inside, like a bookmark, lay a thin and beautifully painted square notepad with two sheaves left inside, the rest ripped out and used up long ago. Its spine shone very bright against the creamy pages, its edges filigreed with silver and stars. It read:

MAGIC RATION BOOK

MAKE DO WITH LESS, SO WE ALL CAN HAVE MORE.

CHAPTER IV

A Door Shaped Like a Girl

*In Which September Meets the Sibyl, Has Her Hair Done,
Acquires a New Coat, and Takes a Step into the Dark*

*L*et us say that the world is a house.

In that house, a wide and lovely place where all is arranged just so, the world that you and I know, the world which contains Omaha and Zimbabwe and strawberry ice cream and horses with spotted rumps and Ferris wheels and wars in Europe, would be the front parlor. The first thing you see when you arrive, the room which stays clean for company's sake. Fairyland would be a richly decorated bedroom, full of toys and gold-stitched blankets and the walls all painted with dancing green scenes, connected to the parlor by a long, cluttered closet and several stairs.

There may be other rooms, too, that we have not visited yet, exciting kitchens and thrilling dining rooms, positively breathtaking libraries, long sunny porches soaking in light. But we are not investigating those other rooms today. Today we, and September with us, are looking for a certain door, set far back in the wall. It is a little door, painted gray, with a silver knob that desperately needs polishing.

Most houses worth their windows have basements, and the world does, too. Dark spaces under the busy rooms, lit only with lightbulbs hanging from the ceiling by lonely cords at the bottoms of creaky staircases. The world keeps a great number of things down there—liqueurs and black beers brewing for summer, barrels of potatoes and apples, jams glowing like muddled gems in their jars, meats curing, pickles pickling, bundles of long green herbs, everything working, everything steeping, everything waiting for spring. So, too, are there boxes kept down in the cellar of the world, all nicely labeled with pretty handwriting, all the things the dear old planet packed away from its previous lives, pyramids and ziggurats and marble columns, castles and towers and burial mounds, pagodas and main streets and the East India Trading Company. All of it just sleeping down there in the dark, tucked away safely, until a fuse blows in the upper house and somebody, a little girl, perhaps, has to venture down those creaky stairs and across the lumpy earthen floor to turn the light on once more.

Fairyland-Below is such a cellar, and the Sibyl is that little gray door, so small you might miss it, if you were not already looking so carefully.

The land between Moonkin Hill and Asphodel is called the Upside-Down. No one ever named it that in an official capacity—no one ever cut a ribbon over the place and put in a plaque. But everyone who passed through called it so—and September did, too. So would you, if you found yourself wandering around in it, for it looked just as though some mischief-minded giant had ripped up the land and put it back inside out and upside down. Roots grew up like trees from soil as rich and soft as whipped butter; bright orange carrots and golden onions and purple turnips and ruby beets sprang up everywhere like hard, squat flowers. Here and there yawning pits opened up where hills might properly have risen. Even more rarely, the foundations of little houses sat squarely on the ground, a glimpse of their green or blue porches just showing, disappearing down into the earth like crowns of radishes. A low mist gathered, dampening September and everything else. The mist, too, traveled upside down, but that makes little difference when it comes to mist.

A road wound through the Upside-Down, made all of bright, cheerful blue cobblestones. The painted side faced down, and September walked upon naked gray stones. She tried to be cheerful, but the mist dispirited her. How she would have preferred to ride through this sad, backward place upon Ell's bright red back! Fairyland seemed altogether stranger and colder and more foreign than it had before—was that September's doing? Or worse, was this the natural state of Fairyland, to which it returned when the Marquess left her throne, no longer demanding that it make itself into a marvelous place for children to love?

She could not believe that. She would not. Countries had regions, after all, and how foreign would her own world seem if she returned to Alaska rather than dear, familiar Nebraska? It was winter in Fairyland now, that was all, winter in a province or state or county far from the sea. And not the pristine snowy winter, either, but the muddy, wet sort that meant spring was coming, spring was right around the corner. Winter is always hungry and lean, and the worst of it comes right before the end. September cheered herself with these thoughts as she walked through the rows of root vegetables with their showy colors glinting in the mist. She thought, briefly, of simply tearing out a ration card and magicking herself to Ell's side—but no. *Wasting rations hastens hunger,*

Mrs. Bowman always said when a poor soul had no more bread cards and the month only half done. September would have to spend her magic ration carefully. She would have to save it, as her mother had saved all those sugar cards to make her birthday cake. She would spend her magic only when the time was right.

September bent and snapped off a carrot, munching it as she went. It was quite the most carrot-like of any carrot she had ever tasted. It tasted like the thing other carrots meant to copy. She picked a few onions and put them in her pockets for roasting later. Sooner or later, she would get to make that fire; September had little doubt.

Once—but only once—September thought she saw someone on the upside-down road with her. She could hardly make them out in the low, glittery fog, but someone had been there, a rider in gray. She thought she glimpsed long, silver hair flying. She thought she heard four huge, soft paws hitting the cobblestones in a slow, steady rhythm. September called out after the shape in the mist, but it did not answer her, and the thing it rode upon—something enormous and muscled and striped—sped off into the clouds. She might have run, might have tried to catch them, to best her performance in the wheat field, if Asphodel had not reared up out of the drizzling, smoky wet and caught her swiftly in its tangled streets.

★

The sun always shines in Asphodel. Hanging big and golden-red as a pendant in the sky, it hands down its warm gifts as to no other city. September blinked and squinted in the sudden brilliance, shading her eyes. Behind her, a wall of swirling fog hung as if nothing unusual had happened, and what was she looking at, really? But having stepped upon the great avenue of Asphodel, September bathed in sunshine. All around her, the city rose up into the cloudless air, busy, shadowless, dazzlingly bright.

Asphodel was a city of stairs. Seven spiral staircases wound up from the street like skyscrapers, so huge that in each pale, marble-veined step, September could see windows and doors with folk bustling in and out of them. Little black sleighs ran up and down the bannisters, carrying passengers and bags of letters and parcels from one gargantuan step to another. Smaller staircases dotted side roads and alleys. Cupboards opened in their bases out of which bakers or tinkers or umbrella makers waved their wares. Some of the stairs whorled with delicate ironwork, some creaked in the pleasant wind, their paint peeling, their steps dotted with dear little domestic window boxes dripping with green herbs and chartreuse flowers. Though each staircase towered and loomed, September had a strange feeling that they were not meant to go *up*, but rather *down*. If she had been big enough to walk down those giant's stairs, she imagined that she would be compelled to begin at their heights and walk downward, to the place where the steps disappeared into the earth. She felt certain for no particular reason that the natural direction of travel in Asphodel was not to ascend but to descend. It was a strange feeling, like suddenly becoming aware of gravity in a social way, sitting down to tea with it and learning its family history.

No one took the smallest notice of September as she walked among the great staircases. She thought of asking after the Sibyl from any number of fauns or duck-footed girls with mossy hair that she happened by, but everyone seemed so furiously busy that she felt rude even thinking of interrupting them. As she passed a pale-green spiral staircase, a handsome brown bear with a golden belt on climbed into one of the black sleighs and told it very loudly and clearly, "Eighteenth stair, second landing, please. And make it half speed; I've a bellyache from all that honey-beer down on twelve. S'Henry Hop's birthday lunch. I hate birthday lunches. Spoils the whole office with silliness."

The sleigh rolled smoothly up the bannister, and the bear settled back for a little nap. An empty sleigh clattered down the other jade-colored bannister and waited, empty, patient. September looked around. No one got in or even looked at the lovely thing, with its curling runners and silver ferns and little flowers embossed on the door. Carefully, as if it might bite her or, more likely, that someone would suddenly tell her she wasn't allowed, September opened the sleigh door and sat down on the plush green seat.

"I'd like to see the Sibyl, please," she said slowly and clearly, though not as loudly as the bear.

The black sleigh bounced harshly, once, twice. September winced, sure she had broken it. Instead, as she clung to the smooth, curved bow of the thing, it detached from its bannister and unspooled four long, indigo vines from its belly. The vines splayed out on the ground like feet, and thick, fuzzy lemony-white flowers opened up where toes might usually find themselves. The sleigh rose up totteringly on its new curlicue legs and, with a jostling, cheerful gait, darted off between the staircases, the sun glinting on its dark body.

The Sibyl did not live in a staircase. The black sleigh brought September far beyond the city center to a square of thick grass full of violet and pink crocuses. Hunched up against the beginnings of a stony crag sat a great red cube the size of a house with a filigree brass gate closed firmly over its open end. The sleigh bounced again as if to discharge itself of its responsibility and jogged back off toward Asphodel proper.

September approached the cube gingerly and hooked her fingers into the swooping metallic patterns of the gate. She peered inside but saw only a vague redness.

"Hello?" she called. "Is the Sibyl at home?"

No answer came.

September looked around for a bell-pull or a door knocker or something whose job it might be to let visitors in. She saw nothing, only the scarlet cube standing improbably in that open field like a dropped toy. Finally, ducking around to the side of the square, her fingers fell upon a row of huge pearly buttons, ringed in gold and written upon with bold red letters. September gasped with wonder.

The Sibyl lived in an elevator.

The buttons read:

THE SIBYL OF COMFORT

THE SIBYL OF COMEUPPANCE

THE SIBYL OF CRUEL–BUT–TRUE

THE SIBYL OF COMPLEXITY

September hesitated. She did not need to be comforted nor, precisely, did she feel she deserved it. She thought she probably ought to choose comeuppance, but she was already trying to make it right! She did not want her punishment now, before she had even a chance to fix it all! September frowned; she probably did need to hear things which were cruel but true. If they were true it did not matter if they were cruel, even if all her mistakes were laid out before her like rings in a jeweler's box. But she could not bear it, quite. She could not bring herself to volunteer for cruelty. That left only the last.

"Well, surely everything is always more complicated than it seems, and if the Sibyl can help unravel it, that would be best. But what if it means the Sibyl will make it all more complicated? What if it means I shall not be able to understand her at all?"

But her finger had chosen before her head could catch up, and the button depressed with a very satisfying *click*. She dashed around to the gate just as it rattled open and the most extraordinary creature appeared, seated upon an elevator operator's red velvet stool.

The Sibyl's face was not a person's face. It was a perfectly round disc, like a mask, but without a head behind it. Two thin rectangles served for eyes, and a larger one opened up where her mouth should be. The disc of her face was half gold and half silver, and all around it a lion's mane of leaves and branches and boughs, each one half gold and half silver, sprouted and glittered around her strange, flat head. Her body had odd carved half-silver and half-golden joints, like a marionette, and she wore a sweeping sort of short gold-and-silver dress that looked like what little girls wore in paintings of ancient times. But September saw no strings and no one else in the red elevator, and the disc of the Sibyl's face made her shiver in the sun and clench up her toes in her shoes.

"Are you a Terrible Engine?" September whispered. "Like Betsy Basilstalk's gargoyle or Death's mushroom lady? Is there someone else back there hiding behind you, someone less frightening and more friendly?"

The Sibyl tipped her head down to look at her, and nothing gleamed in the black bars of her eyes. Her voice emerged from the slash of her mouth, echoing, as if from somewhere very far away.

"No, child. I am only myself. Some things are just what they appear to be. I am the Sibyl, and you are September. Now come in out of the light and have a cup of tea."

September stepped into the great elevator. The gate closed behind her and a momentary panic rose up in September's breast—the elevator was a cage and she was caught in it. But the Sibyl touched the walls as she walked into her house, and wherever her hand fell a pearly button lit up with a number on it, illuminating the room like welcoming lamps. 6, 7, 9, 3, 12. The inside of the elevator shone with redness everywhere: red couches, red chaises, red tables, red curtains. The Sibyl settled into a red armchair whose back had creases like a seashell. Before her a little red tea service had already been laid out on a low table the color of a sunset. Above her head a jeweled brass half circle hung on the wall—an elevator arrow, and it pointed toward the second floor. But the room and its clutter seemed a bit shabby and threadbare, patches of worn velvet and tarnished brass, as though once it had all been much grander. Even the Sibyl's terrible face, now that September felt she could bear to look at it for a full moment, was peeling a little at the edges, and thin cracks shone in its surface.

All around the chair and the table and the tea service and the couches, the elevator was filled with the most extraordinary heaps of junk. Weapons glinted everywhere—swords and maces and cudgels and bows and arrows, daggers and shields and tridents and nets. Besides these September saw armor and jewelry, bucklers and tiaras, helmets and rings, greaves and bracelets. An immense necklace of blue stones lay draped over a long golden rod, and both of these rested against a woman's dark breastplate. Clothing peeked out here and there, plates and bowls and long plaits of shining hair only a little less bright than the metal, bound beautifully with ribbon and arranged in careful coils. In the midst of all this, September sat frozen on a soft red couch made for a girl just her size.

The Sibyl poured tea from a carnelian pot with a little

three-headed stone dog prancing on the lid. One of the dog's legs had gotten snapped off in some tea-related incident years past. The liquid splashed purple and steaming into a ruby cup. The parchment tag of a tea bag dangled from the lip of the cup. In square, elegant writing it said:

All little girls are terrible.

"Are your sisters about?" September asked, trying to keep her voice from shaking. She felt suddenly that she had chosen dreadfully wrong, that this alien, faceless woman did not mean well to anyone. Taiga had called her an awful old lady, and perhaps she was right.

"What sisters?"

"The Sibyl of Comfort, perhaps? I'll take Cruel-but-True if I have to."

The Sibyl laughed, and it came out all wrong, jangling, crashing, crackling somewhere inside her strange body.

"There is only me, girl. My name is Slant, and I am all the Sibyls. You only had to choose which me to talk to, for, you know, we all change our manners, depending on who has come to chat. One doesn't behave at all the same way to a grandfather as to a bosom friend, to a professor as to a curious niece. I was impressed with your choice, so if you take it back now, then I shall have to be disappointed in you, and make you write 'I Shall Not Chicken Out' a thousand times."

"Why . . . why would you be impressed? It's only that I could not bear the others. It was cowardly, really."

The Sibyl's head turned slowly to one side, and kept on turning until it had rotated all the way around like a wheel. "Most people don't like complexity. They would prefer the world to be simple. For example, a child is whisked away to a magical land and saves it, and all is well forever after. Or a child goes to school and grows up and gets married and has children, and those children have children, and everyone enjoys the same cake for Christmas every year and all is well forever after. You could get yourself a sieve the size of the sea, sift through half the world, and still find not two together who would choose a complex world over a simple one. And yet, I am a Sibyl. Complexity is my stock in trade."

"What is a Sibyl, exactly?"

"A Sibyl is a door shaped like a girl." Slant sipped her tea. September could hear it trickling down her metallic throat like rain down a spout. It was a pretty answer, but she did not understand it.

"And how do you . . . get into that line of work?"

September believed the Sibyl might have smiled, if her mouth worked that way.

"How do you get any job? Aptitude and luck! Why, when I was a girl, I would stand at the threshold of my bedroom for hours with a straight back and clear eyes. When my father came to bring my lunch, I would make him answer three questions before I let him pour my juice. When my governess came to give me a bath, I insisted that she give me seven objects before I let her enter my room. When I grew a little older, and had suitors, I demanded from them rings from the bottom of the sea, or a sword from the depths of the desert, or a golden bough and a thick golden fleece, too, before I allowed even one kiss. Some girls have to go to college to discover what they are good at; some are born doing what they must without even truly knowing why. I felt a hole in my heart shaped like a dark door I needed to guard. I had felt it since I was a baby and asked my mother to solve an impossible riddle before I would let her nurse me. By the time I was grown, I had turned the whole of our house into a labyrinth to which only I had the map. I asked high prices for directions to the kitchen, blood and troths. My parents very sweetly and with much patience asked me to seek out employment before they went mad. So I went searching all over Fairyland, high and low and middling, seeking the door that fit my heart. You know how questing goes. You can't explain it to anyone else; it would be like telling them your dreams. I looked under a rock, but it was not there. I looked behind a tree, but it was not there, either. Finally I found Asphodel. The ground is thin here, and a little cave greeted me with all the joy a hollow rock can manage. A thousand years later, most breaths spent in Asphodel are concerned with trade with and transit to Fairyland-Below. The Sibyl industry has boomed all over Fairyland, in fact. There are two other gates now, two! I have even heard of a third in Pandemonium itself. What a degenerate age we live in! But still, I was first, and that counts for something."

"You're a thousand years old?"

"Close enough for mythic work. A Sibyl must be more or less permanent, like the door she serves. The door keeps her living, for it loves her and needs her, and she loves and needs it."

"Is that why you look . . . the way you do?"

The Sibyl Slant stared out of her slit eyes, the disc of her face showing no feeling at all. "Do you suppose you will look the same when you are an old woman as you do now? Most folk have three faces—the face they get when they're children, the face they own when they're grown, and the face they've earned when they're old. But when you live as long as I have, you get many more. I look nothing like I did when I was a wee thing of thirteen. You get the face you build your whole life, with work and loving and grieving and laughing and frowning. I've stood between the above world and the below world for an age. Some men get pocket watches when they have worked for fifty years. Think of my face as a thousand-year watch. Now, if we've done with introducing ourselves—by which I mean I have introduced myself and you've said very little, but I forgive you, since I know all about you, anyway—come sit on my lap and take your medicine like a good girl."

September found herself climbing up into the Sibyl's flat gold-and-silver lap before she could even protest that she was far too big for laps and, anyway, what did she mean by medicine? She felt very strange, sitting there. Slant had no smell at all, the way her father smelled of pencils and chalk from his classroom, but also good, warm sunshine and the little tang of cologne he liked to wear. The way her mother smelled of axle grease and steel and also of hot bread and loving. The smell of loving is a difficult one to describe, but if you think of the times when someone has held you close and made you safe, you will remember how it smells just as well as I do.

Slant smelled like nothing.

The Sibyl lifted a comb from a table that had certainly not been there before. The long gray comb prickled with gray gems: cloudy, milky stones and smoky, glimmery ones; clear, watery ones; and pearls with a silvery sheen. The teeth of the comb were mirrors, and September saw her own face briefly before the Sibyl began, absurdly, to comb her hair. It did not hurt, even though September's brown hair was very tangled indeed.

"What are you doing?" she asked uncertainly. "Am I that untidy?"

"I am combing the sun out of your hair, child. It is a necessary step in sending you below Fairyland. You've lived in the sun your whole life—it's all through you, bright and warm and dazzling. The people of Fairyland-Below have never seen the sun, or if they have, they've used very broad straw hats and scarves and dark glasses to keep themselves from being burned up. We have to make you presentable to the underworld. We have to make sure you're wearing this season's colors, and this season is always the dark of winter. Underworlds are sensitive beasts. You don't want to rub their fur the wrong way. Besides, all that sun and safety and life you've stored up will be no use to you down there. You'd be like a rich woman dropped into the darkest jungle. The wild striped cats don't know what diamonds are. They'd only see something shining where nothing ought to shine." The Sibyl paused in her combing. "Are you afraid of going below? I am always curious."

September considered this. "No," she said finally. "I shall not be afraid of anything I haven't even seen yet. If

Fairyland-Below is a terrible place, well, I shall feel sorry for it. But it might be a wonderful place! Just because the wild striped cats don't know what diamonds are doesn't mean they're vicious; it just means they have wildcat sorts of wants and wealth and ways of thinking, and perhaps I could learn them and be a little wilder and cattier and stripier myself. Besides, I haven't yet met anyone who's actually been to Fairyland-Below. Oh, I know Neep said there were devils and dragons—but my best friends in all the world are a Marid and a Wyvern, and anyone in Omaha who met them would call them a devil and a dragon, because they wouldn't know any better! Fairyland itself frightened me at first, after all. It's only that I wish I did not have to do it all alone. Last time, I had such marvelous friends. I don't suppose . . . you would want to come with me, and be my companion, and tell me things I will promise to find extraordinary, and fight by my side?"

The Sibyl resumed her combing, stroke by long, steady stroke. "No," she said. "I do not go in, I only guard the door. I have never even wanted to. The threshold is my country, the place which is neither here nor there."

"Sibyl, what *do* you want?"

"I want to live," the Sibyl said, and her voice rang rich and full. "I want to keep on living forever and watching heroes and fools and knights go up and down, into the world and out. I want to keep being myself and mind the work that minds me. Work is not always a hard thing that looms over your years. Sometimes, work is the gift of the world to the wanting." At that, Slant patted September's hair and returned the comb to the table—but in the mirrored teeth, September saw herself and gasped. Her hair was no longer chocolate brown but perfect, curling black, the black of the dark beneath the stairs, as black as if she had never stood in the sun her whole life, and all through it ran stripes of blue and violet, shadowy, twilit, wintry colors.

"I look like a . . ." But she had no words. *I look like a Fairy. I look like the Marquess.* ". . . a mad and savage thing," she finished in a whisper.

"You'll fit right in," said the Sibyl.

"Will you make me solve a riddle or answer questions before I go in? I am not very good at riddles, you know. I'm better at blood and troths."

"No, no. That's for those who don't know what they're looking for. Who feel empty, needy, and think a quest will fill them up. I give them riddles and questions and blood and troths so that they will be forced to think about who they are, and who they might like to be, which helps them a great deal in the existential sense. But you know why you are going below. And thank goodness! Nothing is more tedious than dropping broad mystical hints for wizards and knights with skulls like paperweights. 'Do you think you might want to discover that you had the power in you all along? Hm? Could shorten the trip.' They never listen. No, what I want is this: Before you go, you must take up one of these objects and claim it as your own. The choice is yours alone."

September shuffled her feet and looked around at the piles of glittering junk around her. "I thought," she said meekly, remembering her books of myth, in which ladies were always leaving their necklaces and crowns and lords were always leaving their swords as tribute, "folk were meant to leave things *behind* when they went into the underworld."

"It used to work that way," admitted the Sibyl. "It's the proper sort of thing. But the trouble is, when they leave their sacred objects, I'm left with a whole mess of stuff I have no use at all for. Good for them—they learn not to rely on their blades or their jewels or their instruments of power, but for me it's just a lot of clutter to clean up. After a thousand years, you can see it heaps up something monstrous and there's just no safe way to dispose of magical items like these. I met up with the other Sibyls a few centuries back—and wasn't *that* a sullen meeting!—and we decided that the only thing for it was to change our policy. Now you have to take something, and maybe in another thousand years I'll have space for a nice bookshelf."

September looked around. The swords shone suggestively. Swords were useful, certainly, but she did not relish the idea of taking up another knight's bosom friend, a sword no doubt accustomed to another hand, and to being wielded with skill and authority. She did not really even look at the jewels. They might be magical, might even be pendants of such piquant power that they bore names of their own, but September was a plain and practical girl. And her plain and practical gaze fell upon something else, something dull and without glitter, but something she could use.

Out of the heap of heroic leftovers, from beneath the wide necklace of blue stones, September pulled a long coat. She had been shivering for days in her birthday dress, and it would no doubt be colder underneath the world. A girl raised on the prairies does not turn away from a good warm coat, and this one was made of ancient, beaten beast-hide, dyed a deep, dark shade, and dyed many times over, the color of old wine. Creases and long marks like blade-blows crisscrossed the cloth. Around the neck, a ruff of black and silver fur puffed invitingly. September felt a pang as she ran her hand over the long coat. She recalled her emerald-colored smoking jacket, and how it had loved her and tried its best to be everything she needed. She could not imagine where it might be now, if it had fallen off between the worlds or found its way back to the Green Wind somehow. She wished it well, and in her heart whispered, *I am sorry, jacket! I shall always love you best, but I am cold and you are not here.*

She pulled the wine-colored coat on. It did not immediately tighten or lengthen to fit her as the emerald smoking jacket had. Instead, it seemed to regard the new creature within it coldly, guardedly, as if thinking, *Who are you, and are you worthy of me?* September hoped that she was, that whoever had owned the coat before had been someone she had a hope of matching for bravery and wiles. The fur felt silky and soft against her cheek, and she tightened the coat herself. September felt taller in the coat, sharper, more ready. She felt like Taiga with her reindeer-skin on, armored and eager to bite things. She grinned, and somehow she felt the coat was grinning slyly with her.

The Sibyl stood from her chair and pivoted smartly to one side, like a door swinging on its hinges. Behind her, a crevice opened in the wall of the scarlet elevator, a stony, lightless crack. A long staircase disappeared down into it, curving away into the shadows.

CHAPTER V

You Are Free Beasts

In Which September Leaves Fairyland-Above, Encounters an
Old Friend, Learns a Bit of Local Politics, and Changes into
Something Very Exciting, but Only Briefly

*T*he stairway wound around and around. The wooden
steps creaked beneath September's feet. Several slats
were missing, crumbled away with age and use. Just as her
eyes adjusted to the total dark, little freckles of light spattered
the gloom before her. As she went deeper, September saw that
they were stars, small but bright, hanging like old lightbulbs
from the stony ceiling, dangling on spangled, bristly cables.
They lent a dim, fitful light, but no warmth. The bannisters of

the staircase prickled with frost. September trailed her hand along the cave wall. *I am not afraid,* she reminded herself. *Who knows what lies at the bottom of these steps?* And just as she thought this, her idle hand found a smooth, slick handle set into the wall, the kind that forms a huge switch with which someone might start a very great machine. September could just barely see the ornate handle in the dark. It made her think of the one that, when flipped, animated Frankenstein's monster in the film her mother quite regretted taking her to. For a week afterward, September had run about the house, turning on the lights in every room and booming out what she considered a very scientific and professional cackle.

September threw the switch. She could hardly have done otherwise—the handle invited her hand, carved delicately but with a real heft to the wood, as perfect and solid and enticing as if it had been made just for her. Some switches *must* be flipped, and some children cannot help turning off to on and on to off, just to see what will happen.

This is what happened:

The lights came on.

Fairyland-Below lit up at the bottom of the staircase like a field of fireflies: Streetlights flared; house-windows flushed ruddy and warm. A million glittering specks of light and sound flowed out as far as September could see and further, not one city, but many, and farms between them, a patchwork of rich, neatly divided lands. She stood as if on a cliff, surveying the whole of a nation. Above it all, a crystal globe hung down on its own huge, gnarled cable. The black, slippery rope disappeared up into a gentle, dewy mist. The great lamp glowed at half wax, a giant artificial moon that turned the silent underground blackness into a perpetual violet-silver twilight. On its crystalline face, a ghostly smoke-colored Roman numeral glowed: XII.

September could no longer see the walls or ceiling of the cave, only sky and hills and solemn pearl-colored pine trees, as though this were the upper world, and the Fairyland she had known only a dream. Voices filled the silence as quickly as light had filled the dark, and bits of music, too: an accordion sputtering here, a horn sounding far off. Behind her, the long staircase wound up and up, vanishing away in the distance. Below her, only a few landings down, a pretty courtyard spread out, dotted with graceful statues and a little fountain gurgling inky water. She had not seen how close she was to the bottom in the dark! A park bench all of ancient bone perched invitingly next to the fountain, so that one might sit and look out at the view and have an agreeable lunch.

And off in the corner of the courtyard, rather poorly hidden by a statue of a jester juggling little jeweled planets with rings of copper and brass, stood a very familiar shape. A shape with wings, and an extremely long tail, and great hindlegs, but no forelegs.

"Ell!" September cried, and her heart ran all the way down the steps ahead of her, around and around, until she could barrel across the courtyard and throw her arms around the Wyverary's thick, scaly neck.

We may forgive her for not seeing it right away. In the gentle twilight of the crystal moon, many things look dark and indistinct. And September was so terribly glad to discover her friend waiting for her after all that she clung to him for a long time without opening her eyes, relief flooding through her like a sudden summer rainstorm. But eventually she did open her eyes, and step back, and realize the truth of it: The creature she hugged so fiercely was not A-Through-L, her beloved Wyverary, but his shadow.

"Hello, September," said Ell's shadow, gently, shyly, the rough, happy *baroom* of his voice soft and humble, as if certain that any moment he would be scolded. He seemed solid enough when she hugged him, but his skin no longer gleamed scarlet and orange. It rippled in shades of black and violet and blue, shimmering and moving together the way a shadow does when it is cast upon deep water. His eyes glowed kindly in the gloom, dark and soft and unsure.

"Oh, September, you mustn't look at me like that," he sighed. "I know I am not your Ell—I haven't big blue eyes or a fiery orange stripe on my chest. I haven't a smile that just makes you want to hug me. But I have been your Ell's shadow all his life. I lay there on the grass below him when you met, and on the Briary grounds when we found Saturday in his cage, and on the muffin-streets in the Autumn Provinces when you got so sick. I worried with him for you. I lay on the cold stones in the Lonely Gaol, and I was there at the end when you rescued us. I have always been there, and I love you just the same as he did. My father was a Library's shadow, and I also know all the things that begin with A-Through-L. I could be just as good to you as he was, if you can overlook the fact that I am not really him at all, which I admit is a hurdle."

September stared at him, how he ducked his head so shyly and seemed almost frightened of her. If she frowned at him she thought he might actually run away. She wanted to think this was her Wyvern. She wanted him to be A-Through-L, so she could stop feeling so alone. But when she tried to hold out her hand to him once more, she found she could not quite. "Where is Ell, then?"

"In the Civic Library of Broceliande, I expect. He's, or, well, *we've* got an internship and a Studying Curse from Abecedaria, the Catalogue Imp. After you left, we, well, *he* felt it'd be best to perform a few Literary and Typographical Quests before presenting himself to the Municipal Library of Fairyland. Even the Civic Library spoke gruffly to him, for Libraries can get very stuck in their ways and hostile to new folk, especially when new folk breathe fire at the Special Collections. But we got a lunch break every day and read the new editions before anyone. We were happy, though we missed you with a fierceness. We kept a file of wonderful objects and happenings called Things to Show September When She Gets Back. But one day when we were shelving the new A. Amblygonite *Workbook of Queer Physicks, Vermillion Edition,* which has to go quite high up so little ones won't get ahold of it and make trouble, I fell off of myself. Of him. Of A-Through-L. Pronouns are a tough nut when there are two of you! I can't describe it better. It didn't hurt; I felt a strong sucking, as though a drain had opened up in my chest. One moment I was in the Library, the next I was half flying and half tumbling head over tail above the cities down here, and many other shadows fell after me, like black rain."

The shadow-Ell shifted from one violet foot to the other.

"At first, I was very upset. I'd lived with my brother since we were born! What would I do without him? I only knew how to stomp when he stomped, sing when he sang, roast shadow-apples with my gloomy breath when he roasted real ones with his flame. Do you see? Even I thought of *him* as real, and *me* as false. *My* wings, *my* scales, *my* apples—I didn't even know how to say mine back then! Everything was his. Well, that's not right at all. *I'm* talking to you. I am *an* A-Through-L, even if I am not *the* A-Through-L. And who is to say I am not *the* A-Through-L, and he my shadow—if a rather solid and scarlet-colored one? That's what Halloween says, anyway. Shadow Physicks are fearfully complicated. A. Amblygonite has *no* idea. When I finally landed safely down here, I found I was solid, and hungry, and ready to turn flips in the air of my own making! Ready to do my *own* sorts of magic! Ready to stand on my head if I liked, and speak without him speaking first! I was so happy, September. I cried a little, I'm not ashamed to say. And Halloween said, 'Be your own body. I've vanished your chains, just like that! Jump and dance if you want. Bite and bellow if you want. You are free beasts.'"

September winced. She did not want to ask. She knew already. "Who is Halloween?" she whispered.

Shadow-Ell uncoiled his neck and turned in a circle, dancing a strange umbral dance. "Halloween, the Hollow Queen, Princess of Doing What You Please, and Night's Best Girl." The Wyverary stopped. "Why, she's you, September. The shadow the Glashtyn took down below. She says when the parties are, and how to ride them true."

September pressed her lips together. It is very hard to know what to do when your shadow has gotten loose in the world. Just think, if another version of you, who had not really listened when your parents tried to teach you things, or when you were punished, or when the rules were read out, decided to run off and take a holiday from being sweet and caring about anything at all? What could you possibly say to your wilder and more wicked self, to make your wanton half behave?

"Where do I live?" September said uncertainly. "I would like to talk to myself."

Ell scrunched up his blue-black muzzle. His silvery whiskers quivered. "Well, she's not *your* self anymore, you see. That's the point. But she lives in Tain, which is the shadow of Pandemonium, in the Trefoil, which is the shadow of the Briary, all of which is right under the Moon-Below. But really, she's so busy, September! She's hasn't got a moment for visitors. There's a Revel tonight, and she's hardly got a dress picked out, let alone balloons enough for all."

"What's a Revel?"

Ell smiled, and it was quite unlike any other smile September had seen on Ell's dear, sweet face. The smile curved across his muzzle and his silver whiskers: sly and mysterious and secret. The kind of smile that has kept a froggy, dark sort of surprise in its back pocket, and won't spoil it too soon.

"You'll love it. It's just the very best thing," Ell said, and corkscrewed up his tail in delight, letting it uncoil languorously around September. Finally, this old, familiar gesture was too much for her. Perhaps she ought to have been more guarded and careful, but she missed her Wyverary so. She missed him being hers. She missed being his. And so she let the great violet swirling tail enfold her and gave it a great hug, shutting her eyes against Ell's skin. He smelled like Ell. He looked like Ell, apart from the deep patterns of lavender and electric turquoise turning under his onyx skin. He knew everything Ell knew. That had to be good enough. What was a person, if not the things they knew and the face they wore?

"Let us go and do magic, September!" The Wyverary suddenly crowed, nearly howling up at the crystal moon with gladness that she had hugged him at last and not sent him away. "It's *such* fun. I could never do it before! Apart from fire-breathing and book-sorting. And later you will come to the Revel, and wear the spangliest dress, and eat the spangliest trifles, and dance with a dashing Dwarf!"

September laughed a little. "Oh, Ell, I've never seen you like this!"

The shadow of A-Through-L grew serious. He dropped

his kind face down next to hers. "It's what comes of being Free, September. Free begins with F, and I am it. I like *spangles,* and I like to *dance* and *fly* and have *Wild Doings,* and I do not *ever* want to go to bed again, just because a great lug attached to me has gone to bed. I shall Stay Up forever!"

September twisted her hands. "But I can't go to Revels and do frivolous magic! I've come to clean up my mess and restore Fairyland's shadows, and that's all. After it's done, I shall go right back Above and put in a request for a proper Adventure, the kind with unicorns and big feasts at the end. I didn't know you'd be here, and I'm glad for you, because you seem to be very happy about being your own Beast, but it doesn't mean I can let Halloween keep on taking things that aren't hers."

Ell's eyes narrowed a little. "Well, they aren't *yours,* either. And anyway, don't you want to see Saturday and Gleam? I thought you loved them. Not a very good love, that only grows in sunshine. And if, on the way, we happened to trip and stumble and just accidentally *fall* into magic, well, who could blame you? Come on, September. You didn't used to be such a pinched little spinster about everything."

September opened her mouth a little. She felt as though the Wyverary had actually stung her, and the slow poison of it spread coldly under her skin.

"You didn't used to be cruel," she snapped back.

A-Through-L's eyes grew wide, and he shook his head vigorously, as if he were a shaggy dog shaking off water. "Was I cruel? Oh, I didn't mean to be! Only I'm not used to being the one who talks! The other Ell took care of all that, and he was so *good* at it—why, he made friends with you in just an instant, without really even trying, that's how sweet and clever and good at talking he is! I would have made a bumble of it, and you would have found some burly old Dragon with four proper limbs to have Adventures with. And now I *have* bumbled it! And you'll never think I'm handsome or wise or worthy of walking about with you. I am wretched. I am woe! Those begin with W, but today I know what they mean, and they mean Hurting; they mean Gloomy and Disconsolate!" Huge orange tears spilled from the beast's eyes like drops of fire.

A curious thing happened inside September, but she did not know its kind. Like a branch that seems one day to be bare and hard, and the next explodes with green buds and pink blossoms, her heart, which as we have said was very new and still growing, put out a long tendril of dark flowers. Hearts are such difficult creatures, which is why children are spared the trouble of them. But September was very nearly not a child anymore, and a heaviness pulled at her chest when she saw the poor shadow quivering with distress. Hearts set about finding other hearts the moment they are born, and between them, they weave nets so frightfully strong and tight that you end up bound forever in hopeless knots, even to the shadow of a beast you knew and loved long ago.

September reached into her red coat and drew out her ration book. The coat did not quite want to let it go, and pulled on her hands as she plucked it out, but September prevailed. She showed it, reluctantly, to Ell.

"I know your magic would be a sight to see, and if I had a ration to spare I'd put it on the barrelhead . . . only I don't, Ell. I mustn't squander! I've resolved not to squander. If you eat up all your sugar today, what will you do when your birthday comes around? And there's nothing wrong with spinsters, anyway. They have nice cats and little bowls full of candy. Mrs. Bailey and Mrs. Newitz are the kindest ladies you'll ever meet, and they have nips of whiskey in their tea like cowboys."

Ell swore he would never call her names of any sort, but sniffed curiously at her ration book. A rather sullen-looking King Crunchcrab peered out from the front, holding a shield emblazoned with two crabs joining claws over a glittering jeweled hammer.

"But you don't need that here, September. Why would you need it? That's the whole point, isn't it?"

A-Through-L's beautiful shadow leapt up and spun around so fast he seemed a great black blanket thrown up into the air. He bent down like a bull, pawed the earth, and bolted— running around September in three quick, dark, tight circles. A crackle shivered up around her; all the hairs on her skin stood on end. She had the thick, swollen, hardening sensation of her whole body falling asleep like an arm or a hand. Strange fiery lights flickered around her, glittering and dancing and darting at abrupt angles. Ell skidded to a stop, his face lit with rapture and mischief and high humor.

And suddenly September was not September anymore, but a handsome Wyvern of middling size, a bright fur ruff around her neck where her red coat had been, her skin flushing a shade of deep, warm, flaming orange from whiskers to tail.

A Wyvern's body is different from the body of a young girl in several major respects. First, it has wings, which most young girls do not (there are exceptions). Second, it has a very long, thick tail, which some young girls may have, but those who find themselves so lucky keep them well hidden. Let us just say, there is a reason some ladies wore bustles in times gone by! Third, it weighs about as much as a tugboat carrying several horses and at least one boulder. There are girls who weigh that much, but as a rule, they are likely to be frost giants. Do not trouble such folk with asking after the time or why their shoes do not fit so well.

September quite suddenly found herself with all of these things: the tail, the wings, the tremendous weight. In addition to all that, she had a fetching ridge of white-gold plates along her back, which female Wyverns possess but males do not. At first, September nearly tipped over. Then she felt horribly dizzy, then queasy, and finally gagged miserably, fully expecting to throw up.

Green fire bubbled out of her mouth in a neat circle.

This, however, seemed to sort out the quarrel her equilibrium was having with what we might call her sense of September: that feeling of personal permanence most of us enjoy, knowing that our bodies and ourselves are on roughly speaking terms, have come to grudgingly understand each other, and that we are very unlikely to turn into a wombat or large bear anytime soon.

Her squat hind legs said to her wings, *I am a Wyvern now.* Her tail said to her spine-ridge: *No use complaining.* Her whole being swelled up like a great orange-and-gold balloon to say the next most logical thing: *I can fly.*

All thought of shadows and Revels and rations fled from September as she took a heaping, thundering start: one step, two, three, and up, up! Her great pumpkin-colored wings, veined with delicate green swirls, opened out and caught the air, flapping as naturally as her legs had ever walked. The night-wind of the underworld buffeted her beet-bright whiskers. September's enormous, seven-chambered Wyvern heart boomed deep in the depths of her chest. Flight was not a thing she did, it was a thing happening inside her, a thing thrilling through her reptile blood and her armored skin, a thing jumping in her bones and reaching up to catch the heels of the air. The crystal moon shone down warmly on her scales—the ceiling of the world seemed so terribly high, even when she turned huge, lazy circles around clusters of hanging stars. Up close, she could see the stars were jewels, too, with sharp prongs like shards of ice. The difference between a ceiling and a sky was only where you stood. September wanted to shoot up to the very top, bash through the earth, and erupt like a giant fiery mountain into the blue Fairyland air.

She might have done it, too, but A-Through-L sailed up underneath her, easily flying on his back, his indigo belly turned up toward her.

"Natural flier!" he harroomed. "Try a flip!"

And below September, the Wyverary executed a gorgeous backward somersault, spraying a nearby star with an arc of dancing emerald flame as he did. September laughed and her laugh sounded like a roar; as if she had never been able to properly laugh in her whole life, only giggle or chuckle or grin, and now that she could do it right, now that her laughing had grown up and put bells on, it had become the most boisterous, rowdy roar you ever heard. She pitched forward and thought for a moment she might lose altitude and fall, but her body knew its paces. Her wings folded tight as she turned over and flared open again as she came upright. September roared again, just for the big, round joy of it.

"It's all so small from up here, Ell!" she cried, and her cry had gotten deep in the baritone range, such a rich, chocolatey voice she thought she might talk forever just to hear herself. "How can Fairyland-Below be so big? It must be quite as grand and huge as Fairyland itself—maybe bigger, even!"

A-Through-L turned a slow spiral in the air as they dodged stars on wires and looked down on the star-map of cities below them. Still, September could not even see stone overhead that would mark the end of the underground kingdom—only mist and gloam. The Sibyl's staircase must have been in a shallow part of the world, for the rest of it was as deep as the sea and twice as full of life.

"Ever seen a mushroom?" Ell said, flexing his shadowy claws.

"Of course!"

"No, you haven't. You've seen a little polka-dotted cap or an oystery bit of fungusy lace. What a mushroom *is,* what it really looks like, is a whole mad tangle of stuff spreading underground for miles and miles, tendrils and whorls and loops of stem and mold and spore. Well, Fairyland-Below isn't separate from Fairyland at all. It is our cap. Underneath, we grow forever secretly outward, tangling in complicated loops, while what you see in the forest is really little more than a nose poking out."

Somehow, a thought squeezed through the radiant shriek of flight in September's veins. She stopped short in the air, pumping away with her fat saffron feet, four claws clutching at the night.

"Why didn't you have to use a magic ration? Why can you do this? Ell can't do this—he would have, if he could have. We had to walk so far! Tell me you have been studying hard and have gotten a diploma from a Turning-Girls-into-Things school. Tell me I have not tasted something wicked by letting you change me—I do not want it to be wicked! I want to feel like this always!"

A-Through-L's face made a complicated expression. It looked shamed, then thought better of it and looked proud, then cunning, then filled up with so much love that all the other quirks of his mouth and angles of his brow smoothed together into one beaming, jubilant frown.

"We're the mushroom, September. Why would we ever need to ration magic down here? Shadows are where magic comes from. Your dark and dancing self, slipping behind and ahead and around, never quite looking at the sun. Fairyland-Below is the shadow of Fairyland, and this is where magic gets born and grows up and sows its oats before coming out into the world. The body does the living; the shadow does the dreaming. Before Halloween, we lived in the upper world, where the light makes us insubstantial, thin, scraps of thought and shade. We weren't unhappy—we made good magic for the world, sportsmanlike stuff. We reflected our bodies' deeds, and when our brothers and sisters went to sleep, we had our own pretty lives, our shadow loves, our shadow markets, our shadow races. But we had no idea, *no idea* how it could be under the world with our Hollow Queen. And now we shall never go back. The more shadows join us in the deep, the more our cities get soaked in magic, just sopping with it, and you don't even need a book of spells or a wand or a fancy hat. Just want something bad enough, and run toward it fast enough. The rations are for Above-Grounders. They can't have it without us, and they've been drinking from our hands for far too long."

September's huge jaw hung open. Her red whiskers floated beautifully on the cave-winds. And in a moment, as fast as it had happened, her Wyvern-body vanished. She fell, tumbling through the sky—only to land softly on A-Through-L's broad belly. He held her gently with his hind legs. September cried out miserably—her body had gotten small again, like a dress that has shrunk in the laundry. Her skin felt so tight she would surely die of tininess. Her bones groaned with loss, with longing to fly once more.

"It doesn't last long," Ell admitted. "Not yet."

After a long while of feeling sorry for herself and worrying over what the Wyverary had said, September whispered, "If Fairyland-Below is Fairyland's shadow, what is the shadow of Fairyland-Below? What's under the underworld?"

Ell laughed like thunder rolling somewhere far off. "I'm afraid it's underworlds all the way down, my dearest, darling flying ace."

Now, just as there are important Rules in Fairyland, there are Rules in Fairyland-Below, and I feel I must take a moment to curtsy in their direction. These are not the sorts of Rules that get posted in front of courthouses or municipal pools. For example, underworlds, on the whole, encourage rough-housing, speeding faster than twenty-five miles per hour, splashing and diving. Unattended children, dogs, cats, and other familiars are quite welcome. And if September had come underground at any other time, she might have seen handsome, clearly lettered signs at every crossroad and major landmark kindly letting visitors know how they ought to behave. But she came underground at just the exact time that she did, and Halloween had had all those friendly, black-and-violet-colored signs knocked down and burned up in a great fire, which she danced around, giggling and singing. Halloween felt it quite logical that if you destroy the rule-posting, you destroy the rules. The Hollow Queen hated rules, and wanted to bite them all over.

But some Rules are immutable. That is an old word, and it means *this cannot be changed*.

Thus, both September and Halloween did not know something on the day our heroine entered Fairyland-Below. September did not know the Rules, and Halloween did not know that the Rules still ran on like a motor left idling, just waiting to roar into motion.

I am a sly narrator, and I shall not give up the secret.

CHAPTER VI

THE ELEPHANT'S FIERY HEART

*In Which September Is Introduced to High Society,
Is Granted a Certain Rank, Finds a Friend Somewhat Different
Than She Remembered, and Has a Spot of Tea*

A-Through-L's gleaming shadow set September down
on a broad brown lawn. It was not a nasty, unkept,
dying sort of brown, but the very rich and beautiful shade of
good dark coffee or expensive chocolate or perhaps a deeply
steeped tea. The wired stars and the great artificial moon
shone down on little brown leaves and little brown buds and
little brown flowers. Cinnamon-colored peapods rattled;
russety weeds puffed clouds of toast-colored fluff into the

twilit air. The blades of brown grass rippled in the myrrh-scented underworld breeze, all bending in one direction, toward an extraordinary house in the center of the field.

The house stood tall and gleaming, a sort of elaborate pear-shaped silver pot crowned in a flourish of golden branches bearing copper flowers and long, slender bronze leaves. The pot stood on four golden claw-feet. It had four golden spigots arching gracefully around its big, curved belly. Ribbons of a red metal September had never seen before curlicued all round the polished crown of flowers, and in the loops of ribbon several pretty silver teacups peeked out. One of them puffed friendly chimney smoke. On account of the chimney, September knew it must be a house—and one with someone at home in it!

As she and Ell's shadow walked closer to it, September could see a delicate porcelain porch and porcelain stairs leading up to it. A thin line traced a round door in the belly of the pot, so thin she wouldn't have noticed it if the crystal moon hadn't shone just so.

"Where have you brought me, Ell?" she asked.

"Oh, oh, I am so *bad* at keeping secrets and making surprises! They begin with S's! Two of them!" Ell could hardly contain his excitement, hopping from one blue-black foot to another in the long chocolatey grass. "It so happens, this place begins with S, too. But I come here a great deal, whenever I want something to pick me up and make my heart shake the rain off. So I know all about it. It's called the Samovar—that's a nice old word for a teakettle. The Duke and the Vicereine live here."

September wondered quietly whether a Duke was very much like a Marquess and what in the world a Vicereine was to begin with. This Ell wouldn't take her to a wicked Duke in a wicked house, would he? She simply could not be sure.

The whipping violet whiskers on Ell's dark muzzle quivered with delight. "No, I mustn't spoil it for you! The other Ell wouldn't; he'd wink and wait, because that's how you make a surprise, and so I shall, too." A-Through-L winked one great, hopeful black eye at her and sped up his chicken-like gait. Quite soon they had reached the porch. September could hear a bubbling mix of murmuring and laughing and clinking inside.

Ell knocked his shadowy head gaily against the door of the Samovar, exactly like the other Ell had once knocked into the trunk of a persimmon tree to shake down breakfast. From within a rich, musical voice trilled, "Recite the Periodic Table of Teatime, in correct order, with Elemental Symbols, please."

A-Through-L sat back on his handsome black haunches,

shut his eyes, and said: "Hot Tea (H), Herbal Tea (He), Lingonberry Scones (Li), Berry Jam (Be), Butter (B), Cream (C), Napoleons (N), Orange Marmalade (O), Frosting (F), Nettle Tea (Ne) . . ."

"Well enough, well enough!" The voice laughed. A lock and bolt slid open with a merry ring and the door to the Samovar swung open to admit them.

A plume of fragrant steam whistled out of the silver doorway. Out of the mist emerged a handsome, round, brown-cheeked face framed in curling brown and green leaves. The leaves gathered together into fat rolls and a little ponytail tied with linen string like an old-fashioned wig. His eyes shone warm and amber and liquid; he wore a fabulous suit of hundreds and hundreds of tiny white flowers. Two crisp, sweet-smelling teabag epaulets told September that this was most likely the Duke. He beamed down at her.

A-Through-L did a Wyvernish curtsy and introduced her. "May I present my friend September of Nebraska? September, the Duke of Teatime, and his wife, the Vicereine of Coffee."

As the tea steam cleared, the Vicereine seemed to appear out of mist beside the Duke, though of course she had been there all along. Her dark brown hair piled up in a complicated crown not unlike the golden bouquet on the roof of the

Samovar. Red berries and green, unripe coffee beans, studded her curls like gems. She wore a shimmering hoopskirt of a creamy, swirling caramel color, with a single black bean at her beautiful brown throat. All around their feet scampered children with the same rosy brown cheeks and berries or leaves in their hair. Behind them all the great belly of the Samovar opened up before September's eyes as a curtain of steam wafted toward the ceiling and the chimney.

A great party whirled within. Luxurious couches of every color lined the walls, and little samovars stood between them, exact copies of the house in red or green or purple. On every couch lounged a well-dressed lady or fellow. Some were shadows and some were not. September saw a handsome old man with deep red-violet skin whose clothes looked like the iron-bound slats of an oak barrel. A girl leaned in to whisper something in his ear—she was completely and utterly white from her sleek, brilliant hair (out of which poked two neat little cow horns) to her frothy, creamy lace dress to her pearly feet. Everyone laughed and talked in elegant voices, their accents crisp and sharp, like movie actors when they played someone very fine. A boy with bright blue hair, a suit of silver bubbles, and a collar of huge jade stones like olives danced on tables swathed in velvet. A big, happy girl with golden skin and golden eyes and long hair that was not hair, but stalks of wheat and curly sprigs of green, played the spoons in a dress of deep brown and vermillion and gilded yellow. Others piped on penny whistles or sang snatches of songs. A smartly dressed, spike-haired lady-gnome played a black cello made of raven's feathers so fast September thought the pair of them might soon take flight. The Duke and the Vicereine were undeniably not-shadows. But several dark shapes spun around the ceiling in a dizzying reel. The shadow of a mermaid carefully dipped her inky tail into the topmost glass of a champagne fountain, turning all the fizzing falls of wine black, one by one by one.

"Most welcome, Maid September!" cried the Vicereine, and September recognized her musical voice as the one that had asked for the password at the door. She kissed September's cheeks; a lingering scent of spice remained as she pulled away. Her children looked eagerly at September with bright, interested gazes. "These are my darlings—Darjeeling, Kona, Matcha, Peaberry, and of course, the pride of my pot, the Littlest Earl."

Darjeeling, the oldest girl, wore a flapper dress of thin, glittery silver chains, dozens of them, each ending in ball-strainers full of tea leaves. The Littlest Earl, youngest and smallest of them all, stopped scampering and smacked the ball-strainers of his sister's dress to watch them whack against each other like abacus beads. His hair was all a tangle of thin black leaves pinned into curls like his father's, with thin bright orange rinds and wrinkled mauve flower petals. He pointed at September with one fierce finger.

"It's the Queen! The Queen's come to see me! Has she come to give me presents?"

The Duke and Vicereine blushed with embarrassment and hushed their son.

"But she *is* the Queen!" insisted the Littlest Earl. "Look at the mole on her cheek! And the pretty blue stripes in her hair!"

"What have we said about shadows?" admonished the Duke sternly. "You mustn't embarrass her that way."

The Littlest Earl squinted at his father. He did not seem convinced.

"So she's the Queen's shadow, then," the child said with finality.

"The other way 'round," said September with a gentle smile, but this idea seemed to frighten the Earl terribly, and he hid behind his mother's skirt.

The Duke of Teatime spread his hands. "It's a difficult thing to explain to children, you understand! The shadows have been coming down so thick and fast we can hardly keep up with the ethics of it all. But now that the boy brings it up, what does that make your rank, my dear? Certainly you are not a Queen, but I'm hard-pressed to say you're not nobility of some sort. . . ."

"Oh, no, Sir, I'm not in the least noble! I'm not a . . . a maid, either. I'm just September, that's all."

But the Duke was already deep in thought, tapping his temple with a ringed forefinger. He mused while leading the troupe of them further into the massive, crowded central hall of the Samovar. "Rank is defined by one's relationship to the Queen, so naturally you've got to be called *something*. Or else how should we know how to treat you? We might commit some grave breach of etiquette! Just September won't do at all. We could call you the Princess of Nebraska. That might sum up the speed of things nicely."

The Duke shooed a pack of sleek black dog-shadows off a cerulean couch so that Ell could sink onto his haunches and lap at a barrel of fine, hot tea. September perched on a golden chaise and accepted a black porcelain cup from the Lady Grey. But the cup was empty. The child called Matcha, whose long green hair floated around her head as though it was underwater, waited with several lacquered teapots balanced in her hands.

"Our family supplies all of Fairyland with tea and coffee," said the Vicereine with clear pride. "Morning and Teatime are our Duchies. Without us, no tea plant would bloom, no coffee cherry would grow, no pot would whistle, no leaf would steep. Our families were once savage enemies. How vicious and cruel were the Wars of Cream and Sugar! Hardly a soul lived who did not take a side. I met my husband on the battlefield, in my Roasted Armor, my Clove Mace held high over his head—but I saw the gentle face beneath that Oolong Helm, and I was lost. I offered him my hand instead of my blows, and the houses joined. Heralds trumpeted the Afternoon Treaty! Our marriage was celebrated with full cups all round!"

The Duke wiped away tears of memory. "Please, precious bean, we must determine her title before we proceed further, or I shall become terribly uncomfortable. This is a Royalist House, after all. And we cannot serve her until it's settled! Imagine if I were to pour you the blend we call the Redcap's Ruby Whip, and you were not a Princess at all but a Viscountess! It would taste foul to you, and you would have bad dreams."

"Husband, she may prefer something stronger," the Vicereine interrupted haughtily. "But, of course, if you were really and truthfully a Baroness, and I brewed the Grootslang's Plunder for you, with its bite of cardamom and cayenne? Why, it'd taste like licking a penny, and you'd develop a nasty case of wanderlust."

September had only had coffee once, when her Aunt Margaret had snuck her a sip while her mother wasn't looking. It tasted bitter, but wild and strange. She rather wanted to taste it again. "Why do I have to be anything? It's only a cup of tea. And I'm not the Princess of Nebraska, I'll tell you that for certain."

A-through-L laughed. It was almost the same laugh September remembered. A little darker, a little heavier. The shadow of a laugh. The Vicereine of Coffee sat daintily on the arm of the golden chaise.

"Did anyone ever read your tea leaves, back home where you live?" she asked. A green berry came loose from her hair and rolled lazily down to the shining floor where Kona picked it up and flicked it at one of his sisters.

"No," September admitted. "Though my mother used to pretend she could do it. She put a scarf around her hair and peered at the cup and said I was destined to fly to the moon or be the captain of a beautiful golden sailing ship." September blinked and laughed a little. "I suppose I was the captain of a sailing ship, if you look at it sideways!"

"That's the only way to look at things, I always say," propounded the Duke. "Slantways, sideways, and upside down."

The Vicereine put her brown hand on September's arm. "Tea leaves are nothing to the reading of coffee grounds, if you want the unvarnished truth. Coffee is a kind of magic you can drink."

"My caffeinated bride! You malign me!" the Duke protested. "Tea is no less high enchantment! My family are all great and learned wizards of tea, and our children will carry on the family lore," he assured September.

"They will sing the Carols of Wakeful Working!" insisted the Vicereine. "They will cast the Jittery Runes!"

"Not before the Glamours of Soothing Souls!" roared the Duke. "Not until they have mastered the Calm Crafts!"

Darjeeling kicked the carpet with a dainty foot. "I'm rotten at Turkish, you know," she confessed.

Peaberry tossed her nutmeg curls. "Well, I *loathe* the Lemon Sabbat," she sniffed at her sister.

"They will know both," the Vicereine said, laughing and holding up her hands for peace. "You see how it all went so wrong! In the old days, the Robust Cavalry and the Chamomile Brigades tore each other to bits. We are Wet Magicians, all of us royal bodies. We are loyal to our bailiwicks. We've lived in Fairyland-Below since before they hung the stars up, and we'll be here after they burn out. After all, coffee plants come up from under the ground, and yes—tea plants, too! We're the ones who coax them along, who tell them who to be when they grow up strong. There's loads of us down here. That's Baron of Port." She gestured to the man with the violet skin. "That is the Waldgrave of Milk with the horns and the pale hair, the Pharaoh of Beer with the wheaty hair, the Dauphin of Gin dancing up on his table. And the dark lady reclining with cacao seeds around her waist is the powerful and sought-after Chocolate Infanta. We practice our Wet Magic, deep and mystic and difficult, hard to hold in the hand but sweet in the belly. Coffee is the best of them, obviously. It's a drink that's a little bit alive—that's how it makes *you* feel so alive and awake."

Matcha tugged her mother's shimmering skirt. "Tea is alive, too, Mummy. That's why we have tea parties. So the teas can play together, and tell each other secrets."

The Vicereine picked up her green-haired girl in her arms. "Yes, of course, my little leaf. And when you speak of tea or coffee or wine or any of our liquid spells, the drink must be matched perfectly with the drinker to get the best effect. If the match is a good one, the coffee will get to know you a little while you drink it, to know you and love you and cheer for your victories, lend you bravery and daring. The tea will want you to do well, will stand guard before your fear and sorrow. Afternoon tea is really a kind of séance. And at the end of it all, the grounds—or leaves!—left in the bottom of your little cup are not really prophecies but your teatime trying to talk to you, to tell you something secret and dear, just between the two of you. So my husband is being a bit boorish about it, because he is a Duke, and Dukes are the wild boars of the noble kingdom, but he only wants to know what tea is your tea."

September thought about her pink-and-yellow teacups in the sink back home, and how she had hated them and their slimy clumps of leaves. She felt poorly on it now, thinking of tea as a thing alive, which wanted only the best for her.

"I don't want to be a Princess," she said finally. "You can't make me be one." She knew very well what became of Princesses, as Princesses often get books written about them. Either terrible things happened to them, such as kidnappings and curses and pricking fingers and getting poisoned and locked up in towers, or else they just waited around till the Prince finished with the story and got around to marrying her. Either way, September wanted nothing to do with Princessing. If you have to mess about with that sort of thing, she reasoned, it's better to be a Queen, anyway. But the thought of a Queen made her think of Halloween, and her hand tightened on her cup.

"I suppose we could just call you September, Girl of the Topside. That doesn't sound very grand, though." The Duke scrunched up his long nose.

"What about a Knight?" suggested Ell shyly.

September brightened for a moment, but the memory of her shadow still hung in her mind, and she slumped again. "I used to be a Knight," she said. "It's true. But a whole year has passed. And I haven't a sword anymore, not even a Spoon, and I haven't a quest, except for a hope of fixing things that I broke myself, and questing is really about fixing things that other people break. I don't know that I *am* a Knight any longer. A Knight should feel triumphant about their adventures, and I suppose I do, but I also feel strange and sorry because of all that happened after."

"It doesn't trouble me to tell you," said the Vicereine, in the tone mothers use to talk children out of too-expensive toys, "Knights are a dreadful sort, when you get to know them. Oh, in storybooks it's all shining armor and banners, but when it comes to it, they're blunt weapons, and always wielded by someone else."

"Perhaps. . . ." An odd idea was forming in September's heart like tea slowly steeping. "Perhaps, if I am to look at everything slantways and sideways and upside down, as the Duke says, and I'm not a Knight any longer, I could be a Bishop instead. In chess, Bishops go diagonally. They're surprise attackers, and you hardly ever see them coming."

"I feel a Bishop ought to have a Bishopric—that's like a

Duchy for priestly sorts. And a really spectacular hat." The Duke of Teatime pointed out a small teapot from his daughter's collection, a steel-blue one with etchings of clouds and winds upon it. "But you are closer to the Hollow Queen than any of us, and I expect that earns you the right to name yourself. September, Fairy Bishop of Nebraska, for you I steep the Crocodile's Long Dream."

"Nonsense," snapped the Vicereine, who clearly felt she had been patient enough. She chose a deep-red pot from the lot, with roaring tigers engraved upon it. "She does not need sleepiness or gentleness! She needs to wake up, the brightest and hottest waking that has ever rubbed its eyes. For her, I brew the Elephant's Fiery Heart!"

The Duke held his hand to his mouth as though he meant to blow a kiss, and blow he did, but instead of kisses, indigo- and holly-colored tea leaves spun up from his palm, dancing through the air toward September's cup. The Vicereine made an outraged noise and snapped her fingers. Out of her hand whirled flaming rose- and tangerine-colored coffee beans, which ground themselves to powder in midair and outraced the tea to hover over the little cup, scorching the blue leaves as it shot by them. Matcha shrugged and decided for her mother, pouring scalding water from the red pot over the glowing grounds and offered cream or sugar. September took both.

The coffee bloomed black with a crimson froth, and in its depths garnet flames flickered. The cream made strange pink clouds in the brew, and when it was done, a slim strand of silk spooled up and out of the coffee, as though it had really been tea all along, draping over the side of the cup and growing an exquisite parchment tag, which read: WHAT GOES DOWN MUST COME UP. The Duke smirked.

"The Sibyl had a teabag like this!" she exclaimed.

The Vicereine nodded. "Our blends go everywhere, even to Fairyland-Above."

September drank. A huge, thundering warmth filled her from bottom to top. Even the roots of her hair went hot and seemed to crackle.

"You know, September," said Ell, who seemed content to observe as her own Wyvern had rarely been in Fairyland-Above. He rested his enormous dark chin on her shoulder. "Bishop begins with B, and Chess begins with C, and I know a few things concerning the history of Bishops. . . ."

But Ell did not get a chance to tell her what he knew about it, for a great ruckus went up from one of the other tables, upsetting teacups and saucers. The various music that had tinked and plinked lazily burst out in a sparkling cloud of noise, then skittered about, looking for the rhythm again. The Ducal family, Ell, and September all turned to see what was the matter. All of them saw what September saw, but only September gasped and covered her mouth with her hands.

The shadow of a Marid was dancing on one of the tables with the Dauphin of Gin, throwing his long, inky arms up in the air, kicking his smoky legs in a graceful pattern. His charcoal topknot came loose and flew wildly, whipping in time to the gnome's quick cello and the Pharaoh of Beer's clacking coffee spoons. Swirling electric-blue spirals moved over his skin, and September knew immediately that it was Saturday, her Marid, even as he leapt into the air and boldly spun three times as she could not imagine her Marid daring to try.

When he landed, Saturday's shadow saw her. He leapt nimbly across the room, laughing, and spilled September's tea onto the couch when he clapped her up into his arms and kissed her right on the lips. September felt as though she had suddenly fallen off a great cliff, and at the same time, just as she had when she tasted Fairy food for the first time. Something sweet and frightening and mysterious had happened, and she could not take it back even if she wanted to.

"Oh, September!" Saturday cried. "I knew you would come! I knew it! I have missed you so much!"

"Saturday!" said September, and it did not matter that he was a shadow; her heart was glad. But her heart also saw that he did not apologize for spilling her tea, did not even seem to notice that he'd done it. Her heart was bruised by the kiss, smashed and surprised and unsettled by it. September thought kisses were all nice, sweet things asked for gently and given gladly. It had happened so fast and sharp it had taken her breath. Perhaps she had done it wrong, somehow. She put the kiss away firmly to think about later. Instead, she smiled at him and pulled a carefree mask over her face.

"What are you doing here? Don't tell me you are the Count of Something!"

"Don't be silly! But I do love hot chocolate and spiced milk, loyal talk and music and dancing—but you are *here*! Who needs any of that rot now? We shall have *such* fun together!" Saturday's shadow laughed, twining her hands in his beautiful sloe-black fingers. "The games and songs we will play! The tricks and riddles we shall make! Oh, I want to show you everything, everything—the Redcaps' iron castle, the Goblin Market, the Mole Circus, the wild Hippogryphes' hunting grounds! I will show you how to climb up to the bottle-trees atop the Grapelings' vineyard towers and we will drink under the woolly, waxen light of our jeweled moon!"

"I don't believe I have ever heard you put so many words together in one place," said September, who felt a powerful shyness rise up in her, perhaps to replace the shyness Saturday's shadow had left behind.

"It's only because I have waited so long for you, September! I have been saving up exploits for us! Wait until the Revel—you'll never want to leave."

September put her shyness away and hugged him tight. He smelled just the same as she remembered, like cold sea and cold stones.

"I'm not here for the Revel, Saturday. I'm not here for castles or Hippogryphes—only they do sound wonderful, don't they? I am here to bring the shadows back into Fairyland. Things are not at all well there. Magic is being rationed! People are so frightened and lost! I know you don't want people to be frightened; I'm sure you just haven't thought of how they must feel, that's all."

Saturday drew away from her. His expression fell into something more like what September knew—sad and sorry and hopeful, but not terribly hopeful.

"But we don't want to go back to Fairyland. We like it here. We have new friends and have been doing ever so much now that we're free."

The Duke broke off from wrangling his brood into a rough luncheon of dark-purple frosted cupcakes and sugar-dusted scones to say, "They come in waves these days, but they do seem to be a jolly lot, just cracking with magic and savagely hungry for everything. Fairyland-Below has been a going kingdom for half an eternity, and all us Dukes and Ladies and trolls and bats and sleeping dreamworms and long-nosed tengus have tended our gardens and replaced burned-out stars since forever. The shadows are nouveau riche, of course, but we don't turn anyone away." His voice had gone oddly quick and nervous, as if he meant to prove something.

"I thought about it," mumbled Saturday, looking up at her with deep black eyes. "How they must feel. How . . . the other Saturday must feel. Confused, I suppose, and upset, and helpless. But I *always* felt helpless when I couldn't do anything on my own and had to forever follow him and do everything he did. Sit in that lobster cage with him, even though on my own I could have just slipped through the bars and been free. Be quiet and shy all the time because he was, even though I didn't feel shy at all! Wrestle you even though I didn't want to. Maybe it's *his* turn to be helpless and have no magic of his own! You don't have to wrestle for wishes down here. Everything is easy—it just happens. And!" He took September's hands again, breathless with excitement. "The best part is that I have you down here with me, and he doesn't! The other Saturday doesn't even know you've come back! I can hold your hands and kiss you just as he always wanted to and never had the courage. I have *so much* courage, September! Oh, I shall never go back! I shall be a free shadow forever and dance at every Revel, and you, you will dance with me!"

September did not know what to think. A bashful Ell and a madcap Saturday—everything truly had turned upside down and slantwise. She did not know yet how sometimes people keep parts of themselves hidden and secret, sometimes wicked and unkind parts, but often brave or wild or colorful parts, cunning or powerful or even marvelous, beautiful parts, just locked up away at the bottom of their hearts. They do this because they are afraid of the world and of being stared at, or relied upon to do feats of bravery or boldness. And all of those brave and wild and cunning and marvelous and beautiful parts they hid away and left in the dark to grow strange mushrooms—and yes, sometimes those wicked and unkind parts, too—end up in their shadow.

September, of course, didn't have a shadow anymore. But she had worn most of her bravery and cunning on the outside. Her wildness though, her powerful colors, perhaps those she had not taken out often enough, to breathe in the sun. And though she did, very much, want to accomplish her great deed, she had missed Saturday so much, and somehow just being among the fay, dancing shadows made her skin prickle and her blood beat faster.

"Well, I suppose I could have just a *little* look at a Hippogryphe," she said finally, "I don't have the first idea how to find Halloween, anyway, or what to do when I do find her."

"I do!" said the Littlest Earl, his mouth still half full of cupcake.

September startled.

"Don't meddle in Politicks with your mouth full, dear," said the Vicereine gently.

"But I do know!" The Littlest Earl, his black-leaf hair bouncing, jumped up and put his hand over his heart, as if reciting poetry. "You've got to stick yourself back together with her. Girl and shadow!" He smacked his little hand against his chest.

Saturday looked down at her teacup. She had guessed that much. She wasn't a fool. But how do you stick a dancing, reveling shadow to yourself and hope to have her stay put?

Scarlet-black grounds clumped and drifted on the bottom of her cup. They moved into a shape, growing sharper and deeper as the specks of coffee swirled and drifted. Finally, they formed a face, a sweet, gentle face September did not recognize. The leaves glowed with a dim, wet fire. The face was deeply asleep, its coffee-eyes shut.

The Vicereine looked into the cup and gasped, her hand

fluttering to the black bean at her throat. She seized September's arm and turned her deftly away from the others. The lady inclined her head and her face grew dark, fear clouding in like cream. She whispered: "You mustn't show anyone what your cup wanted to tell you. Especially shadows. We're all Royalists here—we're loyal! You see how we have parties and dance and sing just as the Queen likes it."

"Who is it?" September asked. "I've never seen that face before."

"That is Myrrh, the Sleeping Prince, who might have been King of the Underneath, but that he never wakes. He dreams at the bottom of the world, in an unopenable box in an unbreakable bower. You mustn't speak of him, or think of him—Halloween is our Queen and we love her, we do. She says History is just a Rule ripe for breaking. We believe that, truly!"

September trembled a little. The force of the Vicereine's whispers made her do it, and she did not like it at all.

The Vicereine leaned even further in, so that no one might possibly hear her. The music had struck up again, and Saturday was tugging Ell out of his couch to dance. "And now that we've taken you in and given you back your friend and made you a nice coffee—made you a Fairy Bishop to top it all!—you'll put in a good word for us with the Queen, won't you?"

"I hardly think I have any influence!" protested September.

"You do though. You must. You *are* her, really, even if you don't think so. Even if *she* doesn't think so. You must vouch for us." The Lady's hand grew tighter and tighter on September's arm. "Tell her we're loyal. Tell her we make Baroque magic and throw Rococo fetes. That we were so good to you. Tell her to keep the Alleyman away from us, please, September. Please."

Two Crows

In Which Two Crows Called Wit and Study Leave Our
World for the More Thrilling Climes of Fairyland

*P*erhaps, being hungry for exciting tales of the underside of
Fairyland, you have forgotten by now about the two
curious crows who chased September into Fairyland. That is
certainly forgivable! They seemed so ordinary, and who gives
crows a second thought? But I have not forgotten them, and it is
by far time to tell you what befell those two brazen birds who
have broken into our story as if it were an unlocked house.

Firstly, their names were Wit and Study. These might seem quite fanciful names for a pair of common crows, but those are the sort of names all crows have. All modern crows are descended from their royal Scandinavian progenitors, Thought and Memory, who got to fly about with a very fine fellow indeed and sit on his shoulders and tell him their opinions about everything. Most people would never listen to a crow who sat on their shoulder—they wouldn't even know how. Still, those are the very highest and most respectful names a crow can earn, even today. All crows set aside a berry or a scrap of grasshopper for Auntie Thought and Auntie Memory at their suppers. It's the family thing to do.

Like all crows, Wit and Study found themselves drawn irresistibly to the glittering and glowing, and on the day September tumbled over the low stone wall in the glass forest, they glimpsed the tiny tear in the world that tripped her up. Nothing they had ever known had glittered or glowed or shone or shimmered the way that tiny tear did. First, they saw the rowboat with the man in the black slicker and the silver lady in it vanish through the tear, and then they saw the little girl disappear slightly less gracefully, and within two caws, they knew this was the thing for them. Wit and Study folded their wings in tight and darted through just as the world righted itself and the wheat resumed waving gently in the deepening twilight.

Even birds long for adventure. Even birds who have gotten nicely fat on farmers' seeds long for the world to be made of more than things to eat and things to nest on.

"Where do you suppose we're headed, Wit?" cawed Study to her brother in the secret language of crows.

"I don't know, Study! Isn't it *something*?" keened Wit to his sister.

They flew faster.

And when they finally burst through the borders in a puff of feathers and slightly frostbitten beaks, they found themselves not in the glass forest in which September was even then trying so hard to make a fire, but in a peculiar city made of clouds. This suited them just fine, being creatures of the air. Cloud bridges and cloud houses and cloud roads puffed and blossomed around them. The two crows took turns somersaulting through garlands of cloud roses and seeing how many cloudhips they could fit into their feathery cheeks at once.

They rocketed through the empty cloud cottages and cathedrals, not quite paying attention to anything but how delightful it was to find a whole town in the sky, all to themselves. They did not think at all about a girl named September, or her troubles beneath the ground, or where everyone who lived in that cloud village might have gone.

CHAPTER VII

GOBLIN ECONOMICKS

In Which September and Her Friends Acquire Transportation,
Learn a Great Deal About the Stock Market, Drive a Hard Bargain,
and Get New Clothes and a New Companion Out of It,
Both More Extraordinary Than They Look

As they left the Samovar, saying an uneasy good-bye and walking out past the edge of the chocolate lawn to a tidy little road ribboning off into a broad twilit country, September and her friends were being watched—no, *stalked*. They had no notion of their hunters, of course. Saturday danced down the path, his black-turquoise feet leaving silver prints, singing about the times they would soon have. Ell stayed close to September, his great head drooping near her shoulder in case she spoke. She stared after Saturday, unable to get used to this boisterous, talkative shadow-boy.

They did not know that a thing hunted them in the dark because between the three of them they actually had very little in the way of knowledge about formal magic. They knew it was delightful fun and rollicking, and had a rough guess as to how to make it happen, but that is like saying you know all about how airplanes work because you once rode in one all the way to the sea. There are many different kinds of magic in Fairyland. Light and Dark were just not enough to satisfy everyone's needs. In the very old days, magic in Fairyland was like a blanket too small to cover everyone's feet. So magic broke itself up obligingly into patchworks: Dry Magic and Wet Magic, Hot Magic and Cold Magic, Fat Magic and Thin Magic, Loud Magic and Shy Magic, Bitter Magic and Sour Magic, Sympathetic Magic and Severe Magic, Umbrella Magic and Fan Magic, Wanting Magic and Needing Magic, Bright Magic and Dim Magic, Finding Magic and Losing Magic.

Marketplaces use Thin Magic to hunt and pounce. And a small, hungry Market moved just behind and beyond September and Ell and Saturday's field of vision, for it had caught a whiff of their Thinness.

You see, a Marketplace is like a lithe, hungry dog. It can sense when you need something and have even the littlest bit of money, just like a dog knows when a plump little rabbit is wriggling her nose in the forest. They can smell it when you have a great deal of money and very little sense, or when you need something very specific, but might be enticed by something enchanting and just beyond your reach. A Market can make itself any sort of shape or size in order to capture its quarry, fill itself with this or that, depending on how it has decided to have you.

No sooner had they passed the rich brown grass of the Samovar's estate and into a broad obsidian plain than music spun up all around them like sudden smoke and fire. Bright, pale tents unfolded and puffed up, long ebony tables full of glittering things and groaning with food rolled out, and long strands of starry colored lights spooled along tall spires. A little creature toddled from tent to tent, her eyes huge and luminous and moon colored, her ears long and heavy, her skin dark and mossy like a tree's trunk, her hair decorated with every kind of jewel and feather.

Saturday clapped his hands.

"A Goblin Market! Oh, September, you see, I told you fabulous things were waiting for us just round the bend! They're just the very best kind!"

The little creature seemed to finally notice them. She bent double and slowly, deliberately somersaulted across the courtyard to September, turning over and over again like a determined boulder. She came up squat and green-black, her skin thorny and smooth in complicated swirling patterns. Agates, bloodstones, and tiger's eyes stuck all about her hair and face, a dull, glinting mask.

"Come buy, come buy," she said beguilingly. Her long, pale lips drew up into a smile. She pushed her graceful, many-knuckled fingers into her heavy black waistcoat and came out with a bunch of shockingly bright carrots, shining as though they had been panned from a creek of gold, large and gnarled and pointed as knives. "Come buy, come buy, come hear my cry! Oh, hark, oh, hark, oh, heed and hark, sweet child of sun and fable, come rest your feet, come share your heat, and sup your fill at my table!"

"No, no, none of that," said A-Through-L as September looked at the vegetables calmly, without once reaching for them. She had learned her lesson with regards to tasting things without examining them thoroughly and asking a goodly number of questions. "You must look out for Goblins especially hard when they rhyme, September. Rhyming means *up to no good*!" He said the G very hard, so that September would know he knew what he was talking about.

"But then again," Saturday added thoughtfully, "*up to no good* may mean *up to something interesting*! The other Saturday got to ride a velocipede; I should at least get some carrots."

"Come now," purred the Goblin girl. "Why do you malign my Goblin's wares? My silk is fine, come sip my wine, and are not my prices fair?" The Goblin cleared her throat and gave them a bemused look out of the rims of her silvery eyes. "Forgive me, it's a habit. And I durst say most folk appreciate a bit of effort! Patter isn't easy, my great brute! It's a fine bit of Loud Magic, and I learnt it well. Goblin universities are very competitive! Anyhow, if you'll have it plain, I'm Glasswort Groof, and I've got such things, anythings, everythings, allthings, and nothings, whatever you've lost at the tiniest cost, just the thing you're lacking—" Groof laughed at herself again. "Well. Everyone's lacking. We could smell your lack over the hills and through the hanging stars. And my carrots would bring the flame to her cheeks, no doubt on it—his, too!"

"No doubt," huffed Ell. "And have her so full and fiery of living she'd dance till her heart burst and thank you for the song! Or forget her own name and lie down in a swoon? Or perhaps turn into a Goblin girl for you to look after."

The Goblin shrugged silkily. "Mayhap, mayhap! It's only business, nothing personal. I wouldn't Goblin her up though, thank you very much. I've quite enough on my plate with my Market all out of sorts!"

A brisk wind plumped the iridescent tents and sent shadowy weeds rolling between them. Dresses fluttered, amulets rattled.

"Why is it out of sorts?" asked September, who, while not overly fond of carrots, did feel hungry. Coffee is not much of a lunch. The Goblin did not seem nasty or frightening to them at all—and was she not here to sort out the out of sorts?

Glasswort Groof beamed. Her tiger's eyes twinkled. "Well, a Goblin Market isn't like a usual sort of Market, that's first and firmly. When a Goblin's born, if she wants proper work and not to just lay in wait under bridges (which is sheer laziness if you ask me), she goes down into the Ten-Cent Forest with treats in her pocket and her best clothes on—and, of course, a Florid Flintlock or five. Those beasts aren't tame, no, not in nature or name, not in tail or in mane—ahem. Well, your own humble Groof, sixth of that name, went down when she was but a slip of a Goblin maid of two or three hundred, guns in her slingers and coins in her hair. In the tin-bark trees of the Ten-Cent Forest many Markets came sniffing up to me—mostly fruit-selling fairs, that's to be expected—but I'm no common Goblin, and all my sisters were in the fruit business already. I can't stand the stuff.

Strawberries have no *depth,* you know? Plums are insipid. But further into the Forest, where the Nickel-Briars wrangle and the Thruppence-Vines tangle, there you can find spice bazaars and tinkers' carts, fishmongers' barks and smugglers' trade-posts, liquor-fountains and leather-and-iron houses just wandering around the wood on their thick owl-legs, pecking at last year's leaves with the tips of their booths and roofs and counters. They hoot at the moon and gruffle at strangers— poor lambs don't know how to whisper and wheedle *come buy, come buy,* they only know how to scrape and creak and buffle, and all but the bravest would run from their thundering displays. I knew a Goblin boy who tried to rope a Market too big for him, a linen-fair all full of damask and satin, and it threw him, just dashed him on the earth like a dog, whipping him with bolts of grosgrain. You have to know which one matches you—and which you're strong enough to mount. I saw mine out in the Sixpenny Wilds, a fine cheeper with flags aflutter. I plied her with coins and rhyming, I wiled her with new wares and nimble timing, and then I shot her through the money-box and trussed her right there. We've been tight as tills ever since—only lately, only lately . . ." Groof leaned in toward September, avoiding the gazes of Marid and Wyvern. Her Market seemed to lean with her. "Only lately, with the shadows coming down, well, they've no money at all, and they need so much. And they just *reek* magic. They just shed it everywhere they go, and my poor Market gets buffeted in the wake of it. No one needs to buy magical items anymore. They just haul off toward something, and it happens for them. My Market can't sleep at night; her bones have got brittle and her coat has no suppleness. She's just falling apart, poor darling."

And now that Glasswort Groof had said it, the Market silks did seem rather tattered, the booths splintering, the whole place groaning and sorry. Had it been that way before? September could not be sure.

"But you! You're wanting *something*. It's all over you, like musk and brume! And whatever it is, we have it, there's simply no possibility that we don't." Glasswort licked her lips.

"And what are we lacking, if it smells so strong?" said September. Her stomach growled after the carrots, though she knew better, she *did* know better. "What kind of Market did you catch out in the woods?"

"Why, can't you tell? It's a Grand Arcade of Bones' Desire!"

"My bones don't want anything!" September laughed.

"I don't think shadows have any," Ell murmured.

"Shows what you know, sunny-girl! I'm sure you've heard people talk about their Heart's Desire—well that's a load of rot. Hearts are idiots. They're big and squishy and full of daft dreams. They flounce off to write poetry and moon at folk who aren't worth the mooning. Bones are the ones that have to make the journey, fight the monster, kneel before whomever is big on kneeling these days. Bones do the work for the heart's grand plans. Bones know what you *need*. Hearts only know want. I much prefer to deal with children, boggans, and villains, who haven't got hearts to get in the way of the very important magic of Getting-Things-Done."

September tried to feel what her bones were needing, but they only felt tired.

"As for what you're lacking, I think I know, I do! Groof's nose knows a hundred wants and more. My nose is my wand— for selling, for buying, for longing, for sighing, for striking a bargain on the bone-bald barrelhead! Come, come!"

They followed her into the little Market. It made itself over especially for them, trying to hide its shabbiness and put its best face forward. Each stall showed hints of wonders dug out of the depths of their yearnings: vials of ocean water and delicate silver mechanisms for sending messages between Marids, who float in time as in a tide. A bouquet of glittering lemon ices in sheet-sugar cones, a dashing red coat of scales just so very like skin, and a full, illustrated, ribbon-marked leather-bound set of encyclopedias labelled M through Z.

Saturday and Ell looked longingly at them. September tried not to see the girl-size wings and caps of darkness and real swords guaranteed to slay eighty-five percent of Dark Lords— and even her mother's dear, dusty chocolate cake on a tarnished silver pedestal.

"Not that I am totally obsessed with merchantry!" said Glasswort Groof as she led them in an artful circle round the Market. "Goblins are well-rounded, though you'd never think it from the dastard tales folk tell of us. For example, I enjoy stamp collecting as well as haggling. The stamps that pay our letters' way Above are works of art, practically bigger than the envelope! I've an early Mallow three-kisser with a rampant rhinocentaur on it in pewter paint. Pride of my collection. And it goes without saying I'm quite the gardener. Goblin vegetables pack twice the punch of fruit with half the delicacy of a simpering little apricot. Soon turnips will be all the rage!"

"I'm afraid," September said softly, then cleared her throat and tried it again. She refused to be ashamed—she'd been swooped up without so much as a suitcase, after all. "I'm afraid we haven't any money. As you said."

"Nonsense!" cried Glasswort, and she laid her finger aside her nose, which was hard and bony and covered in bits of jade. "Who do you think you're talking to? I smelled you across the black plain. Had to wait til you were out of the Duchy's Protection, but I knew you'd pay for the wear on my pocket watch. You're rich as a bowl of beets."

Saturday frowned. Shimmers of blue moved like water in his shadowy forehead. "We're not that," he said. "We're not *paupers;* I'm sure I've got a pint of breath here or perhaps a teaspoon of tears, but rich is pushing it."

The Goblin girl clucked, her frog-colored cheeks puffing out and in. "I don't know, Marid, Breath is down this week, but Tears have made a strong showing. Voices are up, up, up, Firstborns are at rock-bottom basement prices, and Blood has suffered a bit of a drop since the Winds came back. Still, it's a bull Market and you've got plenty. Pity about that kiss, though."

September started, then colored, remembering that Saturday—Saturday! The shyest boy in the world!—had kissed her in the Samovar.

"Oh, yes, girl. First Kisses are currency standard! If I'd only caught you sooner you could've bought up half my stock for one pucker-up. Too bad—but that's what comes of hanging about with royalty. They bleed you dry. Now, I believe this is your stop."

They had come to a booth wound about with bolts of dark silk and fringes of bluebuckwheat and heavy luckfigs.

Two pedestals tipped with violet velvet pillows stood inside. Languorous tangerine-colored lights curved up in an arc that read, NECESSITY IS THE MOTHER OF TEMPTATION.

"We don't need anything," said Saturday indignantly. "We're going to Tain for the Revel! Everything we need will be there!"

"Ah, but how will you get there, my little blue man? Tain is far away in the center of Fairyland-Below, and the Revel begins at midnight. I'm afraid you need Tickets, Direction, Aid and Abetting! But, of course, my human friend is much more interested in an audience with the Queen than with Reveling about and mucking up her shoes."

On one of the violet velvet pillows, three elegant-looking tickets swirled into being, painted parchment with their names stamped upon them and a curious dark serpent wending through the decorated capitals and edgework. September's own ticket said, under her name: THE WEEPING EEL, 7:35 EXPRESS, COACH CLASS.

"What am I bid for the tickets?" chirped Glasswort Groof with a grin. She had her quarry and she knew it. "Now, don't go thinking you can hoof it. There's no faster travel than by Eel, no more thrilling or willing, and you'll never make it even by Wyvern wing, which, if you'll forgive me, young sir, is not half as fast as phoenix or pterodactyl. It's only the truth

I tell! And it just so happens that while we've been jawing, my girl has been moving us toward the station—we'll be there before you know it, and I'll have you all ready to go with fine, legitimate tickets—looking a little shabby for a Revel, I admit, but at least you'll be punctual!"

"I . . . I don't know!" said September fretfully. The Goblin spoke so fast, but surely they needed those tickets—and now. Her heart beat wretchedly with fear, and Ell rocked from foot to foot with anxiety. "I haven't got anything but a rind of moonkin and a couple of onions, and you were talking about standard currencies and breath is down and tears are up, and I've just no idea what you mean by any of that."

"Goblin futures," said Ell, settling down now that he had something to lecture about. "The math is frightful. I think it might actually fall under Queer Physicks. In terms of pure buying power, two Kisses make a Phial of Tears, three Phials make a Pound of Flesh, Five Pounds make a Maiden's Voice, eight Voices make a Prince's Honor, and sixteen-and-one-half Honors make a Firstborn. But they're all traded on the Grand Market, and some days a Prince's Honor isn't worth your best Kiss. They trade other things, too. Breath, Blood, Wishes, Hours."

"How can you trade an hour?" September asked.

"Oh, Hours are delightful." Glasswort sighed. "You can

pile them up in a vault with Half Hours, Quarter Hours, Minutes and Seconds, and what a sight to see, all the colors, the shapes, one on top of the other! Of course not all Hours are worth the same. An Hour from a great battle is far more lucrative than a Sleeping Hour. A Queen's Hour will trump a Stray Cat's Hour every time. And, Mr. Wyvern, I must correct you, the Firstborns have been taken out of circulation. You would not believe how the Market got flooded! Parents these days! After the Incident, the currency was completely devalued. You-Know-Who and his stupid straw-into-gold trick. I myself barely survived the crash. You won't meet a Goblin who doesn't have a passel of children to look after these days. I've got three of my own. Now the tickets," said Glasswort, without missing a beat. She held out her thumb, squinted her eye, and clucked again at each of them, sizing September and Saturday and Ell up.

"I'll have your moonkin rind and three hours off you," she finally said.

"What about us?" asked Ell.

"No need. That'll pay for the lot."

"But we could split the hours, one for each of us," insisted Saturday. There he was, thought September, the boy who wanted to protect her. Who gave her his favor.

Glasswort Groof laughed. It sounded as though it came

from underwater. "I don't want *your* time! I want hers. She's got a Heroine's Hours to barter with, and that's worth ever so much more than you could shake out of your pockets, even if you had them, my jolly shadow-boys. As for her rind, it's had the sun on it. Fat and gold as a pat of butter. I want it, and I will have it."

"I'm not a heroine," September said softly. "Not this time. I'm a Fairy Bishop. I've work to do."

"Bishop's Hours are fine by me, however you want to call yourself, upsider." Groof leaned back on the rail of the booth, in her element.

September sniffed and picked at something imaginary on the ruff of her coat. "Well," she sighed, "the rind you can have, but how about we settle on a half hour and call it clear?" September had a shrewdness in her she'd hardly begun to use, and out it came with banners flying. She was not about to give up three whole hours—why, that was forever! She'd gone with her mother to buy seed and feed and greens plenty of times. She knew the price on the barrel was rarely the price you had to pay.

Glasswort clapped her hands. "Good girl! Oh, Skinflint-Pan bless my generous heart! Humans never want to haggle it down these days. Firstborn? Yep, spit in the hand, deal's done. Never thought of saying, 'What about the second-born? Or better yet, let me keep my blubbering, clumsy children and will you take a nice armoire from the hall?' Now. I can't take less than two Hours, my sweet little celery root. You'd be leaving me bereft and cheated. Times being what they are."

September pretended to consider it, picking at some invisible fluff on the ruff of her wine-colored coat. "How about fifteen minutes and a kiss? I'm not feeling terribly weepy at the moment, but I'm sure I could think of something sad and summon up a Phial or two to seal it."

Glasswort frowned deeply. The corners of her mouth glittered. "Tears must be genuine, my dear, or they're worth nothing at all. I could make you weep, if I liked. Making children weep is easy, as easy as pulling potatoes. But I don't want your crying. I want your time. An hour and a half, and not a minute less, and I'll have that kiss, too. Second Kisses aren't as premium, but they're steady money."

"I think we could hitch the Eel." September shrugged. "I saw a man jump the rails into a grain car out on the tracks by the creek. Didn't look that hard."

Glasswort Groof bawled laughter. "You try it! I'd love to watch. I'd be telling that tale for ages. You'll end up fried as dinner, kid. You don't want to know what an Eel's third rail looks like. An hour and a quarter, the kiss, and a lock of your hair—final offer, take it or leave it."

September made a gargling, sniffing, spitting noise in the back of her throat as she'd seen her father do when he didn't want some butcher to know what he thought of the price of beef. "Show me a line of folk waiting to buy those tickets, and I'll take the price *you* set. No?" She turned around, looking behind her. September was enjoying the pantomime. It occurred to her that this was a grown-up pleasure, a game like jacks or rummy. The older, wiser part of her thrilled to it. "Nobody? The rind and one hour, then. No Kiss, no Tears, and my handshake on the deal." September stuck out her hand.

Groof hooted in delight, spat in her hand (her spit globbed bright magenta), and shook on it.

"Well," September said somewhat nervously, now that it was done. "What's an hour in the scheme of things? Can I choose when to spend it?"

"'Fraid not," the Goblin admitted. "Buyer's Market. But like you say, what's an hour?"

September squeezed her eyes shut and nodded. She expected it to hurt, as it had when the Glashtyn took her shadow, but all she felt was the warm hands of the Goblin girl on her forehead, and a single sharp *tick* of pain, like a hand snapping into place on a clock face.

"But child, you can't go to the Revel looking like that," Groof whispered confidentially, now she had the Hour safe in hand. "You'll shame your folk back home. Do you want everyone to think your world is a no-account country whose chief export is grimy, determined girls?"

"I look fine!" September protested. The red coat pulled defensively around her, quite huffy at the implication.

A-Through-L grinned through his great long whiskers. "Oh, but don't you want to dazzle Halloween when you see her? When we—well, when *he*—goes to see his grandfather finally, he'll make sure he has been bathed up right! He might even invest in a cravat! Oh!" Ell stopped as though he had just thought of a terrible, wonderful thing. "Do you think there's a shadow of the Municipal Library in Tain?" He sat down suddenly on his dark haunches as though the thought had never occurred to him before, swirls of worried, hopeful violet moving in his tail.

September had not thought much about what might happen when she met her shadow. *Did* she want to dazzle it? *It's really like seeing a school-friend who moved away years back,* she thought. *You want to look nice, but you don't want to make them feel poorly. Not if you want to make friends again.*

While she considered this, the Market went to work.

On the other pedestal, on the other violet velvet pillow, a dress slowly formed out of mist and shadow.

It was like no other dress September had ever seen. Just

looking at it made her feel shabby in her faded, re-sewn birthday dress and old red coat. It was orange, to be sure. No dress that was not could tempt her. But it was a dark, reddish, grown-up orange, stitched with droplets of gold. Garnets hung on its plunging neckline. The shimmery copper-crimson skirt had soft, draping tiers held up by jewelled black rosettes. A deep, dark green silken rope circled the waist three times and a pair of bright copper pocket watches dangled from the slim bustle.

It was too old for her. It was too fine and knowing. September, a practical and still very young girl from the fields of Nebraska, found that, for no reason at all, it felt to her strangely dangerous. Her red coat's fur collar bristled and it drew in close around her as if to say, *You don't need that trussed-up thing. I can keep you safe. I don't want company.*

"That's a *lady's* dress," whispered September.

"It's a Watchful Dress," beamed Groof proudly. "Made in the Blunderbuss Bluffs by Banderos of the first rank. It'll never let you down—and I'll pin a pretty brooch on it for no charge. When the stone goes dark, you'll know your Hour's gone." With a flourish, a pin appeared in the Goblin girl's hand and she stuck it on the breast of the Watchful Dress. It *was* very pretty, silver, with a glowing misty white stone surrounded by tiny, tiny gems like speckles of hoarfrost.

"September," said Saturday gently, "let me buy it for you. I've tears enough for it, I'm sure."

"This dress costs much more than tears, my lad," Groof said sadly, shaking her great green jeweled head. "More than kisses and hours. And no haggling—you haven't the time. Listen!" And they could hear, like a train whistle in the distance, a low, sweet melancholy moan. "The Eel's coming into the station."

All around the Market, blue lamps lit up out of the dark mist. A bell tolled softly. A hanging, swaying sign swung into sight: FEVER-ROOT STATION.

Glasswort Groof planted her large, thorny feet. "I told you about the Firstborns. We're swimming in them! They're not a bad lot, but I never wanted children. Let my brothers handle that; they love bonnets and bassinets! My bairns keep the Market up all hours with their whining for home. Take one off me and the dress is yours. It's worth it, trust me—it may seem a pretty, useless bauble, but that's what they say about upsider boys and girls, and they have some good uses all the same. Aubergine, get out here!"

The bell chimed louder. From behind the stall, a shy thing emerged, quite tall, taller than Saturday, but not by much, with great, sad, dark eyes and a long, thick, curving beak.

"Aubergine's a Night-Dodo," Groof said quickly. "Nothing

like them for hiding and sneaking about. She's too old to fob off on a troll who doesn't know better, and I've got two others to feed besides." The Night-Dodo's feathers shone a piercing shade of purple, with dark emerald underdown and a showy fall of black tail feathers like a dark fountain. Her legs looked strong, gray as old stone.

"Goblins always hold back the best trick for last!" said Ell.

"I'm not a trick," said Aubergine softly. Her voice thrummed deep and echoey.

"You take your wares and you take your chances," Groof shrugged. "I didn't rhyme once when I offered her, if that's worth a thing. Why should I cheat? I have a good sterling Hour in my sack! My Market's starting to perk up already!" The wood of the stall smoothed and polished itself, looking as proud as wood can look.

"Oh, Ell, she's just a poor lost thing!" said September, and held out her hand to the bird. September had no natural defense against lost things, being one herself. She could not quite have put it into words, but she felt profoundly, at the bottom of her new, shining heart, that she could *find* lost things. She could make them *un-lost* if she were brave enough. After all, if enough lost things band together, even in the darkest depths, they aren't really lost at all anymore. "Even for nothing, I'd take her along as far as the capital," September said finally, and the Night-Dodo, ever so lightly and briefly, pressed her big beak into her palm.

Saturday kicked the earth. Perhaps he did not want company, either.

"I'd have bought the dress." He sighed. "I could've. *He* never bought you anything, but I could."

Aubergine nosed September's shoulder with her great dark beak, and suddenly the Watchful Dress hung snug and soft on September's body, as though it had been made for her and her alone. The wine-colored coat wrinkled with distaste, most perturbed at suddenly being draped over an obvious intruder. The coat immediately puffed out and grew long to hide the dress, cinching tight.

Four tickets rested snugly in its pocket.

CHAPTER VIII

THE NIGHT-DODO'S QUIET TALE

In Which Our Motley Gang Travels to the City by Eel,
Meets Someone They Do Not Expect, and Hears a Sad Tale
Involving Guns, Dodo Racing, and Goblin Bargains

*T*he Market and Glasswort Groof disappeared in a pop of
smoke and spangle.

The four of them stood on a station platform, railroad
bells ringing madly around them. A kind of wet thunder
shook the planks of the station. They did not even get a
chance to say a proper word to each other before a great, salty,
steaming rush of water splashed and surged across the black
ground below the platform. It flowed indigo and frothing, a

narrow, sudden river—and on the river rode high the Weeping
Eel. He slowed to a perfect, graceful stop.

He was, quite clearly, an Electrick Eel. Longer and taller
than a train, his livid lavender flesh lit up with hundreds of
balls of crackling peacock-colored electricity floating like
balloons on his flanks. Wafting, delicate pale fins floated out
on either side beneath the electricks, fully as long as his
body. His enormous, gentle, smooth face bore stout whiskers that glowed with light, blinking on and off to signal
that he had docked at the station. His immense translucent
eyes, half covered by heavy, bruise-colored lids, overflowed
with indigo tears, spilling onto the earth to make his own
watery tracks.

His name was Bertram.

All along his endless back folk crowded with suitcases and
valises, laughing and drinking and discussing what seemed to
be very important subjects with much gesturing. Tea-and-
luncheon carts rolled back and forth, and various brownies and
selkies and bluecaps hollered for service. They seemed to all be
having a lovely picnic on the Eel's back as he traveled along.

And on the head of the Weeping Eel, a beautiful orange
lamp floated, pale green legs descending from her base and
pale green arms extending out of the crown of the lantern. A
green tassel hung down around her knees. If in the history of

anything, a lamp ever smiled, this one did, and in the soft, fleshy side of the Eel, a little staircase formed to let them up.

"Gleam!" September cried, and fell into the green arms of her friend. Several passengers burst into applause, though they were not sure why, really; it just seemed like a good time for it, while they were having such a jolly afternoon. Among the nixies and nymphs, however, glowered one or two boys with dark horses' heads, and they watched September with baleful eyes, neither clapping nor speaking.

"But you're not a shadow!" September said finally, when the hugging had worn itself out, and Ell and Saturday had had their turns. Aubergine hung back shyly. With a choked sob, the Weeping Eel began to move again, smoothly sailing down the track of its own tears.

Elegant, golden writing spooled across the face of the orange lantern.

I don't have a shadow anymore.

"Whyever not? Did you trade it away like I did? It hurts dreadfully, doesn't it?"

I died.

"Oh." September colored. She had actually forgotten.

My light went out. You can't have a
shadow without light.

"But you're all right now!" said Ell. "Remember, we went to see the Trifle-Wights in Cockaigne together. We did just as you asked, September: We took her to see the world. Or some of it. The world is very big."

Yes. Big and wide and wild.
But my light was out. I could not be a
lamp without my light.
And the shadows kept falling into the ground.
So I followed them.
Wherever they were going, that was the place for me.
Where no one needed light.

"Poor Gleam!" September exclaimed. "I'm so sorry, it's only that it took so long to get back, and everything was so terribly complicated once I got here . . ."

The golden writing interrupted her, streaming around the skin of the lamp with excitement.

No!
I am happy, September!
I met the Weeping Eel, and he was so lonely,
without a conductor
to talk to him and tell him stories.
Everyone just uses him the way they used to use me,
when I was just a lamp.
Bertram's really a very interesting fellow.
He likes to play checkers.
*And now I get to see **everything**.*
All of Fairyland-Below, one station after another!
It's wonderful here, September, you'll see.
Almost everything is over a hundred years old.
I am so useful.
I am not alone.
And neither is he.

"It must be nice," said Aubergine suddenly, "to have a friend like that, and like things so much."

Yes.

"How far is it to Tain, Gleam?" A-Through-L asked, his chest swelled up, full of happiness for her. "So many things in the underworld seem to begin with rather late letters in the alphabet."

But it was Aubergine who answered. "Tain is Pandemonium's shadow. It moves with the capital of Fairyland-Above." She blushed. A creeping frost spread over her feathers. "Or it did. Pandemonium isn't moving anymore. I'm . . . I'm sure you all know that. Even before the shadows started falling, Tain was always here, a perfect shadow of the city above. It used to be the Marketplace watering hole. They'd snug up all round it and sell anything to everyone. But after a while, the big city stopped moving, and Tain did, too. We'll be there presently. The Eel wouldn't let all these people miss the Revel."

"How can you tell what time it is? There's no sun!" September said, for she felt she needed a good dose of sunshine. The gloaming and moonlight made her feel heavy and sharp all at once. She missed her usual feeling.

"How do you tell time with the sun?" asked Aubergine innocently. "The crystal moon makes it easy—look up, it's half past ten in the evening."

They did look up and saw that a rosy dark shadow shone faintly on the surface of the moon: x. It flickered faintly, not quite bold and true yet.

Gleam tucked her arms and legs back inside her lantern and floated down to discuss something with her enormous friend, and the foursome settled in on the not-at-all-unpleasant skin of the Weeping Eel, which kindly made slightly moist lavender seats and cushions for them. The tea cart came trundling up, but September had had quite enough to drink. She asked for a nice mustard sandwich after Ell assured her everything was quite safe when not purveyed by Goblins. She got, instead, a towering confection that might have thought about becoming a sandwich at one point, but had gotten greater ambitions along the way. Sweet ice-colored leaves layered upon dark, smoky spreads and oozing honey-cream, with black plums and blacker figs and very blackest inkfruit peeking out, crushed between slices of something that was decidedly not bread. It was fluffy and wholesome-seeming, but dove-gray, and tasted a little of pastry and a little of cider and a little of snow.

"Do you know," said September as she ate her sandwich thoughtfully and carefully, sharing with Aubergine and Saturday by turns, "everyone seems to know what they are about but me! When I met the Sibyl, she said that she guarded doorways even when she was a little girl, younger than I! And Glasswort Groof went hunting her Market when she was a maid, and even Gleam has grown up and gotten a profession. I suppose I ought to be thinking about that sort of thing, but I've no idea what I shall do when I am grown! I don't suppose there is much call for Knights or Bishops or Heroines in Omaha or even Chicago. And I'm sure other girls are much better at it than I. I don't believe I have done anything forever and ever the way the Sibyl did." September turned to the Night-Dodo, about whom she really was terrifically curious, but had not wanted to be rude. "Do you know what you'll do now that you're free of Groof? Not that she was so bad. She seemed rather nice. Because, you know," she cleared her throat, slightly embarassed, "where I come from, Dodos are somewhat . . . extinct."

This was a very impolite thing for September to say, and she oughtn't have brought it up until they were better acquainted, but the Night-Dodo just nodded sadly, fluffed her feathers, and settled down on her haunches. September noticed that Aubergine was shaped a little like Ell, squat on two powerful legs, only excepting a different sort of tail and scales and a fiery breath.

"It's very far from here, where I was born," she said shyly. "In the city of the Dodos, which is called Walghvogel, far away over the Bitter Stout Lagoon where the dunkel-fish sing, further than the Squashflower Desert where the giant Alifanfaron dwells with his beautiful wife, further even than the Isles of the Lotus-Eaters or the Balalaika Wood on the shores of the Forgetful Sea."

"Is Fairyland-Below so big?" asked September wonderingly. *And how deep does it go, if there is a Prince sleeping at the bottom of it?*

"As big as Fairyland. It must be—they are twins, mirrors, each country with its mate up above and down below. But Walghvogel is hidden well, in the center of the Forgetful Sea, on a sweet island full of juicy grasses and gnarled, spindly tambalacoque trees that bear good berries and fat seeds. In the center of the island stands a small mountain of which we are very proud, with many caves for hiding in. When the wind goes howling through Walghvogel, the mountain sings. Sweet September, Dodos are extinct everywhere, or very nearly. Only on Walghvogel do we live and squawk and waddle as we will. Everywhere else, men hunted us most fierce, for our eggs."

"Are they marvelous in some fashion?" said Ell's shadow, eager to add to his knowledge of things that began with D.

"I will not say, Mr. Wyvern, for that very thing was so desired by all that they drove us into the sea to get at our nests, shot us from our beloved tambalacoque trees, cracked the shells of our young and fried them in skillets. No, I cannot tell the secret now. But it happened that Wuff, the Great Ancestor, for whom my mother was named, fled from a boisterous hunt and came upon a cleft in the mountains where he lived. Standing in the cleft was a most beautiful lady, so beautiful that even though Wuff knew to fear people, he did not run from her. She wore a silver soldier's coat, and a silver pith helmet, and a silver sash, and silver snowshoes. She had long silver hair and silver skin and sat upon a great tiger, who, strangely enough, did not terrify bold Wuff either. And she said, 'You seem a poor and beset little beast. How would you like to come away with me and be safe forever?' Well, Wuff squawked his most secret and alarming squawk, which would call his flock even from the highest crags, and they came running. The lot of them squeezed through the cleft after the tiger's tail just as the first shots of the hunting party spattered the side of the mountain. And that is how Dodos came to Fairyland."

"It must have been the Silver Wind!" said September joyfully. Again, the passengers behind her burst into applause and cheering, as if they shared her glee. Again, the horse-headed boys merely stared. September remembered all the colored Winds from Westerly, not only Green but Blue and Black and Silver and Red and Gold. Silver had gotten into some sort of trouble, if she recalled it right. Oh! But hadn't the lady in the rowboat had silver skin and silver hair? Perhaps she had come by Wind the second time, too, and not even known it!

"Really, they're so excited to be Eeling along they'd cheer at anything," groused Saturday.

"Oh, I wonder if the Green Wind has a shadow I might meet here in Fairyland-Below?" said September. "I do so miss him, and he has been nowhere to see me, which I think is a *bit* rude, but Wind manners are like that I suppose. Come to think of it, I don't believe I've ever seen a billow of wind cast a shadow, so I oughtn't get my hopes up. Still, how wonderful that we both came into Fairyland by Wind!"

Aubergine clucked mournfully. "Oh, but upsider-child, it was worse in Fairyland! For Fairies do love to gamble. They cozened Wuff and just about all the rest into becoming mounts for their Oathorn Races, which used to be held every full moon round a great track that ran the border of Fairyland. That is how fast Dodos could run, once upon a time. Racing Dodos was all the rage in Fairy society. Such saddles they made, dripping with fringe and lace and boughs of cherries, piled up so high with magic carpets and cushions and chairs enchanted for every kind of advantage that the Fairy Jockey and her Dodo never had to formally meet. They raced poor Wuff until, on the last lap of the Creamclot Derby, his heart just burst. His Jockey, a blackthorn Oread who flaunted her one-sixteenth Mabish blood to anyone who asked and most who didn't, came tumbling down off her high seat and broke her neck. The Fairies howled for Dodo blood, for vengeance is also a great hobby of Fairies, even if they didn't care much for the dead maid in question. In the stables that night, Wuff's sister Scuff called all the flock together, and they made their desperate choice: They flew south for Asphodel and disappeared under the world forever, carrying their magnificent saddles with them, mercifully empty.

"The saddles still rest in Walghvogel, a little orchard of Fairy furniture where we bring our chicks to tell them the tale. So that they know they must keep silent and secret in the center of the Forgetful Sea, the only safe place in all the worlds."

"The Fairies don't hold Races anymore," began Ell quietly.

"Good," finished Aubergine for him. She had no interest in the strange mystery of the Fairies' disappearance—as far as she was concerned, they could disappear forever.

"But if it is so secret and safe, how did you end up traded to a Goblin?" asked Saturday. The gentle darkness flew by outside the light of the Eel's Electricks. The great beast swayed lightly from side to side.

"Well, that's the trouble with Goblin Markets and Bones' Desires." The frosty blush crept up Aubergine's throat again. "They can find you anywhere. Scuff and her band, their legs still powerful but awfully sore and broken from use, had hardly roosted in Fairyland-Below before the Markets scented them and came running. Well, we didn't want any dresses or spinning wheels or magic shoes or philtres or powders or even fruit—well, we did want fruit, really, but we had learned a little of Fairy food by then. The Markets howled and whined, but cleared off. Leaving only Glasswort Groof and her Bones' Desire."

September held her breath. "What did she offer you?"

Aubergine's tears finally fell, spilling onto the lilac skin of the Weeping Eel and trickling off to join his own tears on the great salt track below.

"Walghvogel," she whispered. "I have described it to you—but I have never been there. Glasswort had it in one of her booths—the only booth—when the others scattered and left her knowing she had the only thing we truly needed. It sat in miniature on her violet velvet pillow: the tambalacoque trees, the mountain full of caves, the sweet grass, the freshwater ponds. And all in the midst of the Forgetful Sea, so that anyone who did find it would forget it by the time she reached shore again. It was perfect. A place to rest. But how," the Night-Dodo's gaze turned back where they had come, toward the Goblin and the stalls that had long vanished in the Eel's rushing progress. "How could we pay for it? Those were heady days, the days of the Bustard's Market (the Bull and the Bear are nothing to the mad prosperity of a Bustard), and Groof didn't want kisses, she didn't want time, and, oh, we had tears to enrich the lowliest sprite, but, no. She wanted a Firstborn. A Firstborn female, of course. No one in Fairyland yet knew the secret of the egg, but the Goblins knew others wanted it, so it must be valuable. Groof would have it first of all Goblins, and there was no dissuading her. You cannot blame anyone for what happened next. For Walghvogel, anything would have been a bargain.

"All the Dodonas brought their firstborn squabs for Groof to choose from. My mother tried to hide me, to give me a great long tail so I would look like a Dodono, but Groof is a canny buyer, and she was not fooled. She looked at me and only me. We both stood very still."

September and Saturday and Ell sat very still, too, holding their breath, even though they knew how the story must end. The passengers behind them craned forward to hear.

"Well, the trouble is, you're right, September. Sometimes you know what you are when you are very young. Not always—don't worry yourself, kind sunny-girl! But sometimes. And I was even then a prodigy of Quiet Physicks. I stood very still, and this was a mistake, for when I stand very still—not only very still but the stillest it is possible to stand—strange things occur. Sometimes I vanish. Sometimes I become a statue of black marble. Sometimes I glow with a terrible light that freezes all it touches, so that those things become as still as I. A true Master may control it and do so much more. In my time with my Goblin mistress, I have become a Journeyman only, though no Quiet Quorum would acclaim me. I vanished, and Glasswort crowed delight.

"Groof raised me as her own. She stayed up all night and drank pennywine and stole stamps from any poor postman she came across—but she wasn't cruel. She named me for her favorite vegetable, along with Parsnip the Ouphe-lad and Endive the Greencap-girl, who she'd got in other bargains. She taught me to count currency and follow the speculations and futures Markets and her own Loud Magic—which I was always hopeless at. You cannot go against your nature. This was, naturally, before the Market crashed and we Firstborns lost all our value.

"In the end, Groof chose me, my flock got Walghvogel and a fleet, sleek Goblin Schooner to take them there without suffering the effects of the Forgetful Sea. I turned to my mother who was also named Wuff. I said good-bye. Quietly."

CHAPTER IX
THE WOEFUL WIMBLE

*In Which a Friend Bids Farewell, the Capital City Is
Explored, an Enemy Is Sighted, and September Has a Lesson
in Both Underworld Geography and Quiet Physicks*

*F*olk flowed off of the Eel as if in a single body. Bells and
guitars struck up; a chorus or three rose then died as
the revelers' hearts lifted and they descended upon the city in
a colorful, delighted cloud. Nearly everyone pulled a mask
down over their features as soon as their feet hit the road.
When the gates of Tain opened, a wave of music boomed out,
so sweet and dark and strange it caught September's breath and
tied it in a bow.

"Come with us, Gleam," she said finally, looking back up at the lavender wall of Bertram the Weeping Eel and the crackling light of his electric globes. The orange lantern hanging near his great sad eyes looped her golden writing once more.

I cannot.
I am happy.
I have my Eel and the whole world to see yet.
One day I shall turn two hundred.
And what adventures then!
Do well, September.
You always have.
Don't let them tell you you haven't.

September knuckled tears out of her eyes. She missed her friend, who had once held her in the dark. Who would hold her now? Her new friends carried darkness with them, and she had hoped—oh, she had hoped for a little light. But one of them, at least, should know where she stood in the world, and that was enough.

Oh, September! It is so soon for you to lose your friends to good work and strange loves and high ambitions. The sadness of that is too grown-up for you. Like whiskey and voting, it is a dangerous and heady business, as heavy as years. If I could keep your little tribe together forever, I would. I do so want to be generous. But some stories sprout bright vines that tendril off beyond our sight, carrying the folk we love best with them, and if I knew how to accept that with grace, I would share the secret. Perhaps this will help, if we whisper it to our September, as she watches her friend dwindle in the gloamy lilac breeze, borne away on a track of quicksilver tears: "So much light, sweet girl, begins in the dark."

If Pandemonium is a city of silk and soft cloth, Tain is a city of stone.

The frothing tear-tracks of the Weeping Eel still trickled and eddied in the main station long after Bertram and Gleam had surged away. The station glimmered empty and clean, a fragile-looking building of a pale-blue cream stuff that might have been spun sugar, but A-Through-L knew better.

"That's lace agate—that's what it is. There's brothers, up northways, in the Pillow Bobbin Alps—they spin it out from the raw stone on great diamond wheels, just like it's wool. Spin it so fine you can pass the agate through a needle or so thick you can build a cottage out of it for wintering. Nothing like it. They say the brothers met the Fates once, and they had a spinning contest."

"Who won?" asked Saturday, lighting off the swirling stone pattern of the station platform with his shadowy feet.

"It's still going," shrugged Ell, and floated off of the platform on his shadowy wings. "Shall I tell you about Tain, September, before we go in?" The gates stood open and inviting, and they could see a long silver road leading into a lane full of shops, packed with people in red silk and high feathered hats. Masks of long bony noses and arched black eyes peeked around the corners. Bronze-beaked bird masks glittered; hard-cheeked tragedy masks glowed. Some had long horns like unicorns or antelopes; some boasted wild straw hair knotted through with black stones. Yet though a sweet dark music played from some unseen tower, though the air fairly fogged with excitement, the place seemed oddly quiet.

The moon showed a pale, barely visible ix.

"It begins with T, though!" September protested. She touched her hair self-consciously, suddenly reminded how black and streaked with electric colors it had become. What must she look like among all these wild folk? The red coat pulled close around her, as if to say, *We look just fine, thank you very much.*

"Cross-reference!" A-Through-L said happily. "You taught me, remember? Fairyland-Below is F and B, and Capital is C, and I've got it: Tain!" His black face and violet whiskers and big dark eyes shone, so eager to have this moment with her just as it had been before, to experience it again, but this time for himself and not as a silent shadow, to wrap it up and hold it to his heart the way he imagined the other Ell had. He didn't even wait for an answer. "The Capital of Fairyland-Below is fed by two rivers, the Amaranthine and the Gingerfog, both of which roll down from the Phlegethon in the Firehorse Wastes. It consists of four districts, Glassgarlic, Anisegloam, Gallopgrue, and Nightonion. Population estimate: unstable and unavailable. The highest point is Shearcoil, a hollow narwhal horn which houses the Physickists' Rookery, the lowest is the Nuno's Hollow, and mind your feet around their grave-mounds, no matter how easy you might think it to steal black honey from their hives. Common imports: rice, lodestones, rain, spare engines, unwanted children, spring maidens, heroes with something to prove, ghosts, and shadows. Common exports: magic, tea, coffee, and pomegranates. The two rivers cross in the center of the city, where the royal residence, called the Trefoil, stands on high amarine legs (that's a gem that looks like an ice-cream cone, September, all pinkish purple and yellow) and tapers into a sharp-pointed tower, a patchwork of every sort of metal except iron: bronze and copper and gold and silver and embertin and beetlelead besides. Two great pearl leaves, one white, one black, open forth from it, descending into staircases that end in the great Floatstone Pavilion. Hard to miss!"

"Thank you, Ell," said September simply. It was too much to think, how different and yet alike this place could be from Pandemonium! Her mind spun, and she wanted Gleam's pale green arms to hold her.

But the shadow of A-Through-L fretted. "You're supposed to say 'skip to the part where it says I am this many miles from a girl named September.' Or at least, 'skip to *some part* since it's *zero miles* and we're here.' You let me get through so much of it without interrupting! That's not right at all!"

"I shall interrupt more in the future, just to make you happy, Ell." September smiled and wanted to hug him and comfort him, because he was not so unlike the Wyverary she adored. She did not, then thought better of it and did. His shadowy skin beamed warmth. All four of them stepped together under the filigree agate gate into Tain.

Just as they did, a grinding, jingling noise erupted from the crowd ahead of them. A weird, dreadful sort of concertina played—not badly or without skill, but with so much dread in every note that Ell hid his face behind September, which did not hide him in the least, and Saturday grabbed her hand. Aubergine stood very still, so terribly, awfully still that when September turned to include her in their family embrace, the Night-Dodo had disappeared.

The crowd parted. Feathers and hats and even shoes were

left where they lay as a great dark truck came creaking up the silver road of the capital. It was a Fairy truck, no doubt, covered in mad rainbows of lights, some colors September could not even put a name to—perhaps *viollow,* or *crimsilver,* or *oreen.* Brambles, their vines speckled with glow-worms, and vast dark flowers wrapped over the bed like the canvases on army trucks. The headlights were glass globes with flickering gray candles floating in them. The engine, if it had one, made no sound, but the dark-green squash-rind wheels made wet crunching sounds on the street, and the terrible concertina played on.

"Whoever is driving that cannot be here for the Revel," said September. "I don't believe whoever is driving that could Revel about anything, ever." And indeed, when she peered with all her might, September could not see a driver in the cab of the Fairy truck, only a strange pointed red hat with two long striped feathers in it, floating where a head should be.

From beside her, where Aubergine had recently stood, came a low Dodo's voice.

"That's the Alleyman," it whispered.

The truck rolled to a stop. From the top of the brambly canvas, a long silvery ladder grew like something alive, higher and higher and higher. It did not have a color, really, but glowed like water. Finally, the door of the truck opened, and the red hat emerged, looking redder now that September could see it clearly. The two feathers stood up high like horns, pheasant's feathers, or perhaps some strange, awful parrot's. The hat moved up the ladder, and the rungs creaked as though someone's heavy feet climbed them, but no feet did. The ladder had grown so high that September and all the rest of Tain had to crane their necks and shade their eyes to see where it might end. The red hat floated somewhere up beyond where they could see, in the heights of Fairyland-Below, where its ceiling met the floor of the world above.

Aubergine whispered, drawing invisibly nearer to September so that she could feel her soft feathers on her bare hand, but still, the Night-Dodo could not be seen. "Listen. He is taking out his Woeful Wimble. The stars glint on its blackbone handle. He got it from Halloween as a birthday present, along with the other, the Sundering Siphon, and a belt of custard glass to hang them on either side of his hips like pistols. These are his tools; these are his emblems. The Alleyman is putting the Wimble against the rock ceiling of the world. The Wimble bites in, then he begins to turn the crank. One, twice, three times, he turns it. A crack opens, not very big, no wider than your littlest finger. Under the crack, the Alleyman presses the belly of the Sundering Siphon, and a shadow flows in like smoke. The shadow flows down and drifts through the crystal belly of the Siphon and further down, down past the ladder until some kind or unkind wind catches it and it goes to find its place in Fairyland-Below."

"How can you see all that? I can't even see his hat!" Saturday whispered.

"I listen," whispered Aubergine, even more softly. "That, too, is part of Quiet Physicks. A very difficult part, which I studied under the Great Grammophone of Baritone Gulch while my Goblin mistress sold him a pelican. If you can learn to listen deeply and completely, listen not only to words and sounds but also to the pneumo-dynamicks of hearts and light, the partickles of sorrow and gladness, the subtle fluid dynamicks of regret, there is nothing you cannot uncover. I listened to the stars reflecting, the Wimble turning, the shadow falling, and the slow, steady breath of the Alleyman. He weeps as he turns the Wimble, you know. He weeps as the shadows seep through. He thinks no one hears, but I hear. The Alleyman is a Lutin, a kind of invisible hobgoblin whose red hat is like his heart. It is his strength and his self, the only part of him he wears where anyone can see it. And a Lutin weeping is the quietest weeping of all. Invisible tears from an invisible man."

The ladder receded, sliding back into the truck, and the red hat came with it. Somewhere off behind him, a black wisp floated off to its destiny. All around, September saw folk clutching their bodies, their bellies and backs, sweating and trying desperately to remain silent. The shadows looked unconcerned and impatient, but the rest of Tain trembled. The red hat paused at the cab of his bony black truck, as if appraising them all. No one breathed. Then, it lowered into the driver's seat, and on those acorn-squash wheels the Alleyman trundled, slowly, away.

"Surely," said September as shaking breaths sucked in all round and nervous laughter wriggled out over the street, "surely, he cannot hurt anyone down here. He's taking shadows from Fairyland-Above and that is terrible. It must be stopped, but who could he harm in Tain?"

A-Through-L stared at her, a little shamefaced and a little defiant, his tail whipping back and forth like a cat's. "Well, you know, there's plenty who live here who aren't shadows. Like any place. The Duke of Teatime and Aubergine and Glasswort Groof and all of them. The Glashtyn. Nunos. And sometimes, just sometimes, not terribly often, you know? The Alleyman takes their shadows, too."

"They want to keep their magic," mumbled Saturday. "You can't blame them. But when the Alleyman comes, it's better just to hold still until it's over."

September thought this a sad, rotten thing to say. She

remembered the awful sawing that cut her own shadow from her, and she might have dwelt on that terrible pain and what it cost her, had not the Revelers struck up their singing and laughing and talking and dancing once more. They shouted and whooped even louder than before, dancing as if to erase the memory of the Alleyman and his great dark wheels.

Aubergine, feather by feather, reappeared, her solemn dark eyes shining.

CHAPTER X

THE REVEL

In Which September Learns a Great Deal, the Queen Engages,
a Feast Is Demolished, and the Wild Revel Finally Begins,
but Not Necessarily in that Order

I find it reasonable to suppose that some of you, dear readers, have been to a party or two in your young lives. Perhaps you were given a sparkly hat and a bag full of little toys. Perhaps cake was served, and ice cream, too. If you went to especially good parties, you might have played games and won prizes, or watched a fellow in funny clothes pull doves out of his sleeves or make a puppet dance or even play a song on a banjo or guitar or accordion. No doubt you had far too much to eat and drink and needed a good nap after the whole affair.

But you have never been to a Revel.

A Revel is to a party—even that very best party with the doves and the puppets and the accordion—as a tiny, gentle green lizard licking his eyeball on a hot stone is to the Queen of Dragons in full flight, wings out, breath ignited, singing the songs of her nation.

And before every Revel comes a Feast.

The central boulevard of Tain, which A-Through-L could have told them was called Fool's Silver, erupted with long tables full of the delights of a dozen cuisines. Goblin tarts and Nuno honey in rock-crystal jars, steaming Spriggan pies of heartberry and blisspeach and pumpkin and moonkin that got bigger and smaller as you grasped for them, green and healthful Gnome soups overflowing with hexweed, passion-poppy leaves, thrallbulbs, memory-mums, and ropes of good, sweet basil and sage. Glashtyn oatcakes and hay-muffins with golden crusts, Dryad rain-stews and sunnydaise sauces, braided flame-bread for Ifrits and seastone pastries for Marids, genuine cloud-roasts and piles of grilled dunkel-fish and the Järlhoppes' special feverblossom coffee. The Scotch-wights had been saving their best Pining Peat for the occasion—and of course the Wyverns' beloved radishes scattered here and there on the tables like drops of blood, among charm-tortes shaped just exactly like old books, brown and buttered and crackling.

September saw on the table nearest her a great orange-chiffon pumpkin soup with candied almonds, orange sauce in a moat around a castle of carrots and sweet potatoes, and a chocolate cake so rich and dense and moist it shone black and wet the crimson doily beneath it, and the pale plate. It shamed her mother's cake and September blushed. The frosting sparkled in rosettes and ribbons. And all around the plate was written in very nice handwriting indeed: Everything Must Be Paid For, Sooner Or Later. September ran her fingers over the letters. Was it the same hand as the Duke's tea-tag? She could not tell.

To say they ate well is to gloss over the hunger and glee with which the whole of Tain devoured their favorites and new delectables, not minding the mess they made, pitching crusts and rinds at one another, toasting everything they could think of. "Here's to the life of a Gnome!" from one table, "Cheers for my Goblin love!" from another, "Hurrah for the health of all shadows!" from still a third. "So long as they don't crowd my bogs!" bellowed back a teetering Scotch-wight. And from every table, every cup, "Long Live the Hollow Queen, All Hallow's Girl!"

Mischief, too, was on the menu. The watery shadow of a Naiad touched the red clay cup belonging to the bald, golden-scaled girl next to her with the tip of her rippling finger. Blue sparks fountained out, and the wine foamed over, each bubble tipped with a tiny sapphire. The scaly maid yelped, giggled, and then drank it down in one gulp, whereupon her face vanished and blossomed into an elephant's huge, trunked head—though still covered in golden scales, and her eyes flashed garnet flames. She trumpeted, and marigold petals flew from her trunk, becoming tiny scarlet sparrows as they fell onto the shoulders of the crowd. The sparrows sang riotously and disappeared altogether with a loud crash of unseen cymbals. The Revelers burst into applause, and the Naiad's shadow blushed a pearly gray.

"Oh, I want to try!" cried Saturday.

"I've turned her into a Wyvern already," said A-Through-L's shadow, not without pride.

"I should have known," said the Marid, his eyes large and sad. "You have always had the better part of the fun without me, even before. You met her first; you let her ride you—I came along too late to play, and everything went dark and awful so fast!"

"Not I," said the Wyverary gently. "Never I myself, Saturday. I would never cut the line in front of you. And you came right quick anyhow! Don't forget the velocipedes!" He nudged the shadowy Marid with his great head. "Go on, now! It's a Revel! Anything is allowed!"

"Wait!" cried September. "Stop talking about me like I'm a toy you've got to share! I have work to do, I don't want to be—"

But it was too late. Saturday was grinning like he knew a secret, and he had grabbed up both her hands. He kissed them—once, twice, three times. *And there's four kisses I've got in a day,* thought September, who was not at all sure what to make of kissing and at that moment would be granted no time to consider it. Quite without warning, she felt something open up inside her like a balloon suddenly swelling up shiny and bright. She found herself floating lightly above her chair, her wine-colored coat and Goblin's dress gone. September wore instead a delicate gown of grasshopper wings and the smallest spiderwebs, hazelnut shells, and lacy mushrooms, oak leaves and crow feathers and cornsilk, beaded with fireflies and raindrops. Her feet hung bare above her plush seat, and she felt two long, satiny wings beat slowly at her back, as natural as lifting her arms.

September was a Fairy.

September laughed at the same moment that tears came to her eyes—everyone was staring at her, their jaws slack, their gaze uncertain, as though they, too, did not know whether to laugh or cry. How long since any of them down here had seen a Fairy? But tears did not come—instead, she wept black pearls that shivered into luna moths as they fell, their long wings brushing the heads of every Reveling shadow and leaving licorice blossoms in their hair. September's laughter rippled and echoed, spooling out into a bolt of sunshine-colored silk that flapped its seams like wings and spun around twice before winking out in a little swirl of light.

"It was so nice of you to dress up for my party, September," came a sweet, throaty voice behind her, and suddenly the crowd did know what to do. They burst into hollering and ululating, into a long, loud cheer, thumping the table and toasting all over again. September tilted her wings and brought herself around, trying as best she could to neither blush nor look foolish, though she feared she could not avoid the latter. She did her best. Flared her wings wide and shook free her midnight hair. The fireflies on her dress helpfully blazed. Bluebells twined through her bare toes.

Halloween, the Hollow Queen, stared up at her. September stared back. Neither moved first as the Revelers went wild around them.

The shadow *was* September. A shadow-September still wearing the shadow of her old orange dress and worse—the shadow of her beloved green smoking jacket. She wore the shadow of one sweet little mary jane. The Queen's face was just the same as her own, though shaded with azure and lavender and perhaps a little more canny, a little more used to getting her way. When September had watched her shadow go into the water with the Glashtyn, it had been flat and dark and featureless, but now it had weight, shape, dimension. Halloween was a person. Her gaze sparkled with mischief and a secretive glee. On her familiar head rested a wispy crown of autumn mist, and within that misty ring rode a small autumn moon like a crown jewel.

September did not feel shy or cowed. She could not—that was *her* wearing that crown, her own self, left behind and gone quite fey, but her self all the same. It was not like looking at the Marquess in her finery. She felt quite able to speak, and even a little impatient with herself. Had she really been so frightened? This was her own face in a mirror! Herself from a year past, still with only one shoe. No, she was not afraid. But she was not confident either. If only Saturday hadn't turned her into a Fairy! She felt ridiculous. The other Saturday would never have done it, not without her permission.

"Hullo, shadow," said September, and she tried a tiny, hesitant smile.

"Hullo, girl," said Halloween, and smiled identically.

There was nothing for it but to try. September extended her hand, covered with faintly glowing Fairy tattoos. "Come home with me. Don't you want to go home?"

The Hollow Queen laughed. She laughed so long and high and loud that her laughter began to echo around the towers of Tain and come back to her doubled and tripled. The scaly-girl's elephant head shrunk back down, and the shadows all got very quiet. As Halloween laughed, everyone's glasses filled up again, even those drained dry.

"Why would I *ever* want to go home?" September's shadow sneered in her own voice. "Haven't you noticed that home is *terrible* and *boring* and *nothing* ever happens there? Come *on,* September! Tell me you didn't spend all year just waiting to come back to Fairyland, pining away and reading up on centaurs and looking out your window for our Green friend?" Halloween spread her shadowy hands. "Tell me you spent your days just *basking* in the wonderfulness of Nebraska and appreciating its simple joys, having just as many lovely adventures as you would have had here, happy as a clam not to be in a place where magic is real and everyone knows your name! Look me in the eye and tell me it's true, and I'll come back with you right now. I'll tag along like a good little doggy!"

September's heart flooded with shame, and Saturday's

magic chose just then to shrivel up. Her wings wrinkled away. Her heavy wine-colored coat and the hidden dress beneath came rushing back around her with an indignant snap, the rough leather brushing her ankles. She landed on her chair and stepped down from it hurriedly. She and Halloween were, naturally, the same height precisely. The shadow of the green smoking jacket reached out a curious sash to the red coat and stroked its sleeve hopefully. The wine-colored coat allowed its own sash to flow out, just a little, to meet it, and the two girls watched their clothes greet each other.

"I can't say that," September admitted.

"Of course you can't! Come home with you? Never in a hundred thousand evers! I don't want to have to go to school and lie there on the floor while you learn long division! I don't want to wash shadow-teacups while your fingers get all wrinkly from the dishwater! When I can be Queen and have parties whenever I like and eat pumpkin tarts every single day and dance on mushroom caps while the Glashtyn sing and drum the night down? No, thank you! If you thought about it for half a second, you'd agree with me. It's no kind of life being your shadow! Or anyone's shadow! My name is not September, it is Halloween! We are not your tails to wag! We are our own hounds, and we will not be bossed about any longer!"

The Reveling shadows roared approval.

"I might agree," said September, "I might. Magic is powerful fun, and I did want to come back to Fairyland, more than anything. Except what will you leave me to come back to? Or anyone? Don't you know they're rationing magic in Fairyland-Above? It's bleeding away, because you're taking their shadows! Soon there will be nothing magic left up there. All the wildness and fabulous happenings and strangeness will be down here in the dark!"

Halloween smiled, and this time it was not September's smile, but something altogether narrower and more sly. "So? I like the dark."

"You can't just take things without asking," September said, feeling somehow that she was not winning this argument as handily as she had thought she would.

"Since when are you such a rules-minder? You ate Fairy food! You went into the Worsted Wood! You took a sceptre and a sword and all sorts of things without asking! It's all right for a *real* girl, but not a shadow, is that it?" A hot, shrill pain lanced through the Queen's voice, pain and fear and a heap of words that had been waiting so long to be said. September remembered suddenly that a whole handful of years had passed in Fairyland. Halloween was not new at ruling, and in fact, though she looked no different than September, she must be much older now, perhaps fifteen or even sixteen! Almost a grown-up. And she must have been stewing over this, chewing over her fear in the dark, the fear that she was not real. That she was only a reflection of September, a poor, ignored little sister. September felt suddenly sorry for her. But she remembered Taiga and Hreinn and the Sibyl and the magic rations in her pocket, and her anger came rushing back as bright as before.

"I took things I needed, not for fun, but to do what wanted doing! And I didn't keep any of it. You can't just hoard everything for yourself! You've got enough! Stop it! If Mother were here, she'd scold you silly."

A terrible gray blush flared in Halloween's cheeks. September had struck home. The shadow-girl drew close to her and screeched furiously, sounding more and more like a child.

"I can *so* hoard everything! Everything! I can have it all here, with me, and no one will ever leave me for some stupid war or hurt me, because we'll all be together in my city, in my palace, in my Fairyland! I don't care *one bit* for Fairyland-Above! Or Mother, either—did she even notice I was gone? I doubt it! What did Fairyland ever do for me? You threw me away as soon as you got there, you miserable little brat! I hate you, and I hate them, and I *will* have what I want. I *always* have what I want."

Halloween calmed herself. She smoothed her shadow-skirt with her shadow-palms. When she spoke again the child's tantrum had gone from her voice, replaced by something hard and old and strong.

"I am a good Queen, September. I am not the Marquess. You will not find a whole nation of folk happy to see me go. I am the shadows' mistress, and I am loved. I am everything you aren't brave enough to be. I am what you cannot even admit that you want to be—Queen of Fairyland, which is how all the best heroines end up. And this *is* Fairyland. I will make it the *only* Fairyland. Not Above, not Below. Let the rest hang—my country will outshine all." She smiled again and reached out quickly, taking September's hands.

September gasped—she felt the space between their skin shiver and crackle. The weight of her shadow's fingers felt cool and soft.

"But we don't have to bicker like a pair of quarrelsome sisters. You could stay; you could stay here with me, and with Ell and Saturday and whoever your Dodo friend is. You could be Queen with me. You could be Queen for the Undersiders, the others who aren't shadows at all. It would be an elegant arrangement, one Queen for each. The Hollow Queen and the Princess of Wild Beasts—you'd have to be Princess to start, of course. I've been at this longer. But I would teach you, every day like composition class, and it would be ever so much more fun than long division. You could be Queen after you graduate. I wouldn't be selfish and hoard all the Queening to myself. You'd be my sister. We'd share everything. Why bother growing up and having a job or a baby or a house or any of the things you're supposed to have? *We'd* have a Coronation, the greatest Revel anyone ever saw! And if you wanted, if you missed her very much, you could bring our mother here. The Wimble could do it, I'm almost sure. If we found the right spot. At least it could get hold of her shadow. Mother would build us an airplane of cobwebs and moonlight. We'd fly together. Aces."

Oh, how she made it sound! To never have to worry about what she'd be when she was grown, or composition class, to always be wrapped up in magic, to never have to leave or choose which part of herself to lose—to never have to lose anything, because everything was gathered together and happy and no one hurt. And perhaps, if Halloween had not mentioned the Wimble, September would have forgotten all about the Alleyman and been tempted just enough, just barely enough, to give in.

"But it is the *Woeful* Wimble, Halloween," she said softly. "People are frightened of it, and if they are not frightened of you, they are of him, and he belongs to you."

Halloween cocked her head to one side. Secrets sparkled in her eyes. "You know, he's really kind, and gentle, when you get to know him. You'd never believe how gentle."

"To you, perhaps."

"But that's what matters."

Their hands were still joined. September had held out a dim, dismal hope that if they touched, they would simply join together again. She hadn't thought it likely, mind you, but she had hoped. Nothing could be quite that easy in Fairyland. It could be a Rule: *Nothing is easy here. All traffic travels in the direction of most difficulty.* Still, she held on tight.

"You're not like me at all," September whispered. "If you were good and true, the Green Wind would be down here with you, dancing at your party. And he isn't. You can't yell that away."

"Oh?" said Halloween archly. "I thought he was on the side of the ill-tempered and the irascible. Good and true is Fairy gold. It looks lovely, but it turns to junk when you aren't looking." But Halloween's voice shook a little, and she did not deny that the Green Wind was not here, had not set his banner beside hers. The Queen let go of her hands. For a moment, a wild hope leapt up in September's breast, that they would not pull apart, that it really would have happened simply by their touching. She tried to want that as hard as she could, the way Saturday had wanted to turn her into a Fairy or Ell wanted to turn her into a Wyvern. She held her breath, she wanted it so much.

Their skin stuck together for a moment, like two magnets held terribly close to each other, and for the briefest second, September thought it would work. But finally, they slid apart.

"I will not go with you, and you can't make me," the Hollow Queen said. "And don't you try that Wanting Magic on me. You're not a magician of any kind, and I am. It's completely hopeless. I Want things more than anyone. You can't possibly Want harder than I do. You might as well stay, because your beloved Upsider Fairyland is going to be an awfully dull place to have your holidays. It's over before it began. But please, enjoy my food and my friends and my hospitality—naturally, my house is your house."

Halloween whistled, high and piercing, and a shadow fell over the tower-tips of Tain. Down swooped a huge creature, graceful and noble and ridiculous and beautiful: an orange parrot the size of a house, its round beak black and shining, its feathers soft and fiery. The very parrot September had seen in the pet store, oh, a hundred years ago now, it seemed. The one she had wanted so badly to take home and love and name Halloween. Oh. *Oh.* September's throat got thick and hard. She did get everything she wanted. Everything they both wanted. The parrot had a saddle of dark wood and furs, spangled with golden tinsel and nuggets of some raw green gem. He cawed lovingly at September's shadow, who climbed up onto his back and lifted her shadowy arms in the air.

"Let the Revel begin!" the Hollow Queen cried.

Behind her, fireworks exploded, pinwheels of orange and red and blue and purple, green rockets and golden pastilles, starry fountains raining light down on them all. The Queen rose up on her parrot and wheeled around the Revelers as they began their great parade. The wild folk of the underworld danced madly, singing a thousand songs that somehow became one, harmonizing and tying their melodies together, turning somersaults and bouncing high into the air, snapping their fingers until spells and sparks flew from them like rice at a wedding. An Ouphe juggled Pixies; Mermen spat streams of colored water in arcs over the heads of Dryads who drank it hungrily with their rough brown hands. Many folk kissed passionately, which made September try to look away politely, only to see others, an Ifrit embracing a shadow-Lamia, a Goblin courting a young Strega. Bells rang; drums thundered; fiddles sizzled through a million notes and more. September was lost in the crowd, looking up at her shadow disappearing into the night toward the crystal moon. The Revelers buffeted her; some tried to pull her into dancing or simply touch her, their bodies crackling with magic. Their masks swirled; their songs grew louder and louder until the bright cobblestones of the street shook.

And when September could no longer bear the crush of it all, she saw the wildest and most abandoned dancers stamping their feet together up on a steep rooftop: Ell and Saturday, their shadows burning with magic and an untamed, uncaring joy.

CHAPTER XI

Questing Physicks

*In Which September Hatches a Plan of Her Own, Sees a Girl
About a Prince, Hears a Lecture Concerning a Most Unusual
Science, and Learns What Everyone Knows*

*T*he crystal moon beamed a ghostly VII down onto the
sleeping ramparts of Tain. Shadows slept in fountains
and draped over statues of namelessly ancient Kings and
Queens of the Fairyland-Below. In the Floatstone Pavilion
stood a serene-looking man of green marble, holding a pair of
scales in one hand, with a feather resting on one copper plate
and the shadows of several hobgoblins and peris in the other.
A centaur maid, her four legs tucked up underneath her,

snoozed beneath the imploring alabaster gesture of a grieving young man with a lyre on his back. Balloons still floated ghostly through the streets, chasing their own exploits. The air smelled of spent fireworks, and bits of the marvelous feast dripped or slowly slid off the tables, pushed by the cool wind blowing from the twinned rivers.

September herself lay snugly in a marble basket held up by a statue of dark stone—a sly-eyed, canny lady with huge pomegranates tumbling through her thick hair. Saturday slept curled next to her; Aubergine roosted at the statue's bare feet. A-Through-L had wrapped his body and tail about the whole business.

September woke before anyone. The whole city snored. She lay awake, looking up at the dim stars and the teetering tops of towers. Nothing had quite gone to plan. Perhaps if she hadn't felt so sorry for her shadow, the Wanting Magic would have worked. But now . . . now she would have to do something else. Something slantways and sideways and upside down, like the Duke had said. September looked at Saturday as he slept, and at the great bulk of shadowy A-Through-L. Were they her friends, or Halloween's? Her Saturday would stand between her and the world, but the shadows were strangers, really. New people with the same shapes and names. Her Saturday would never have stolen her first kiss without so much as a thank-you. Would never have turned her into a Fairy when she'd told him not to. But did she know that for certain? Some part of this Saturday must live in the other one, just as she saw flashes of her kind, gentle friend in the trickster child sleeping next to her.

September felt suddenly very secretive. The wine-colored coat approved. It closed in tight as if to say, *Yes, tell no one anything. It isn't safe out there.* She must protect herself. There would be no one to do it for her. A plan started to prick up its ears inside her, slowly, but getting stronger.

September quietly pulled herself up out of the basket without waking the Marid. Careful not to wake anyone, she climbed up and out of the basket and scrambled down from the statue, stepping lightly on a hovering shard of frosted rosy-orange rock in the Floatstone Pavilion. Other shards floated here and there about her, making a very strange scene, as though the slabs were sleeping birds, waiting for sunrise to shake off their dreams. She knelt at the feet of the forest-green statue and in the cold morning of Tain and shook Aubergine awake.

The Night-Dodo yawned, showing pink at the back of her feathery throat. She started to squawk up at the day, but September shushed her.

"Hush! You mustn't wake anyone else!"

Aubergine snapped her beak shut and looked up at September with large, soft eyes. Could she trust the bird any more than the others? Perhaps, because Aubergine had no one else, just like September. *I will be right back*, September thought, looking at the dear shadows of the Wyverary and the Marid. *I will come back once I know what to do, and we will all go together.*

"I'm going to go see the Physickists," she said finally. "And I want you to come. You're one of them, after all."

Shearcoil Tower is a perfect shadow of Groangyre, its twin in Pandemonium. Where lumpy, bulbous Groangyre stitches up its heights in cracked leather, Shearcoil is hard and alive, a long, spiraling black narwhal's horn filled with hundreds of clean white rooms in which Extremely Pleasant and Possibly Flammable Physicks might be practiced. At the very tip-top of the horn perches a peculiar library, a peculiar librarian, and a total devotion to the pursuit of Questing Physicks. Along with Queer Physicks and Quiet Physicks, this discipline completes the Three Q's that make up the Noblest Study. When your parents remind you to mind your P's and Q's, these are the Q's they mean, and the P's, too! Children are natural practitioners of the Queer and the Questing, for childhood is nothing but a quest through a queer country. Of course, they often have a good deal of trouble with the Quiet.

When September and Aubergine finally got to the top of the horn, out of breath and aching with the effort of a thousand and more stairs, they saw the Questing Floor stretched out before them, bright lamps lit and a little lunch boiling over the hearth in a burnished pot. Books and scrolls and folios lined the walls in every direction, towering and tapering up to the tip of the horn. Little wisps of clouds played up near the highest shelves. Ladders chased each other lazily around the rotunda. And a little creature lay on her stomach on a stack of diagrams piled up upon a desk much too big for her, littered with papers and inkwells, waggling her feet back and forth while she read. She was quite tiny, little bigger than a footstool, wearing a great wide-brimmed black straw hat and a little caramel-colored monk's habit with ash-colored beads around her neck. She clicked them together idly. Her olive-colored hair was cropped short under her hat. She had a wide brown face and dark green lips to match her hair and fingernails and zebra-like stripes on her skin, peeking out from under her habit.

"Excuse me," said September, when the creature did not look up at them. She cleared her throat.

The small monk arched her eyebrow at them and returned to her book.

"The sign at the bottom of the stairs said to look for

Questing on the one hundred and forty-fourth floor," she tried again, determined to appear as brave as she could. That was what was called for, she was sure of it. "And Ell said that this was where the Physickists lived, and he's never been wrong about anything yet, so I do believe you must be a Questing Physickist. My name is September. I want to go on a Quest."

The monk looked up again. "We discourage casual inquiries. You might try the Bards down on ninety-seven—they dabble in a little of everything, and they'll sing whatever you like for a penny. I believe they've put the Second Law of Dragon Dynamics to some sort of tune. Goodness knows their bassoons keep me up late enough."

Aubergine spoke softly—so awfully softly September could hardly hear her. "But you are a Physickist? A real one? You . . . you went to a university, and they put a laurel on your head, and you turned into a respected scholar, and from then on they let you speak up any time you wanted?"

The little monk slapped her hands down on her papers.

"What a gentle voice you have," she said, her gaze calculating. "I can feel it wrap me up like a woolen scarf, rubbing my cheeks and insisting that it would hardly hurt me to help a poor young girl from out of town." She hopped down from her papers and off the lip of the desk, using her wide black hat to float a little ways before landing before them. She poked her finger up at Aubergine. "You're a Quiet Physickist if I ever heard one," she accused, but she did not seem terribly upset. Indeed, when Aubergine inclined her head to admit that she was indeed, the tiny girl burst out in a brilliant smile. "Why didn't you say so? How wonderful to meet a cousin in the Odd Arts! My name is Avogadra, and you . . . well, I'll confess I haven't seen you at any of the conferences. Are you registered with the union or are you a dabbler like those dilettantes down on ninety-seven? Forgive me, I'm just so excited. I'm the only one here, you see."

"My name is Aubergine, and I have only just begun my Quiet Studies," the Night-Dodo demurred.

"Nonsense, you're *quite* advanced!" Avogadra enthused. "I nearly gave in before I caught myself. And I didn't even hear you on the stairs! *This* one I heard clumping through the lobby, but you? *Silent.* Sublime."

"Where are the other Physickists?" asked September, who thought she had stepped as softly as possible.

"Doing fieldwork, obviously," Avogadra said, and hopped down from her book to finally greet them. "We are nearly all Monacielli—that's what you call a beast who looks like me! We used to hide in the cellars of monasteries, waiting for the brothers to hurry up with the beer-brewing or the mushroom harvest.

We'd upset their inkpots and build our houses out of their hymnals and tap their barrels when they had a nice chocolatey porter coming along. But if one of the brothers got lost in the catacombs or the woods beyond the abbey, or if something dreadful befell one—at sorest need, when they'd passed beyond all human aid—we'd come in the dark and show them the way out. The way home. It's in our blood—we heard their distresses like a rung bell in our bones. We lived reasonably well, but before too long we'd learned a great deal about manuscripts and contemplation, and realized that we had got a fair sight better at it than the monks themselves! So we left. We came to the city, two by two and three by three, and Shearcoil took us in. We made our own rectory, our own cathedral up here. We kept our Complines and our Vespers. When the ink and the beer and the hymnals belong to you instead of to big folk who flap their arms ridiculously when they get upset, it's not so much fun to spoil them as to use them well and put them away after. And no one else is quite as deft at the Third Q as we. We can't cut out the part of ourselves that feels the ringing of the bell when our old brothers are lost or in despair. We learned to Quest by following them into all their black places."

"Humans can quest, too. I'm certain of it. Lancelot and Galahad and Jason who had the Argonauts and those sorts," September said shyly. She felt as she often did in class when she was nearly sure she had the right answer, but could not always make herself raise her hand.

The Monaciello put her hand over her small heart. "Of course, we owe a debt of gratitude to those early theorists! And any number of posthumous doctorates! But they were amateurs, really. They didn't choose their Quests, the Quests chose them. They would have been happy to be done with them, from beginning to end. We seek out Quest-Dense Zones and hop in with both feet. We Experiment. We Prove. Mersenne has gone off into the Jargoon Mountains to work on his thesis, investigating the spiritual connection between dragons and maidens. Candella last reported from the bottom of Blackdamp Lake, conducting experiments on free-range treasure. Red Newton wholly devoted himself to the study of magic apples, immortality causing and otherwise, and that means setting up a year-round camp in the Garden of Ascalaphus. Questing Physicks isn't like the Quiet and Queer branches. You can't do it at home in a comfortable chair—you have to be out in the thick of the business, with your tools on your belt and your heart on your sleeve! It's my turn to stay home and keep the light on for the others, though. I only finished up my Grail Equations in the fall." Avogadra clearly hoped that one or both of them had heard of her work, but finding no recognition on their faces, sighed a wistful weary sigh. "It is my dearest hope that one day I shall be the one to discover the GUT—the Grand Unified Tale, the one which will bind together all our Theorems and Laws, leaving out not one Orphan Girl or Youngest Son or Cup of Life and Death. Not one Descent or Ascent, not one Riddle or Puzzle or Trick. One perfect golden map that can guide any soul to its desire and back again. I will be the one to do it, I know it. I hope I know it. I know I hope it."

"Well, *I* want to go on a Quest," said September stubbornly. "Not for research but because it needs doing. Even if I am human, even if I fail. I have some experience, and I am good at sticking things out till the end. If I am good at anything, I am good at that. I wanted to consult with an expert, but I'll do it myself if you don't want to be bothered. And I'll almost certainly muck it up, and it'll be a mess, but I'll keep going anyway."

Avogadra scratched under her hat. "Well, what sort of thing did you have in mind? An Object Quest is a nice beginner's run. Or a Damsel in Distress. The Conservation of Princesses Law figures in there, but the math isn't hard."

September did her best to fix Avogadra with a steely gaze. "I want to go down into Fairyland-Below and wake up the Sleeping Prince," she said. Aubergine turned to her, surprised. She fluffed her feathers in distress.

"No one even knows where he is, September," she fretted. "Or how to wake him up. Or if he's even real—the Dukes and Countesses like to talk about him, but that doesn't mean anything. It doesn't mean he's a real person who really ought to have been King of Fairyland-Below and who can really stand up to Halloween, even if the rest were so!"

Avogadra put a small hand on Aubergine's purple breast. "Thank you, Sister," she said solemnly. "Well done."

Aubergine bowed. "Most welcome," she answered.

"First Law of Heroics." The Monaciello grinned up at a confused September. "Someone has to tell you it's impossible, or the Quest can't go on. Your friend has volunteered herself as a Non-Euclidean Companion, which is also necessary to proceed to the next stage."

Avogadra darted off toward the towering bookshelves, leaping onto a ladder and riding it like an unbroken pony as it bucked and shot upward. September reached out for a second ladder, but did not manage to catch hold before the wine-colored coat swept open, revealing the beautiful, coppery Watchful Dress beneath. September tried to pull her coat closed again, but the dress had other ideas. The two pocket watches that draped so gracefully from her waist unspooled themselves and shot upward, hooking around the swan-like necks of a pair of gargoyles further up the stacks and swinging her into the air, reeling her up and onto a safe wooden ledge next to Avogadra.

"Well, that's a Useful thing and no lie!" said the little monk.

September could not help herself—she laughed. Her cheeks flushed; her heart beat wildly. Aubergine stared up silently from below, flightless.

"I had no idea!" September exclaimed.

Avogadra nodded as she ran her fingers along the book spines. "That's one of the four Object Types: Useful, Wonderful, Deceitful, and Mutable. Mutable Objects always seem like something silly or plain, when they are actually marvelous. Or they appear marvelous while being secretly useless. But if I'm not mistaken, that's a Bandero dress! I've heard of them, but I've never seen one."

"Is that . . . a wicked thing?" September asked.

"Well, it all depends on how you look at it. Most things do, down here. The Bandero are spies. Girls with bat wings and lion tails and scarlet eyes that can see a thousand yards in the dark. All women—and don't ask me how they make more of them because they keep it a secret. Fiends for secrets, the lot of them. They collect secrets. They have a vault made of whispering glass up in the mountains, past the fireline. Some say they eat them—they need secrets like you need bread.

Some say they sell them at prices only the stars could pay. Perhaps I'll send Mersenne after the secret of their secret! Or go myself. I'm exhausted with all this sitting still. Anyway, they all wear getups like that. To help them in their spycraft. But I've never seen one on a plain girl with no wings or tail at all. They guard those dresses something terrible. Ah, here we are."

Avogadra reached up on her tiptoes, her caramel-colored sleeve spilling down into her tiny face. September reached up to help her and pulled down a large velvet-covered dove-gray book embossed in silver. It read, *Sleeping Royalty and Other Politickal Conundrums.* The Monaciello flipped past beautiful illustrations of sleeping maidens, spinning wheels, a cross-section of a mountain, and one very complex diagram of an apple. The chapter she settled on had no pictures at all.

"Other than revolution and assassination, falling asleep for a hundred years or more poses the biggest danger to royalty these days. They're all at risk, though just try to tell them that! You'd think one of them would keep a Physickist on retainer for these kinds of emergencies but no—it'll never happen to *them, they* invited all the right people to their coronation! *They* don't even have a stepmother!" Avogadra frowned. "Prince Myrrh sleeps at the bottom of the world, yes, yes, we know that," she scolded the book as if it was an erring child. "Why do you vex me?" The book riffled through its pages, embarrassed. It settled on a page thick with text. "Ah, now *there's* something!"

"Does it say where he is?"

"Oh, no, nothing like that. But if my numbers are right, there's a minotaur involved, which lets us know we're running a basic Theseus Quest-model, and that's a great help!"

"Is it?"

"Certainly! It means there'll be a labyrinth somewhere— where there's a labyrinth, there's a minotaur, and vice versa! I can't imagine a decent maze that would be caught dead without a minotaur. It's not done! You don't go out of your house without any clothes on, and a minotaur doesn't go into the world without a labyrinth to keep him warm." The monk hopped to another ladder, which whirled her up and away, further into the heights of the horn. The Watchful Dress suddenly filled its skirt with air, a great balloon, and just as quickly puffed it out through the bustle, shooting September up like a little orange rocket. It repeated this several times until she came to rest once more beside the Physickist, who had hauled out another enormous book. This one was powdery white, with onionskin pages like a dictionary September had once seen in the huge library in Omaha. It read, *A Ryte and Goode Historie of Fairyland-Below (Unabridged)*. This book did not wait to be scolded, but whacked open and flew through its chapters without being asked. The Monaciello beamed at September, as if to say, "Look how well my babies behave."

"Just as there are different types of stars—red and white and brown and blue and dwarf and giant and all that lot— there are different types of Quests, and if we determine what type you face, we shall have a much easier time managing the whole business. We're doing very well. Already we know that Prince Myrrh is an Endgame Object Type W—that's Wonderful, since we have yet to see if he will be any Use in governing. He sleeps suspended in a Theseus-type narrative matrix, however he does seem to have some gravitational pull on events, which is unusual for a T-Type. After all, we still remember him even after all these years. It's far easier to forget something than to remember it. Remembering takes all kinds of magic. No one knows who he is or what he looks like or where to find him, and yet we all know of him. We all know he sleeps in an unopenable box on an unbreakable bower. That's a frightfully strong E.K.T. Field for one little creature!"

"What's an E.K.T. Field?"

Avogadra grinned. "Whilst on an expedition to prove the Rule of Three, my honored colleague Black Fermat hypothesized that certain Quest Objects cast a field around them, like a magnet or a planet—an Everyone Knows That Field. This is how they draw in unsuspecting Heroes. When an E.K.T Field is in effect, everyone within its power will know a good deal about the Object, even if they can't say where they heard about it or why it's so deathly important to remember all that dusty old nonsense. They'll chat about it with any passing stranger like it's sizzling local gossip. 'Oh, the Troll-Goblet of Clinkstone Hall? A Forgetful Whale swallowed it, and took it to her pod so they could bring the Whale-Maiden Omoom back to life. Everyone knows that!— the sword Excalibur? Nice lady down by the lake will let you see it for a dime, swing it for a dollar—Everyone knows that!' Trust me, if you want to know the score, just find out What Everyone Knows, and you'll be on the scent. Of course, the Field might not be on his own account. See here: 'Long ago, a great Sorceress pulled up the earth over the Prince like a blanket, and sang him to sleep in the dark at the bottom of the world. She called on her Powers to guard him, and these were horses and bulls and tapirs and other beasts. Then she whispered in his ear the time and manner of his waking, but only the earth heard it.' So it might be the Sorceress bending the tale to her boy. He might not be a proper Prince at all, I suppose. Being the subject of sorcery tends to elevate one in society."

"Can you find *anything* in these books?" September wondered. "Anything at all, so long as it's to do with Questing?"

"Nearly! Of course, a library is never complete. That's the joy of it. We are always seeking one more book to add to our collection."

September felt a pang of guilt at having left Ell behind in the courtyard. How he would have loved this place!

"Can it tell me how to put a person and their shadow back together again?"

Avogadra peered cannily at her.

"Well!" September said defensively. "It's not so odd a question. Halloween is my shadow! Everyone knows that. At least they seem to."

"Quite so," said the Monaciello, and put two of her fingers into her mouth. She whistled loud and sharp. A book flew off a shelf several feet away and shot toward her—a black one, with a cloudy-pale title. *Rhymes of Knowing and Not-Knowing.* It looked new, only just printed, or written, or however books were made in Fairyland. She flipped it open and licked her thumb as she hunted through the pages.

"Here! 'Not thread nor glue, not nails nor screws, will ever self and shadow wed.' Helpful, those poet-types. Perhaps this one: 'Seek the grimy queen of dread machines, if you your errant shadow miss.' Now that's quite good! As a Prophetic Utterance, Third Class (Vague Hints and Mysterious Signs), you couldn't ask for better. It's downright plain-spoken!"

"It isn't at all! I don't know who it means or what. I'm hardly better off than before!" September cried.

"Well, that's what you get with Third Class. But no book of ours would ever just *tell* you a thing. The Quest would spoil, just as if you added the wrong chemical to a medicine. It would turn poisonous and rancid. A Quest is not followed, it is engineered. Now, in you go."

Avogadra turned several chapters at once and came to a frightening, hideous page: all black, from margin to margin.

"In?" September trembled.

"In. Didn't you hear? You're headed for the bottom of Fairyland-Below. This place is made up of layers like a thick, dark cake. You have to go down—you'll have to sooner or later so might as well get a start. Just hop in—I know it looks dark. It *is* dark. It's a mine, as a point of fact. But that's where you need to go, and I'm opening the door for you."

September peered into the utter blackness of the page. "I can't go without my friends," she whispered.

"No time," the Monaciello said. "A book is a door, you know. Always and forever. A book is a door into another place and another heart and another world. But this one is a real door, too. They float through all the books of the library. At noon, they're in the Biographies, at teatime they flit into the Advanced Slaying section. Dally too long, and they'll go winging off somewhere and it'll take weeks to find one again."

"But I can't just *leave* them!"

"I'm here," said Aubergine softly, and September started. Without a sound the Night-Dodo had slowly and doggedly climbed the ladders to where they stood peering at their book, hooking her beak over the rungs one by one by one.

But Saturday and Ell, still sleeping in the cold Tain morning! She couldn't just let them wake up without her and no note or message to tell them where to find her. Could she? *Can't I? I snuck off without them just fine. Either I trust them or I don't.* A hard, brave, strange voice inside her stood up to have its say. But the voice was not very big yet.

"Then I shall have to get down some other way," September said. "Even if this is easier. Anyway, it's very black down there at the bottom of a book."

Inside the bodice of the Watchful Dress, a little satiny door opened. A small, agitated pocket watch flew out, its chain looping up and around to make a pair of tiny wings. It darted off, buzzing so fast September could not see it at all, down the stacks of books and out of a great round window. A moment passed, then two, then three, as Avogadra glanced worriedly at the open book. The black page rippled, impatient to be on the move.

And then A-Through-L came rising up through the air, his powerful, shadowy wings beating the morning winds. He peered through the window. Saturday sat on his back, rubbing his sleepy eyes and batting at the pocket watch, which jangled alarms in his ear and buzzed all about the poor boy's blue-black head.

"I will smash that thing—see if I don't," he growled.

"Oh, Ell!" cried September. "I wasn't going to leave you, I promise! Hurry, hurry, fly up here!"

The Wyverary did, squeezing through the window with a groan. He marveled at all the hundreds and thousands of books along the way, books he could not stop to read or alphabetize. But finally, all four of them perched or hovered together, an unruly, motley crowd. September hugged them and Aubergine, too. She hooked her arm into Saturday's elbow, and her other around Ell's dark claw.

"You don't have to go, Aubergine," she said, realizing something she ought to have said before. "I know Groof said you had to, but you don't. You don't really belong to us at all. You are a free beast, and should do what you please. You can stay and study with the other Physickists and be happy."

The Night-Dodo said nothing. Quietly, she moved closer to September, that was all.

"Everyone ready?" said Avogadra, beaming under her wide black hat. "I suggest jumping right now."

"Are we going somewhere?" asked A-Through-L.

Before she could answer, the Monaciello gave September a shove, and all four of them tripped into the book. They seemed to fall terribly slowly, and the black page got bigger and bigger beneath them until it swallowed them up completely.

CHAPTER XII

THE MINES OF MEMORY

*In Which September Gets Lost in a Book, Gets Some
Help with Her Memory from a Large Blue Kangaroo,
and Works a Shift in a Mine*

*S*eptember and her friends did not so much fall into the
book as crash.

The black space was not an endless empty hole, but a
tunnel full of rustling, of pages ripping and turning, of heavy
leather spines thunking hard against feathers and scales and
skin. Blind, September tumbled and rolled and stumbled,
pointing downward in a general sort of way, tasting strange
ink as pages flew at her face. The roaring sound of it all

sounded like nothing so much as a great, angry tide surging in, wave upon papery wave breaking over her poor head.

Slowly, ahead of her in the dark, a clanking, bonging, metallic sound grew. The papers thinned and finally blew aside like gauzy curtains. September followed the sound of metal being struck and scraped until, groping blindly, her hands fell upon a wooden frame and a hard, cold doorknob. The door wedged shut somewhat below her, and the papers crushed in behind, pushing on her shoulders with little wordy kisses. September put her shoulder against it and shoved. It came free far more easily than she expected, and with a little cry, she fell down through the door inside the book and tumbled out onto an earthen floor. Bits of paper still clung to her hair and the ruff of the wine-colored coat, which bristled and shook them off.

Avogadra had told the truth—the black path through the book ended in a mine. All around her, sharp rocks and dark bluish boulders bulged. A wooden track ran through the great cavern, and on it rickety cars raced by, some empty, some topful of sparkling gems. Now that September's eyes adjusted to the dimness of the mine, she could see that the light came from the walls. Rich, looping, twisting veins of crystalline stuff shone as though a fire lived inside them, brighter than any jewel September had ever seen—though in truth this was not too many. The harlequin colors mingled and cast a cool reddish purplish greenish bluish goldenish radiance on the bustle of the miners, none of whom noticed that a girl had fallen out of the ceiling.

September stared at the miners: furry turquoise kangaroos with large, inquisitive eyes and powerful tails. They hopped from one cart to another, with pearly lamps on their heads and beautiful long necklaces around their silky throats. They wore brown leather straps in an X over their chests, the better to hold pickaxes and shovels on their backs. They carried gold-pans like little shields on their brown belts. But their chief mining tool was clearly their tails, which they whacked against the rock walls with whoops and trills, knocking loose little falls of rubble, which they panned through and picked through and poked through. One hopped over to the wall nearest September and planted his feet to give it a good thrashing.

"Halloo!" the kangaroo barked, startled by the sudden presence of a girl in a ball gown sprawled in the way of a nice thick vein of peridot. "You came out of the wall." He looked very flummoxed by this, his gentle face scrunching up with worry. *Something* was not right, not right at all.

"Yes." September did not know what else to say. She realized all at once that she was alone—A-Through-L and Saturday and Aubergine had not made it through with her. Her skin prickled with cold.

"Are you a ruby? Or a tourmaline?" The kangaroo did not seem hopeful.

"Certainly not," September said, and peeled herself up off the floor, brushing pebbles and torn bits of paper from her skirt. She pulled the wine-colored coat close around her, shivering a little. She felt safer with its thick sash tied tight.

"Well, if it's work you want, I'm sure we could find you an ax and a shovel and a pan. But this is my seam, see, and you . . . well, you can't have it. I don't mean to be rude. It's only that I've forgotten my mother, and peridot—that's the pretty green spangly stuff you're, er, sitting on—is frightfully good for motherly memories."

"However could you forget your mother?" September asked.

The kangaroo adjusted the brown straps of his harness. His gold-pan reflected the pale green-yellow seam flowing fiery around them. "I'm a Järlhopp," he said proudly. "We're born without memories. They say all babies are innocent, but no one holds a candle to a wee Järlhopp. If not for my Clutch, I wouldn't even remember my own name. Which is Gneiss, if you wondered." Gneiss lifted up the pendant of his long necklace. Dozens of hundred candy-colored stones clung together in a spiky, glittering globe.

September smiled shyly. "But I know about Järlhoppes!"

she said. "Mr. Map told me that they keep their memories on a chain around their necks. One called Leef taught him to make maps when they were in prison together. It seems so long ago now!"

"I don't know a Leef, but that's no shock. I might have known her, and forgotten all about it, if I didn't have a bit of seam nearby to remember her for me." Gneiss nodded his azure head toward the wall. "That's a seam, there. A thick thread of peridot running through the black earth. It's what keeps the world together, you know. That's why they're called seams. Stitches in stone, hemming up the underside of everything. Without them, everything would just fall apart. But down here, in the deep, the jewels are more than the pretty baubles you find near the surface. They're memories— the memories of the earth, hardened and polished by centuries of brooding and dreaming and worrying. A Järlhopp's memories are so small next to the memory of all the whole earth! Ours fill up only the tiniest cracks and flaws in the crystal. See, this here's full of earthy memories of continental drift and megafauna—but the flaw there? That's the first boomer who broke my heart, Märl." The Järlhopp pointed to a sharp dark-red shard in his Clutch. It had a creamy pale flaw in its center. "He ran off with a centaur and threw away the girasol stone that meant me and all his family in the mines, our mushroom and sorrowgrass suppers on stone tables, under stone lanterns. So he'd never even think to come back, see. If you said my name to him he wouldn't even know the G was silent. But I remember how to say his name. If I press his shard to my heart I can live it again as often as I like. But you have to have the right sort of stone. Peridot for mothers, girasol for lovers, sapphire for sadness, and garnet for joy."

"But what if someone took your necklace? It's so fragile!"

"I don't mind telling you we have to be careful—our Being-Careful stone is one of the first we get, a nice fat pearl. But mining is hard work, and sometimes the Clutch gets knocked about, like mine did when I forgot my mother. I know I forgot her because I have a topaz for my father and a bloodstone each for my brothers, and they all know I had a mother, so I must have. Now I'm after a good knuckle of peridot so I can recognize her again."

"Gneiss, did anyone else come in before me? From the wall, I mean. One would look like a great black dragon, and one like a boy with black skin and blue swirls all over him, and one is a very quiet Dodo."

Gneiss smiled, which looked very odd indeed on a kangaroo. "Little ruby, if I didn't cut out a knob of onyx for Remembering Strangers, I wouldn't know it to tell you if the Queen herself came parading through. You have to dig new stones for new memories, and that right quick. I try to only do it for the best ones—the times that please me the most or hurt me the most."

September had been holding on to all three of them when she tripped into the Monaciello's book, she was sure of it. Perhaps they were only late. They'd be along, wouldn't they? She leaned into the rough stone wall, trying to listen for the footsteps of a Wyverary.

"I do wish that I could hold on to my memories like that," September sighed into the flaming green seam. "I forget things all the time. But if I had a Clutch and I remembered to be careful, I'd never forget anything! I'd be able to look just once at my lessons and remember everything perfectly. When I'm lonesome, I'd just press it to my heart and live my mother singing me to sleep over again!"

Gneiss shrugged. "Well, there's a good shallow vein of sunstone just down the way. I can smell the Topside on you— sunstone would be best for a young thing with not too many years to wedge in. And who knows? Maybe your friends fell out of a different bit of cavern! You never know. Let's have a look on both accounts."

September bit her lip and considered whether it was better to wait and hope they came kicking and hollering out of the wall as she had, or search for them deeper in the mine. The hard strange voice woke up inside her again, urging her to keep going, not to stop. This time she listened to it and ran skipping alongside the Järlhopp through the dark kaleidoscope of the mine, trying to keep up with his powerful hops. Other Järlhoppes waved as they went by, and the seams ran through the earth like fine colorful handwriting, but no Marid leapt out to kiss her, no gentle Dodo appeared next to her as if out of nowhere.

Finally they came to a gnarled, thick knot of deep orange stone with coppery sparks leaping hot and bright inside it. Gneiss looked down at her, shining his pearly miner's lantern in her eyes.

"Halloo!" the blue kangaroo exclaimed. "Who are you? Are you a ruby or a tourmaline?"

"No, I'm September! You brought me here to find my friends and make me a Clutch!"

Gneiss looked dubious. "Was it a very long time ago that we set off? Have we had adventures on a wild rocky ocean? Have we fought alabaster octopi together, or crossed axes with the emerald ogre?"

"No! It was only a few moments ago! We've not come half a mile!"

"Ah, my apologies, little ruby. I've only a little space after a thing happens to snatch up a gem for it and add it to the Clutch. If I forgot to do it, well, I've quite forgotten that I forgot to do it, not to mention forgetting the thing I should have remembered not to forget!"

September could not help herself. "Is there really an emerald ogre somewhere?"

"Oh, yes! Her name is Mathilda. She lives up in the north section of the mine and makes a lovely spinach stew. She's a fierce thing for manners, though! If your *please* is out of place, she'll thump you one. I was making you a Clutch? Well, let's have at it. You've got to get your ore yourself, though. No good if I do it." Gneiss handed over his pickaxe—it was heavy, but not so heavy September could not lift it. Gneiss waggled his huge tail experimentally.

"Be ready with the ax when I swing!"

Gneiss swung. His cerulean tail whacked hard into the cavern wall and a shower of dark rock and shimmering gemstone came bursting down on them both. September swung her axe, breaking up the big pieces into smaller ones, and smaller still, until she'd uncovered a rough fist of sunstone of just the size to wear. Gneiss reached into his pouch and came up with a chain. He bit a hole in the jewel with an enormous sharp tooth and strung it onto the chain and around September's neck.

"Now, that'll hold only everything that's happened to you till now. I'll stick on a nice chunk of heliotrope to keep

THE MINES OF MEMORY

you going for the next few days. But if you want to remember more, you'll have to get more seam for it, mind me?"

September nodded, trying to imagine where she'd get jewels back home. They didn't make ration cards for diamonds. Gneiss licked an oblong scrap of green jewel with golden streaks and shoved it through the center of the sunstone. It pierced the gem as if it were a marshmallow and stuck solidly there.

"September!" cried a voice further down the mine shaft.

September turned toward it so quickly she nearly got her legs tangled up in each other. Saturday! She ran down the shaft after the voice, Gneiss thumping along behind her. Following two thin thready veins of amethyst and gold, she darted past carts and rock piles until she found them, all three of her lost friends, sticking half out of the wall of the mine.

Saturday had his head and arms free and was trying to push himself all the way out, the way you might push yourself out of a wet pair of trousers. A-Through-L and Aubergine had gotten buried in the cavern up to their necks, their snouts jutting out of the wall like hunting trophies. September grabbed Saturday by the arms and hauled. She pulled as hard as she could, and then just a little harder, but he would not budge.

"We lost you in the book," Saturday panted with effort. "And we must have been too slow climbing down, because the whole thing closed up right around us! Maybe the door went off into another volume while we were inside." He shuddered. "Oh!" he suddenly cried, and then blushed slightly blue with embarrassment. "I forgot."

The Marid shut his eyes and opened his hands, turning his palms up. "I wish for all of us to be free of the wall," he said calmly.

And they were. The Wyverary and the Night-Dodo stood next to Saturday in a neat little line.

"But you haven't been wrestled!" September cried.

"I told you, I don't have to do that kind of awfulness here," Saturday shrugged. "I just Want it badly enough, and it happens!"

"Then why can't I just want things badly enough? Why can't I just *want* us to the Sleeping Prince, or even better, *want* to know how to put myself back together with my shadow?" September kept herself from stamping her foot in frustration, but only barely. How could things be so easy for him and so hard for her?

Aubergine fluffed her violet-green feathers. "Because you haven't got a shadow," she said. "You can't do magic."

A-Through-L nodded. "You'd never notice what was wrong unless you tried something really savage or magical, but the wild bits of you have been shrinking up and blowing away bit by bit. It's only that you don't really need them in

Nebraska. You probably just thought you were growing up. It's an easy mistake."

"I think I ought to say what parts of me I need and where!"

"But it's all right, September! We can do any sort of magic *to* you. We'll help. Anything you need done, just ask your boys, and we'll be ready with a wish or a spell."

September frowned. She did not feel like anything had gone missing inside her. But hadn't she wondered if staying shadowless so long would cause any trouble? Didn't it make sense that if Fairyland-Above was losing its magic to Fairyland-Below, she would lose something, too, having lost her shadow before anyone?

"I shall do what needs doing myself, thank you," September said finally. "And I'll ask you kindly to stop telling me what I need and what will be wonderful just as soon as I agree with you! And *most importantly* to stop turning me into things I didn't ask to be and kissing me when I didn't ask to be kissed! You stole my First Kiss from me, Saturday. I haven't forgiven you just because I haven't had a shout about it yet. I've been busy! But I think I'm the only one who gets a say about when I get kissed or turned into a beast! Not that it wasn't nice to be a Wyvern or a Fairy. I'm not saying it wasn't nice." September could not help adding the apology.

But she would absolutely not go meekly along relying on everyone else to fight and speak and wish for her. She would not have things done to her when she could do them on her own! She'd done plenty—and shouldn't Ell know that? Perhaps only her own dear red Ell would understand that she could not just let everyone else do her work for her. Her mother did not just hope some other man would come along and take up the work that needed doing in her factory. She did it herself, and so would September. She reached into the pocket of the wine-colored coat and came out with her magic ration book.

"Take me to the Prince!" she said plainly and loudly, before anyone could protest. September ripped off one of the ration cards. With a wisp of green smoke, it vanished in her hand, leaving a sharp smell of sunny grasses and warm winds behind.

A new shaft opened up in the mine, just in front of them, breaking the amethyst and gold veins in two. It gaped wide, leading down into blackness. September looked back at all of them defiantly.

"Are you all coming? Or do you want to sit around jawing about nonsense?" She remembered her manners and turned to the Järlhopp. "Thank you kindly, Gneiss. I shall not forget you, I am sure!"

"Halloo!" cried Gneiss. His blue fur rippled. "Are you a ruby? Or a tourmaline?"

September bent down and picked up a tiny fleck of sunstone. "Remember me, Gneiss. If you want to. It's up to you. Everyone should get to choose their own way, and that's all I mean by yelling. But I shall choose to remember you, and it would be nice if it went both ways. That's how it generally goes in my country." *But does it?* September thought. *If a body is hurt, they try to forget the person who hurt them and never think about the pain again. Remembering aches, like when I remember my father. It'd be so much easier to never wonder about him. I'm sure he remembers my face, but it's hard to remember his, when he's been gone so long! Perhaps memory is a thing that everyone involved has to work at, like stitching up a big quilt out of everything that ever happened to you.*

The Järlhopp took the stone happily, and stuck it onto his Clutch between a piece of jade and a tiger's eye. September hugged him quickly, and then, rather more terrified than she was willing to let anyone see, jumped into the mine shaft with both feet.

"Good-bye, September," said the blue kangaroo.

The others, after only a moment's shocked pause, jumped in after her.

CHAPTER XIII

EVEN THE FLOWERS ARE DUCHESSES

*In Which September Loses Her Temper, Learns Something
Rather Important About Magic-Handling,
and Dances Very Nicely Indeed*

Somewhere in the mine shaft everything flipped upside down so that when September emerged into an empty field, she sprang up out of a stone well and landed neatly on her feet. Saturday and Aubergine shot up after her like cannonballs. A-Through-L got stuck briefly, but with a little wriggling and squashing, popped out in a tangle of dark claws, snarled whiskers, and a slightly kinked tail.

The field spread around them, quite bare and lonely. Black soil ran on in every direction, freshly turned. Here and there, green shoots poked sleepily out of the soil, so pale they shone nearly white. September peered into the gloaming.

"Is that a house? I think it's a house," she said doubtfully. She strode off after it, however, still smarting somewhat and eager to show that she was just as wild as she wanted to be, whether here or in Nebraska. Aubergine hooted mournfully, for she had not done anything to offend, but still worried that she might have somehow gotten lumped in with the others and was making herself quite wretched over it. She even tried to fly and distance herself from them, only succeeding in a few long, respectable jumps. Saturday and A-Through-L followed gamely. But something made September stop a good ways off from the place. A chill rippled over her skin.

It was a house, though a terribly shabby one. It might once have been grand—cupolas like great splintered heads of garlic squatted on top of graying wooden towers. Its clapboards and its window frames and its big cellar doors were all the same gray, petrified color. September knew just that shade of gray from every abandoned farmhouse on the prairie. Every ruined corn patch that had gone to dust and sent its people packing just about the time September was busy being born.

In fact, the whole place looked as though someone had turned the lights off back home. It could have been any farmstead for a hundred miles around September's house, only painted black and empty and starlit.

A wind picked up, and September knew that sound, too, the howling, hollow noise of the night rushing through an empty broken house. She could not see the crystal moon anymore—tall, jagged hills hunched up on the north end of the field, and only the light of the wired stars lit that lonely place.

"I don't think anyone lives here," Aubergine said softly.

"But I used my ration card," September insisted. "We have to be going the right way. This should be the Prince's house."

"Don't worry, darling," Saturday said, putting a warm hand on her shoulder. "I can wish us aright." He paused, biting his violet-black lip. "But only if you want me to. We can even wrestle for it, if it will make you feel better."

September ignored him for a moment. "Maybe we're at the bottom of the world already. It's certainly barren and empty enough." She did not like to think of Prince Myrrh in that dreadful house. Even if he was wicked or lazy or brutish, no one should have to sleep forever in a place like that.

The door of the farmhouse cracked open. The owner of

the house peered out, and then came into the gilded, misty light. It was a man, a tall man with skinny legs and arms. As the starlight dappled the roof and the furrows and the man, September saw that he was not just skinny; his long fingers were straw-colored bones with no skin on them. Stringy roots fell in fringes from his sleeves. The naked bones of his feet gleamed greenish and strong. His suit peeled and crinkled, made of delicate purple onionskins.

His head was an enormous golden onion with no eyes or mouth.

As they watched him, the Onion-Man began to dance, first to one side, then to another, holding his arms above his head and bringing them down with a sharp sudden snap, moving his hips to some unseen onion-music. He ducked his golden head and threw it back, spinning around three times before stopping to sniff the air, though he had no nose to sniff with.

A rumbling filled the night. A grinding, growling sound, growing near. Aubergine ducked behind September, who put her arms around the bird's neck without thinking. A-Though-L looked down in surprise. Perhaps he expected, being very large and good for hiding behind, that September would turn to him for comfort. But she was bigger than she had been, and the older, wiser part of her thought first of comforting the Night-Dodo before comforting herself.

But when the Alleyman's truck came around the skinny, stony black road they had not even seen winding around the farm's crumbly edges, poor September did inch nearer—only a little, for she had not yet forgiven him—to the shadow of her Wyvery. She tried to be brave, tried not to be afraid of that glittering heap of candy-cane lights rolling toward them. Ell put his long blue-violet tail around girl and bird, coiling it tight. They kept silent and hunched down, holding their breath. Ell's and Saturday's shadowy bodies faded into the night, and Aubergine had already gone half invisible with standing so still and quiet. Only September stood out in the lightless field, in her wine-colored coat and her copper-colored dress.

The Onion-Man saw what had come for him. He danced anyway. Up went his arms, out went his graceful long bony legs, bending at the knee, pointing at the toe. He made a ballet dancer's leap, and then spread his skeleton's arms wide, nodding his onion-skull from side to side. The truck stopped. The dark door of the cab opened, and the red cap floated out, its twin feathers like knives stuck into the scarlet felt. The Onion-Man kept dancing, his steps growing more frantic, his leaps higher and more desperate.

"He's going to take his shadow, isn't he?" whispered September.

No one said anything. They all knew. Saturday and Ell stared at their feet.

The red hat bobbed and nodded in time with the onion-man, dancing with him. In his invisible hands, the Woeful Wimble and the Sundering Siphon gleamed. With every turn and pirouette, the red hat came closer. But September thought there was a reluctance to its movement. It approached slowly, though it didn't need to; it dipped and shook from side to side as though the invisible head beneath it were shaking *no*.

The hard strange voice stood up inside September once more. It stood very tall and straight in her chest, and the voice also said, *No*. September let go of Aubergine and pushed Ell's tail out of the way. She marched across the furrows and the crumbly dry soil, terribly afraid and terribly angry.

"You stop it!" she cried, and the onion-dancer stopped. The red hat stopped. They both turned to look at her in dumbfounded amazement. "He's never done anything to you, Mr. Red Hat, and that makes you a bully. Don't you touch him!" The red hat did not move so much as a feather. "Oh, I know I'm not terrifying like you and I can't order people about like Halloween, but I'll have you know my dress is very fierce indeed, and I'm mad enough to burst! I'm the one who put a stop to the Marquess, and she scared me much worse than you do, so if you know what's good for you, you'll just turn around and go back where you came from!" This was not true at all, but it sounded very fine, so September stuck by it. The red hat looked back toward his truck uncertainly. Then it turned back to September. She could almost feel the invisible body beneath it staring at her. She felt suddenly ridiculous in her ball gown and her fine coat and the great jewel at her throat and her blue-and-lilac-streaked hair. But she would not let the Alleyman make her feel small. She would not.

And then she felt her Ell's great strong presence beside her, and Saturday slipped his hand in hers. Oh. *Oh.* They would not abandon her. Of course, they would not. How silly she had been. They were her friends—they had always been. Friends can go odd on you and do things you don't like, but that doesn't make them strangers.

"Oh, I hate you!" September cried, her voice deep and loud with the strength of her folk around her. "Get out of here, you dreadful thing!"

And, somehow, for some unfathomable reason, in the face of them all, the Alleyman did. The red hat recoiled from her like a struck animal. It shook from side to side as if trying to clear its invisible head. The red hat dropped suddenly, and September knew, somehow, that the Lutin under that cap had fallen to his knees in some private trouble. It trembled below her gaze for a long moment.

Then, without a word, it simply rose and floated back

inside the truck. The Alleyman's truck ambled away down the skinny stony road, and September tried to calm her hammering heart. Aubergine came slowly into sight, the wired stars reflecting on her huge beak. The Onion-Man stood, for once, quite still. September tried to guess his thoughts, but his faceless head offered no sign.

Suddenly, she felt a lurching commotion in the pockets of the wine-colored coat. September reached in to see what was the matter. The flaps of the coat rustled and shook as the three small onions she had taken so long ago from the Upside-Downs leapt past her hands and out of the coat, landing joyfully on the ground.

Three little lavender-and-yellow onions rolled to the dancer. They ringed him in a circle, rolling through the dark earth, spinning with pleasure. The onion-headed man bent down and put his bone-hands to them, full of affection, brushing the tuft of onionskin at their heads. They rolled over like round puppies so that he could stroke their plump bellies. Finally, they bounced up and toddled into the gray house.

"I didn't know they were yours," September said by way of apology.

The Onion-Man bent down, for he was awfully tall. He took September's cheeks in his skeletal hands and pressed his onion-face to her forehead. September's eyes filled up with burning tears—as they always did at home when she chopped onions for Sunday soup. The Onion-Man began to move his feet from side to side again, dropping his shoulders and fanning his fingers against her cheeks, tapping out a rhythm. She found that though bones were certainly a little unsettling, they were warm and smelled like growing things and not dead things at all.

"You seem very nice, Mr. Onion," she said. "But I do wish I knew why my ration card sent me here. I said I wanted to get to the Prince, and I don't suppose you are anything of the sort."

"But he is a Prince, a bit," said Saturday. "The way Teatime is a Duke and his wife's a Vicereine. The onions love him—and look!"

Beneath the Onion-Man's tapping feet, tiny pale green shoots were wriggling up out of the dark soil, swaying a little to the pattern of his dance.

"You have to be very specific when it comes to magic," A-Through-L said sheepishly. "You must say things as carefully as you can. Magic is like a machine that only does exactly what you tell it to do. So you have to speak to it in a way it can understand. And magic only understands you if you spell it out slowly. And use small words. You didn't tell the card which Prince or how quickly you wanted to go. For all we know this *is* the shortest path—or it thought you meant our fragrant friend here! Or perhaps the Alleyman is some sort of Prince, too. The word *Prince* is very open-ended. You can't really trust anything that far down in the alphabet."

"I do believe everyone in Fairyland-Below is royalty!" September exclaimed. "Queens and Princes and Vicereines and Emperors—it's like visiting Europe!"

Aubergine nodded. "That's how it is in underworlds. And more so, the deeper you go. Even the flowers are Duchesses, in the deepest dells. Even the raspberries are Khans. In the beginning of the beginning, all the Kings and Queens of Fairyland came from Below. When they needed an Empress or a Tsar, they went to a certain frozen lake in the Hoarfrost Desert, cut a hole in the ice, and sunk a silver pole they called the Kingfisher into the frigid water. All through Fairyland-Below, we would see the great hook descending toward us, and the bait on the hook would tell us what sort of ruler they had in mind. A crown of rowan branches for a Fairy Queen, of obsidian for a Dark Lord, of iron for a Human Hero. It could be anything. So all of us had to be ready. Any day, someone could be called to duty. Everyone had to practice princely ways."

The onion-dancer did not especially seem to care about Aubergine's history lesson. He pulled at September's hands, lifting his arm to twirl her underneath. He prodded her to dance with him, and extended one long arm to invite the others, too. Saturday was already sweeping his arms overhead and making the most curious shapes with his slender limbs, grinning with delight. His eyes flowed with tears, too—they all wept, and laughed at their weeping, for the onion-fumes grew stronger the more excitedly he danced. Ell rocked from hind leg to hind leg, curling and uncurling his tail in an elegant motion. Even Aubergine, her feathers blushing a frosty shade, fluffed up her feathers, flared her wings, and began to hop in an odd but not unlovely dance.

"Come on, September," pleaded Saturday, and the Onion-Man pleaded, too, in his silent way. He was happy, she could see. He had been spared. And though she was deathly shy of dancing, though she could not bring herself to at the Revel, there in the dark, September joined the little tribe in a silent, joyful dance. They held hands and spun in circles, laughing and crying and jumping and somersaulting like little children. And everywhere the onion-dancer stepped, shoots came up out of the ground, growing and curlicuing and corkscrewing upward until the five of them danced in an onion forest, the tops of the trees unfurling strange leaves to catch the starlight.

And through the great onion-trunks, September thought

she saw, only for a moment, a figure all in silver slipping through the wood. She called after it, but it did not pause, so pale and brief it might almost never have been there.

"Oh, tell me you know the way to the bottom of the world," whispered September into what she guessed might be the Onion-Man's ear as he lifted her up at the height of the dance, breathless and flushed, spinning her around and around. The lights of the underworld blurred in her vision.

He set her down and pointed with one long fleshless arm toward the weather-beaten cellar doors.

CHAPTER XIV

THE OAT KNIGHT'S APOLOGY

*In Which September Encounters an Old Enemy,
but Finds Him Rather Nice After All, Offers Aubergine
Her Freedom, and Ends Up in a Bad Way*

September climbed up onto a dune covered in salt-crusted pink grass. She pulled Aubergine by the talon out of the cellar passage and closed the door behind Ell as he shook his scales like a wet dog. On this side, the door was a slab of shining mahogany with a neat brass knocker. The roaring of the sea greeted them all, a sharp marine wind rippling through the coral-colored dune grass. Big, heavy silver bees buzzed sleepily around a few giant emerald-colored flowers clotted with black pollen. Holding her dark hair back from her face, September looked around for anyone or anything—and saw only a heaving, smoky, frost-colored sea below, a shade just like moonlight, its waves swelling up and rolling into shore, where they crashed against boulders and a long dark beach.

She shrugged and headed up over the dunes. *I'm sure to find someone eventually,* she told herself. *Every patch of Fairyland-Below seems topful of folk!* As they walked, September took Saturday's hand in hers and squeezed. *In a day or two, I may forgive you for the kiss,* she wanted the squeeze to say. *So long as you stand by me always as you did back there. I want to think you're my Saturday just as much as the one aboveground. I want to believe it. So I shall, as best as I am able.*

He squeezed back.

They saw the village as they slid and slipped down the face of a dune patchworked with wild licorice and wintergreen, the perfume of it all as heady as the onion-fumes had been. A ways off from the beach, where a few gentle hills protected it from the sea-wind, several bungalows crowded around a tremendous hearth full of flaming driftwood logs. As they drew closer, they got a better look at the bungalows, all built of braided leather like horses' reins. On top of each, a great saddle perched as a stout roof, the pommel dappled with sea moss. The window frames were big silver stirrups tipped in spurs, and over each door a golden horseshoe shone like a piece of the sun.

No one moved between the houses or tended the fire, but as September and her gang stepped onto the sandy meadow, a creature leapt out from behind a wind-warped whitethorn tree and drew a rough bone knife from his belt.

It was a Glashtyn.

His soft black horse's head gazed on them with limpid eyes, his mane wild, wind-tossed, decorated with sharp, jagged shells. The rest of him was naked—a fact September had long since ceased to be particularly embarrassed about—his knees and forearms only sheathed in silver armor. His skin matched the color of the sea.

The Glashtyn made ready to bar them with his knife—though the green-blue flames like pilot lights in his eyes would have stopped them quite handily. But something flickered in those flames, something like recognition. He squinted at her.

"It's you, isn't it?" the Glashtyn whispered. "Yes, it must be. I remember you. Do you remember me?"

He wore a silver ring through his equine nose like a bull. September tried to remember this exact Glashtyn. The Järlhopp's Clutch warmed against her chest. A memory pricked up in the back of her mind.

"I . . . I think so," she whispered back, and Saturday's shadow stirred against her. "I think you took my shadow one day a long time ago. On the river." September tried not to let him see her tremble. He had been terrible on that day, frightening and violent, and she knew the feel of that bone knife.

The Glashtyn bent his noble head and all his fierceness softened. He spoke quietly and kindly. "That I did, human girl. If you would know me better, I will tell you my name is the Oat Knight. I see in your bearing I was terrible to you. I was terrible then because it was my job to be terrible. I aimed for terribleness, and I like to think I often caught it! But the Hollow Queen, bless her name, let me fold up my terribleness at last and put it in a steamer trunk at the bottom of my spirit, quite locked up. You know, before the Marquess press-ganged us to pull the ferry, I was a peaceful boy who wanted to be a poetry farmer. I suppose that sounds strange to you. It's such easy work down here—hardly a Knight's profession. You hoe a blue field and give it a bit of water and moonshine, and poems just come popping out of the earth like winter squash." The Glashtyn snorted gently, reminding himself to make good conversation. "I hear it is harder, where you come from."

September thought of the poems she had been made to

write in class, the hours she had spent trying to find a rhyme for this or that thing. She liked poetry, liked how, in a good poem, the words fit together like a puzzle. But she had not, in her estimation, ever managed a good poem. Hers came out fitting together more like a broken faucet and an angry milk-goat.

"Harder, yes," she admitted.

The Oat Knight nodded. "This I have been told."

Several lithe, young horse-headed boys peeked out of the rein-houses. They stepped nimbly onto the sand and stared at her, standing stiff and tall. The Oat Knight put a cold, blue-gray hand on her arm.

"Come," he said. "We wronged you. Break bread with us and we will mend."

The Oat Knight led them to the bonfire, and the other Glashtyn brought out bowls of clean, fresh water, salads of alfalfa and apples, lumps of sugar dotting oatmeal soaked in whiskey and cream, thick, lush seaweed and round, firm fern heads. Inside the oatmeal mash hid a little roasted puffin, glistening with brown fat. The Glashtyn sat cross-legged on the ground and ate with their fingers—which should have seemed vulgar but instead looked rather nice, when they did it. September even saw a few Glashtyn girls, with rings in their velvety ears rather than their noses. Aubergine enjoyed the food greatly, but she kept looking out to sea, as if she expected something to appear over the horizon. Saturday ate with relish. Ell only sampled the vegetables.

The Oat Knight introduced the others: the Millet Knight and the Corn Knight and the Barley Knight and the Apple Knight and the Bean Knight, and the mares too, called the Buckwheat Knight and the Rice Knight and the Rue Knight. They shook her hand one by one, putting their hands over their hearts as they did so. After supper, the Oat Knight gave them each a clay cup of appley drinking chocolate, and they all walked together onto the dark sand beach. The crystal moon was visible again, showing a bold V on its milky face. Long bleached-wood piers stuck out into the moon-colored sea. September watched the waves break against the shore; they shattered into a foam of tiny black diamonds.

"I chose, you know," September said, embarrassed by the silence and the deference the Glashtyn Knights showed her. "I chose to do it. I could have let you take the Pooka girl and kept my mouth shut—though perhaps I couldn't have. I'm not very good at keeping my mouth shut! But, anyway, you mustn't feel so bad about it. I made the choice."

"But we made you choose," the Oat Knight said wretchedly. "And we meant it selfishly. A Knight should not be so selfish. But we hated the ferry so. We hated the hauling and the endless work of it! We wanted to end it. We would have done anything to end it."

"But it is ended!" Ell said. "You can be happy now!"

September had not thought a horse could blush, but the Oat Knight did, his whole face heavy and hot with shame. How could she have feared this boy so? He was hardly older than herself!

"We are free of the Marquess now. We no longer pull the ferry—we no longer have to. You must not think we are ungrateful. We know what it cost. September, look there and see the emblems of our gratitude."

September looked. It took a long time to see it, like a half-finished puzzle whose picture you cannot guess until it snaps into focus all at once. The pleasant hills that guarded the Glashtyn village were not hills at all, but vast, heavy chains, grown over with grass and moss and kelp, with little hardy trees growing up out of their green links.

Pale scars shone on the Oat Knight's slender chest where once he had borne those very chains. The Knight touched them lightly.

"Someday, perhaps, I may sow my poems as I wished to, because of you."

"Then what's wrong?" September asked. "Why do you

seem so glum, when you have your own lovely town by the sea?"

"I mislike telling a lady that we practiced deceit," the Glashtyn said. She rather liked his formal way of talking. It was how a Knight ought to talk. "In all things we prefer to play fair. Even Fairies obey the letter of their pretty laws."

"I forgive you," September said kindly, even though she had no idea what he meant. But forgiving seemed to be the sort of thing a Fairy Bishop ought to do when faced with a humble Knight.

"We meant to take her down and use her most selfishly," confessed the Oat Knight. "Your shadow, I mean. Our Hollow Queen. You cannot blame us. We needed her, you see. Because one of the rules of Fairyland-Below is *Do Not Steal Queens. A Girl in the Wild Is Worth Two in Chains*. And you gave her to us. Not completely freely, but *mostly* freely, and one has to work with what one has these days. We said we meant to put her at the head of our parades—and we did. I am sure you have seen it. It is the thing to see in Fairyland-Below, the gorgeous Revels she invents night by night. But we also meant for her to go deep, as deep into Fairyland-Below as anyone has ever gone, and find something. Something valuable to us. Something we have longed for. For at the bottom of Fairyland-Below the Prince of the Underneath sleeps. Prince Myrrh,

Who Never Wakes. Princes do that, sometimes, you know. Fall asleep for years at a time."

"I do know, actually," September said.

The Oat Knight did not seem particularly surprised. "Everyone knows that, I suppose. I did not mean to be prideful in assuming you did not, my lady. We meant for Halloween to do what must be done. To find the Sleeping Prince and wake him up for us. But she didn't want to do it. She said, 'I don't want to marry any silly Prince who can't even set his own alarm clock. I shall be Queen for my own sake, and if he doesn't like it, he can have a couple of cups of coffee and come see me about it.'"

"Good for her," said Saturday, and September privately agreed. She did not like the notion that her shadow was just a tool for the benefit of a boy neither of them had ever heard of. But then, she meant to use that very boy as a tool for her own use, didn't she? She looked down at her drinking chocolate, and further, to the waves churning beneath the pier.

"Yes, well, we didn't begrudge her," the Oat Night continued. "Shadows own a wildness we do not. And you defeated the Marquess, anyway, for which we owe gratitude." The Glashtyn saluted her, putting his hand over his heart. "So we didn't strictly need the Prince so much, to go up and free us from her. We might have liked to be the ones to do it ourselves, of course. We don't like to have to say a girl from Away saved us. But that's no matter, in the end. Everything worked itself out, and for a long while Halloween made things such fun that we didn't really mind. We asked if we could just *call* her the Sleeping Prince, to satisfy prophecy and make it all neat and tidy. She said we could, if we didn't mind being thumped. But . . . oh, we were not as strong as our Queen! We got so *tired,* dancing and feasting every night. We needed a rest. So we came here and built our village. We meant to stay for a summer and return to Tain in the fall."

"But you couldn't," said Aubergine. September jumped a little. The Night-Dodo could be so quiet, September was always startled when she spoke. "No matter how you tried to remember how much you liked it in Tain, or that you really did mean to go back, it just slipped away from you. There was such a lot of good grasses and birds to eat, and the moonset made you so sleepy and happy."

"Yes," sighed the Oat Knight. "You understand."

Aubergine clucked lightly. "This is the Forgetful Sea. Over and away in the middle of it is Walghvogel, my home. The sea breeze and the spray makes the mind sleepy, though it's nothing compared to a dunk in the stuff."

"We do *mean* to go back," said the Oat Knight plaintively.

"The Revels were so beautiful. And Halloween loved us specially."

"Of course, you mean to," Aubergine said comfortingly. "It's not your fault at all."

"If we're so close, Aubergine," September said gently, "do you want to go home? I have said it before, but you don't really belong to me at all. I've got terribly fond of you, but you can get away home right here and now. I can go on, we can all go on, and we'll be all right."

The Night-Dodo looked out over the moony waves. "Without a boat, I would not even know my name by the time I got there," she sighed. "I suppose I could build a Quiet Ship, given enough time. And there would be time here. I could resist the spray for long enough." Her plum feathers ruffled in the breeze. "But I don't want to go back," she said with a savage determination September had never heard her quiet friend use. "They traded me to Glasswort Groof, and though I understand they had a desperation, and though Glasswort looked after me decently, they still used me as money, and I can't forgive it. I am not a coin. Besides, I want to go back to Tain when this is all done. I want to go back to Shearcoil and study Quietly, to become the Quietest of all, so that whenever a young thing aims to be a Physickist they will say, 'I want to be just like Aubergine the Night-Dodo,

Mummy! Wasn't she the very best and most powerful Physickist of all of them?' And their mothers will have to say, 'Yes, yes, she was.' "

Once more September marveled that even the Dodo knew what she wanted to be when she was grown. She simply could not think what she herself might do. September expected that destinies, which is how she thought of professions, simply landed upon one like a crown, and ever after no one questioned or fretted over it, being sure of one's own use in the world. It was only that somehow her crown had not yet appeared. She did hope it would hurry up.

September hugged Aubergine, who put her feathery head against the wine-colored coat. "I am glad not to lose you," September said. She turned back to the Glashtyn, her thoughts spinning up to something, though she did not quite know what. "If you love Halloween so and she loves you, why have you not forgotten about the Prince entirely? You live in a forgetting place! I'm only curious, you understand. But the thing of it is, Myrrh might be no better. If I remember my stories, people only tend to sleep that long if they're very beautiful and very stupid and mess about with things they shouldn't, like apples and spindles and such." But she remembered what Avogadra said about the field cast by the

Prince, and how folk would want to talk about him. The Glashtyn certainly did.

September frowned. Everything had rollicked along so fast she had hardly had a chance to consider much of it. But now the considering broke over her like a wave. "It seems rather silly to put all your eggs in one basket, King-wise. Just because he was born to it doesn't mean he'll be a good King, or do what you want. He'll be a real walking, talking person, and maybe he'll be bad. Anyone can be bad. And I warn you, in chess, Kings are important pieces, but they are very weak. They can only move a little, and the smart money is never on them to do much at all. Why not just have a revolution? It's easier. Then you can rule yourselves."

The Oat Knight looked shocked. "We *love* our Queen. We don't want her hurt or banished or embarrassed!"

"She is a little bit violent," Ell said by way of explanation.

"Queens are very splendid things!" the Glashtyn insisted.

"They are!" agreed Ell happily.

"How would we count the time without one? How could we have Coronations or Royal Banquets?"

"You could have a Congress," September said sheepishly. It sounded a very strange word down here under the world. "And a President. That's what we have where I come from."

"What sort of crown does a President wear?" the Oat Knight asked dubiously. "Does she know enough riddles to rule a country? Is Congress where she keeps her magic?"

September hid a smile under her hand. "I suppose Congress is where the President keeps magic," she said. "Laws are a bit like magic. They have a lot of complicated words and they can make you do anything they want."

"You can call your Queen a President if it makes you happy." The Oat Knight shrugged. "It's not that we didn't want the Hollow Queen or the Revels. We only wanted *our* Prince back, too. And though we might forget what we mean to do in the future, what we have done wrong in the past sticks to the heart. We took Halloween and meant to use her, as though she were not her own beast who deserved to choose her fate. I wished to give you my confession, September, for you, too, were wronged in our acts. And I have given it." He put his hand over his heart once more.

"Well." September smiled, putting her hand on his arm. "I do forgive you. And I shall make you a present to show that I do: I am going to wake up the Sleeping Prince." September wanted to say, *Just see if I don't,* but the Glashtyn was so noble and formal that she said instead, "I swear it."

A-Through-L and Saturday stared at her. They hadn't known her plan until now, but they had been so loyal and stalwart in the onion-field, that September judged it safe to let the secret slip.

They had reached the end of the pier. It stretched awfully far from the shore, out into deep water, filled with shadowy fish and dark shafts where the light of the crystal moon did not fall.

September smiled at her wonderful friends, in all their colors and bright eyes and gentle ways. "You know, in Fairyland-Above they said that the underworld was full of devils and dragons. But it isn't so at all! Folk are just folk, wherever you go, and it's only a nasty sort of person who thinks a body's a devil just because they come from another country and have different notions. It's wild and quick and bold down here, but I like wild things and quick things and bold things, too."

Saturday put his hand on her shoulder, and they looked out over the underground ocean toward Walghvogel, far off and invisible. September's heart swelled; it beat hot and happy.

"I'm sorry," the Marid said gently. "I mean well. You can't see that now, but you will. It'll all be wonderful, and we'll live together in a house of pumpkin and gold."

"I'll live there, too," said Ell, tears forming in his great dark eyes. "And bring you all the books in all the world."

"What are you talking about?" September laughed.

But she did not get her answer. Instead, before the Oat Knight could cry out or Aubergine could step between them, her beloved Saturday looked longingly into her eyes, kissed her cheek, and pushed her as hard as he could.

September fell, too shocked to scream, into the foaming depths of the Forgetful Sea.

Two Crows

*In Which We Return to Our Friends Wit and Study, Who Discover
a Number of Things Familiar to Us, but Not to Them, and Pass
Over Something Tremendously Alarming Without Noticing It at All*

*W*hat have our two humble crows been doing all this
while, you ask? Have they been lolling about in the
clouds or have they been eaten up by some Fairy beast?

I shall tell you, for we are becoming good friends, you
and I, and friends may tell each other anything.

Wit and Study flew high and wide over Fairyland. They marveled at what they saw passing by below them. A country all of Autumn and one all of Winter, side by side! A herd of bicycles snorting like bison! A city all of silk and cotton and corduroy without any stones at all! In the late, golden afternoon, a whole flock of cast-iron ducks flew past them in a sharp, impressive V, quacking out a merry hello.

"What an extraordinary place this is, Study!" Wit exclaimed to his sister as they passed over a trio of witches brandishing wands that looked very like—but no, it couldn't be!—long wooden kitchen spoons. "I think I should like to live here forever!"

"I wonder if there are any crows here, or if we should be the first?" mused Study. "Perhaps here, in the future, crows will set aside berries and grasshoppers for Uncle Wit and Auntie Study! Wouldn't that be a thing to caw home about?"

Wit laughed, which for a crow is a loud, rough sound. Crows look down a bit on birds that make pretty, trilling sounds. *Pandering to humans,* they say. *Just shameless.*

The pair of them saw the sea coming up ahead over the curve of the world. Violet waves crashed onto a beach covered in glittering golden junk. Their crow-hearts quickened and the shine and shimmer of the shore made them quite drunk. Their bellies rumbled for the very delicious fish that surely swam very close to the surface in this country, having no idea that two sleek and clever hunters were on their way. Wit and Study flew faster still.

They passed over a meadow full of tiny red flowers. Wit darted down to snap up a fat orange-and-green-striped caterpillar, which he shared with his sister. Study hung behind to peck at a tree full of juicy persimmons that did not taste terribly like persimmons at all. When she caught up to her brother, she brought him a thick scrap of fruit to thank him for the caterpillar. Wit and Study cared for each other a great deal. Crows have dark, vast, secret hearts.

Heading off toward the seashore, where with their keen eyes they could already see fish leaping up out of the water and sceptres crusted with jewels spangling on the beach, the crows passed over a curious sight. They did not give it much mind, since this strange foreign place seemed to be full of every mad and nonsensical thing.

It was a street sign, the same official-looking bright green and white that they knew well from perching on them back home in our world. It was an intersection. One sign said, 13TH STREET. One said, FARNUM STREET.

"Why, didn't we eat a mouse on Farnum Street just Sunday last?" Wit cawed.

"Perhaps we're coming around home again," Study sang.

"But not before I get a good scavenge on!" She swooped and circled further toward the sea, faster and faster.

Neither Wit nor Study could possibly have known that only a few hours before, it had looked entirely different, with four signs which read:

TO LOSE YOUR WAY

TO LOSE YOUR LIFE

TO LOSE YOUR MIND

TO LOSE YOUR HEART

CHAPTER XV

TEMPORARY MAD ASSISTANT

In Which September Gets Some Experience with Deep-Sea Diving, Fairy History, and Practickal Physicks

September plunged through the waves.

The Forgetful Sea grew dark quickly and totally once the moonlight ceased to pierce the water. The cold tide pulled at her with biting fingers, yanking her hair back to get at her face, her mouth, her nose, to get inside her and scrub her clean. Still, September was a good swimmer and had managed to get a deep breath before she splashed down. She kicked powerfully up toward the surface, but her strokes only sunk her deeper into the chill ocean. Very soon she would not have enough breath to get back, but the harder she swam, the faster she fell.

The top layer of her skirt, a gauzy golden veil, snapped up swiftly and covered her face. September clawed at it, panicking. But the skirt flattened against her face like a glittering mask, sweeping back over her skull, flowing up into her nose and down into her mouth. She tried to keep her precious breath, but she couldn't help choking on the fabric as it wormed into her. September braced for the end, for the fast inrushing of salt water and then, well, blackness and as little pain as possible, she hoped. Now that she was certainly going to die, September felt reasonably calm about it. She thought of the fish she had caught and killed on that other Fairyland sea. *Poor fish! Perhaps you can laugh at the joke—both of us perished on the sea. Some sailor I turned out to be!*

September squeezed her eyes shut. Any moment, the ocean would swallow her just as she had swallowed that sad little fish so long ago.

But she could breathe! As easily as if she stood on land in the sunshine with a stiff breeze blowing. The skirt masked her face from the cold water, sending blessed air down into her lungs. The rest of the Watchful Dress swelled up around her like a bright balloon, to keep her safe and the pressure of all those heaps of water off her poor bones. It warmed and glowed slightly with the heat it gave to her clammy skin. The wine-colored coat stretched grumpily around the clever, clever dress. *Thank you, Glasswort Groof!* September thought giddily, relief seeping through her along with the warmth.

Far down below her, September saw a pale, fitful light. At first, she could not be sure it was anything but a great fish flitting by, but as she kicked downward toward it, it grew brighter. *Since I can't swim up, I might as well swim down,* she thought. *Avogadra said I'd have to go very far down, sooner or later. Might as well be sooner.*

The Watchful Dress spat out streams of bubbles, sucking in jets of water through the sleeves and propelling her along as best it could. Still, the light lay deep down at the bottom of the Forgetful Sea, and September's arms and legs ached from swimming. *Saturday pushed me.* Her mind insisted on bringing up this subject. She did not want to think about it. *He meant to* kill *me.* September tried to focus on the light, but her thoughts would not obey her. *No, not kill me—make me forget. Forget everything. He said we'd live together in a house of pumpkin and gold—yes, once I couldn't remember why I'd come to Fairyland-Below, or recall Fairyland-Above, or even Omaha and Mother and Father and any reason not to live in Tain and feast every night! How could he? That's as bad as killing, to take away everything a person is.* September had never been betrayed before. She did not even know what to call the feeling in her chest, so bitter and sour.

Poor child. There is always a first time, and it is never the last time.

But why can I remember that he did it? Aubergine said even the sea spray makes the head fuzzy. But I remember it perfectly! And all the rest, too! Why, I have never been so clear about things! The light shone strong and steady now, a warm, ruddy light spilling up from the ocean floor. It lit every part of September in her balloon-dress and deep-water diving skirt. She was falling very fast. The Watchful Dress spat out a powerful jet from her sleeves and her collar.

The light twitched and wriggled in the dark—September could almost touch it. She kicked harder, swimming after it, and in a moment or two, she could see that the light was a lantern, clutched in the tiny hand of a Monaciello.

Avogadra swam ahead, lighting the way, encased in a smart diving suit with a huge bell for her hat. She held her lantern out to show September the path through the sea. *At sorest need, when a brother passed beyond all human aid, we'd come in the dark and show them the way out.* That was what Monaciello did, their oldest instinct and profession. A tear fell onto September's cheek. The skirt of the Watchful Dress drank it up and wicked it away.

Avogadra set down on a sandy, empty seafloor, where a glass hatch rose up before her in a little dome. She knocked three times on it with her lantern, and then the little monk vanished, leaving September alone on the endless wasteland at the bottom of the ocean.

It doesn't matter what Saturday did or Ell, either. I have to keep going. A Monaciello would keep going, no matter what.

The hatch had a glass wheel, like the steering wheel of a great ship. Warm, buttery, rosy light flowed through the frosty, ice-patched glass. September felt sure whatever lay inside the hatch was much better and more friendly to the body of a young girl than the dark freeze of the Forgetful Sea. And besides, Avogadra had brought her here. This was the way out. The way home. September reached out to turn the wheel. The Watchful Dress had made its sleeves into coppery-red gloves for her when it swelled up. And a good thing, too, for even through the gloves the wheel was so cold as to turn any girl-skin that touched it black and dead.

September leaned her weight into the wheel and pushed as hard as she could. It did not even creak. A few shards of ice broke off and floated slowly upward. She tried again, wincing beneath her golden mask. It refused to budge, as stubborn as a pickle jar. She took hold of a glass spoke to go again.

Beside her hands appeared two new ones—silky, strong,

dark-green hands, made of nothing but the long rope-belt of the Watchful Dress. The two of them pushed the wheel, straining. The Dress tore a little, and then a little more.

Whips of wine-colored leather shot out and wrapped tight around the smooth handle of the wheel. The tails of September's coat, feeling much put upon, shoved with such a force that it nearly knocked September off her feet. But the wheel moved. It ground around in a slow circle, ice splintering off of the thing and drifting up through the miles of black water. The wheel groaned and squeaked in protest. September feared the whole sea would rush in once she opened it, but she could not see how else to manage. She lifted the hatch—and the Forgetful Sea minded its manners.

September sighed with her whole self and climbed down into the hole at the bottom of the sea.

September fell, soaking wet, out of the ceiling of a house and landed roughly on a long worktable. It creaked under her weight, but held. Several pieces of metal and ceramic made themselves understood underneath her, poking her spine and her shoulders. Her vision spun, gone hazy with the sudden taste of real air and absence of a half a mile of ocean pressing in on her. A large, greasy hand grabbed hers and pulled her upright. September pulled the sodden Dress off of her face.

A woman looked at her with curiosity, and for an awful, brilliant, dizzying moment, September thought it was her mother. She had a broad, dear face creased with dirt and motor oil, friendly green eyes, and her hair pulled back in a short ponytail, tied up in a kerchief. Her shoulders squared broad and strong, her fingernails black with work grime. She wore a dark-blue boiler suit with lapels that had probably been crisp and dapper before she'd gone crawling through some huge infernal engine to find the erring part. The suit had a name tag that read: *B. Cabbage.*

But it was not her mother. A pair of iridescent wings poked through the woman's work dress, like a luna moth's wings, with long, drooping tips. So much black machine grease and dust and soot clotted those wings that September could not be quite sure what color they were underneath it all. She took a ragged breath as the hope went out of her that somehow her mother was here with her, impossibly, in Fairyland. Machines and pieces of machines, devices, pumps, motors, wheels, and gears and broken bits of bearings, shafts, cranks, and rods crowded the room on every surface. A small path had been cleared through the floor, but no other inch of space spared.

The Fairy reached into her breast pocket and took out a measuring tape. She hooked the business end into September's shoe and snapped out a length, all the way up to the crown of her head. She put her thumb on the measurement and peered at it.

"One hundred and twenty-odd centimeters," B. Cabbage said to herself. "Thirteen years, born under the sign of the Bull, carrying 2.3 kilograms of hardship and sorrow, rather a lot for your age, second seasonal cycle, recent contact with harsh Q-rays. Missing .00021 of total body weight due to shadow surgery, memory excised via Ocean one hour, fifty-two minutes, and seventeen seconds ago, replaced by Järlhopp Clutch one hour, fifty-two minutes and sixteen seconds ago, unit reads thirty-seven percent Gumption by volume."

The Clutch! September's hand flew to Gneiss's pendant hanging around her neck. It pulsed warm in her hand. Saturday hadn't known about it. He hadn't guessed she had such a thing.

"You can tell all that about me from your measuring tape?"

"Well, I use the metric system. It's the only way to get really exact numbers." The Fairy stuck out her calloused hand. "Belinda Cabbage, Mad Scientist and Proprietor."

"September. I'm . . . sorry about your roof." Where had she heard the name Belinda Cabbage before?

Belinda Cabbage looked up over September's head. The ceiling, though showing several alarming blast-scars, seemed no worse for wear and entirely hatchless.

"Looks all right to me." The Fairy shrugged. All the same, she selected a piece of equipment from the table, one cluttered with delicate colorful antennae and ampules of liquid with varying numbers of bubbles in them. Several etched lines marked measurements on their surfaces. B. Cabbage shook it vigorously, then held the device up to the ceiling and waited for the bubbles to settle. The antennae spun—some of them looked like they might have once belonged to a snail or three.

"Wondrous strange!" Cabbage exclaimed. "Where did you say you came from?"

"I didn't, but I came through a hatch at the bottom of the Forgetful Sea."

Belinda Cabbage smacked her free hand against her forehead. It left a sooty print. "My *foot!* I must have left it there! What a menace that ocean is, I tell you what! The Forgetful Sea is miles and miles from here, girl. And then miles more! But I think, I *think* I might have collected samples, oh, it couldn't have been more than a hundred years ago, and it was so much easier to open up a squidhole than to walk all that way. Ugh, who wants to walk when you can tentacle?"

"Squidhole?"

"Oh, well, you'll be familiar with the basic Physicks of wyrmholes I'm sure. You need a frightful lot of equipment to manage one; the grocery list is hideous. Bee-souls, eel-hearts, about six liters of gnome ointment, a hair off of the head of Cutty Soames, and that old pirate *never* falls asleep, no matter how much gloamgrog he drinks—and that's just for the preliminaries! Anyone with a beaker full of sense goes for squidholes instead. You need a Dread Device and several willing field mice, that's all!" She gestured at a bluish, fleshy sort of engine the size of a bread box. It had been shoved absentmindedly on top of a stack of journals and manuals. Under its eerily undulating skin, toothy gears spun. Several long fleshy tubes extended from its face and hung limply down the stack of books to lie dormant on the table, their ends capped with glass. Inside the glass, tiny, sweet-faced mice slept curled up with their tails in their paws. "A wyrmhole just goes from one place to another place. Dull as a *street*. A squidhole starts in one place—like my shop here—and goes to five to ten other places, depending on how many field mice you managed to get. I suspect I left an end open, and I do apologize for that—sloppy of me, truly sloppy."

September did not like the look of the Dread Device. She felt it prudent to change the subject. And suddenly, she did remember where she had heard the name before. She closed her Clutch in her hand. "I heard about you on the radio," September said. "But I thought you lived in Fairyland-Above. 'Belinda Cabbage's Hard-Wear Shoppe, bringing you all the latest in Mad Scientific Equipment.'"

"That's me!" The Fairy agreed with a wide, frank smile. "And I do, or I did. But my Narrative Barometer started reading *Imminent Katabasis Event,* and I knew it was time to go underground." This time, Belinda Cabbage pointed at a smart brass dial on the wall, sealed in a glass bell. It had hands like a clock's, though there seemed to be at least seven or eight of them, and possible readings of *Katabasis, Anabasis, Incoming Hero(ine), Musical Thrones, Kidnapping, Locked Room Mystery, Coming of Age, Treasure Hunt, Epic, War Saga, Edda,* and many others in concentric rings so small September could not read them. "I built it to track Pandemonium, so I could get home whenever I needed to. But then Pandemonium stopped moving around, and it seemed a bit useless—but I never throw anything away. Jolly way of behaving, no matter what my assistants might say! Want not, waste not! And a good thing too. *Imminent Katabasis Event* means something's going on Down Below, because *Katabasis* means a journey to the underworld. It means put your business trousers on and head underground! I don't mean to suggest you didn't know that! It's only that I am also a Mad Professor, and I often teach, so I'm used to explaining things. Just raise your hand if you don't understand. Anysquid! I've been investigating the shadows and building and thinking down here. I think better by myself, anyway. Broke my heart to leave Eva Lovewool, my first assistant and an Extremely Mad Scientist in her own right. Heart of my heart, that girl. Handsome as an armoire and twice as useful! But she'll keep the roof on the place till things sort themselves out."

September twisted her cold hands. "*Will* things work themselves out?" The Watchful Dress was valiantly trying to dry itself, but having little success. Parts of it inflated and deflated as it shook off the Forgetful Sea.

"They usually do. If you take the long view, as I do. Formally, I'm a Queer Physickist, but I dabble in Questing, too, hence my Barometer. We Queerfolk are big-picture types. You have to be, to see how the Queerness of the World works itself through everything. Queer Physickists are so terribly Queer that most people don't even like to have us for tea. We might wear the tea on our heads to prove our theory on the Gravitationals of Guest Magic. We might be practicing Being a Broom or on a Visibility Fast. So many just shun us altogether. You have to be able to see the world as a whole to bear it—to see the Queerness that moves in every bit of Fairyland, how it threads through every heart and field, how we are all bound together up in the Weird Well of the World. Can't get too upset about folk being wicked. The Queer old world does so love to turn itself on its head on the regular. Anyway, Fairyland has a kind of weight to it. It tends to settle back into its own ways.

Oh, we'll have a wicked Thorn-King for a century or nine, but in the end, where there's a Thorn-King, there's a Rose-Maid to throttle him silly. It might take her a while to get here, but like I said, you have to take a long view."

"That's not much comfort to people who have to live their whole lives with a Thorn-King being wretched to them!"

"Isn't it? *I* think it's comforting. I thought about it a great deal when the Marquess was making her mess. I had a good place to watch it all happen, up in Groangyre Tower. I could see her warping the weft of the world. And I certainly didn't appreciate her telling me to stop my Electricks program or to fire Miss Lovewool just because her Reign Gauge said the old tyrant wouldn't last. Well, I know what loyalty is, thank you very much. And at night I comforted myself by lathing out a Calendar Centrifuge—to whirl out the present, dark day and leave behind only the distant tomorrow when I would be able to breathe again. It *was* comforting. Of course, Fairies can afford to look at things that way. We live so long."

"But . . . Miss Cabbage, do you really? I know something's happened to the Fairies up above. There are rather few of you left. Do you really live so long? If it's something the Marquess did, shouldn't it be all mended by now?"

"You know," said the Mad Scientist, "many years passed between Queen Mallow and the Marquess. She was hardly the only person capable of making dreadful things happen. I am working on the problem. I and all of us in Groangyre and Shearcoil both. You needn't worry about it. What I mean to say in plain Professorial terms is *mind your own business,* begging your pardon. I know humans have sensitive manners."

September minded her business. She didn't know quite what else to say, however. An awkward silence fell between them like a curtain.

"Would you like to see what I'm working on now?" Cabbage said hopefully.

"Certainly!" said September gratefully.

The Fairy rummaged behind her Dread Device, leaning over it to get something on the far side of her worktable, kicking her legs up into the air as she reached. She came back with a most peculiar object which she pointed alarmingly at September, a strange sort of gun made of brass and silver and mother-of-pearl. It had a big barrel, as big as a grown man's fist, and a long pneumatic tube hanging from it, attached to nothing in particular.

"Oh, don't worry!" Cabbage laughed, seeing September's understandable concern at having a gun pointed at her. She had not even known Fairyland had guns, and she would really rather it didn't! "I haven't invented bullets for it yet."

"What is it?"

"Well, it's a Rivet Gun, obviously."

"What is it meant to rivet?"

Belinda Cabbage looked at the Rivet Gun curiously, peering down its monster of a barrel. "That's not how Science works, love. First, you build the machine, then it tells you what it's for. A machine is only a kind of magnet for attracting Use. That's why we say things are Useful—because they're all full of the Use that chose them to perform itself. Understand?"

September didn't.

"Well, take the Dread Device. Do you think I had the first idea what a squidhole was when I invented it? Certainly not! I was just messing about! That's when the very best and very Maddest Science gets done, you know. I thought, *Why, this alabaster octopus looks like it wants a nice transmission inside it,* and fairly soon I had a thing that obviously had a Use, though what that Use could be was a total mystery. I set it out to cool on the windowsill of Groangyre and what do you know, within a year or two it had punched six holes in the damask of space-time (that's what it's made out of, if you didn't know it, and of course, I'm sure you did) and I had a lovely vacation in Broceliande! Take my Sameness Engine over there." She pointed to the other end of the room, where a huge silver-green machine squatted. It looked like a printing press had grown claws and teeth. "I haven't the first notion of what it's for! That's not why I made it—I made it for the sheer joy of making something new! It's getting up to telling me what it wants to do, though, I can just feel it. It's been giggling a lot at night. I expect sooner or later the Rivet Gun will tell me what it's good for, and until then I have patience. Patience is always the last ingredient in any spell, the last part in any machine, whatever your original blueprints say."

All the while the Fairy Scientist talked, the gun's pneumatic tube had crept across the floor toward September like a careful snake. It snuffled at her feet, and at the hem of the Watchful Dress.

"It seems to like you," Belinda Cabbage said. "If you're willing to report back in detail, I don't mind letting you take it for field testing. Sometimes you have to get out in the thick of things to get a really good Use going."

September did not know how to answer. She had seen the veterinarian Mr. Walcott's revolver, when he went out to put down a horse that had broken its knee or couldn't pass a stone, and her swimming coach had a starting pistol, but that was the beginning and end of her experience with guns. Only it wasn't *really* a gun, she supposed, not like Mr. Walcott's revolver was a gun. She knew a little about rivets from her mother, who made use of them on airplane bodies that had to hold together very tightly. But to be sure, a Rivet Gun and

Mr. Walcott's revolver were in the same family, perhaps even siblings. The Rivet Gun looked solid and powerful to her, and she hadn't a weapon to protect herself except for her Dress, whose feats she could never predict. Now that Ell and Saturday had abandoned her—and she winced, remembering that—she had to take care of herself somehow. She held out her hand, trembling a little, shy.

Cabbage tossed the gun up and caught it by the barrel, handing it over grip first. September took it. It felt heavy and good in her hand. The pneumatic tube snaked up to her waist, tucking its loose end in her little bustle.

"See? You'll be fast friends in no time. Be sure to keep good and copious notes, time and date stamped, and if at all possible, collect samples of anything it Rivets." Belinda Cabbage took up a lightning rod and touched each of September's shoulders with it. "I dub thee September, Temporary Mad Assistant."

September holstered the Rivet Gun in a silken pocket that formed helpfully in the hip of her dress, just the right size for it. "Do you know which way I ought to go? To get to the bottom of the world, I mean. Where Prince Myrrh sleeps."

Belinda Cabbage cocked her eyebrow skeptically at September. She turned to the Narrative Barometer and cracked open its glass bell. The Fairy flicked one of the hands to MUSICAL THRONES.

"There's usually a door of some sort," she shrugged. "I'm sure there's one lying around." Cabbage put both hands against a pile of machinery on her left-hand workbench and shoved it to the back wall of her shop. In the rough wood of the bench gleamed a safe-door. She spun the combination and hauled it open.

"Copious. Notes," she said in a tone that no one, even in their wrong mind, would argue with.

September took Cabbage's hand and climbed up onto the bench. "One last thing," she said. "I wonder if . . . being a leader of the Scientifick community, I wonder if you ever knew a . . . a highly puissant Scientiste, who wore the biggest pair of spectacles ever built, and lived with a lady-Wyvern, and had a wonderful Library?"

Cabbage put on her own pair of spectacles, square industrial nickel-rimmed goggles. "Of course," she said. "That's my father you're talking about."

September shook her head and laughed. Then, holding her gun tight to her hip, she jumped feet first into the safe and disappeared from Belinda Cabbage's workshop.

CHAPTER XVI

A Practical Girl

In Which an Old Foe Returns, but Not as Expected

S eptember fell out of the workbench, through the safe, and into a courtyard. She was alone, as she had not been since her first step in Fairyland-Below. The gray and black and muddy white cobblestones of the courtyard stretched out into alleys narrow and vast, cobbles upon cobbles, as far as she could see. A few bare birch trees stood with their wide branches leaning over empty benches and empty shop fronts where no one displayed their wares. Over one, an old painted wood sign read: ANYTHING IMPORTANT COMES IN THREES AND SIXES.

Snow began to fall, quiet and slow.

In the center of the courtyard stood a little garden with a low wall around it. Withered-up basil and sage and crushed mallow flowers tangled together around the black, broken roots of a fig tree. Husks of old fruit hung from the branches, and wrinkled dead toadstools ringed the roots. In the center of the garden sat a dry fountain—a high, dark marble bowl with a statue of a maiden sitting cross-legged in it, cradling a horn of plenty in her arms which must once have overflowed with clean, starry water. September had never been so tired, but still she knew that face.

It was a statue of Queen Mallow.

The wine-colored coat wrapped itself tight around September, its fur collar keeping out the soft, dry snow. She took a step forward—and saw a figure sitting on the far lip of the fountain. A young girl sat with her chin in her hands, kicking her feet in the air. September held her breath and walked a little ways around to get a better look. The girl was a shadow, violet and silver and blue lights flickering in the black depths of her skin. The shadow wore a lacy shadow-dress, with thick shadow-petticoats underneath it, along with elegant shadow-gloves and shadow-stockings and shadow-slippers.

And a very fine hat.

At her side, the shadow of a panther stood guard, quietly licking one massive dark paw.

September didn't move. She wanted to laugh, and she wanted to run, and she wanted to take out her Rivet Gun and fire it straightaway. She didn't do any of that. She just stood there and watched the girl who was the shadow of the Marquess. In the end, she waited too long and the Marquess saw her first.

"Oh!" said the Marquess, dropping her hands into her lap. "It's you."

"It's me," said September.

Iago, the Panther of Rough Storms, turned his great head to look at her. His gaze was as unreadable as any cat's. *Even his shadow would never leave her,* September thought, and it awed her a little.

"I'm only passing through," September said finally. "I don't want any trouble with you. I don't want anything at all to do with you, really. I've had a very bad day, and you are just the last thing I can bother with right this second. I know you must feel poorly about how things went when we saw each other last, but you're just going to have to keep feeling poorly."

The Marquess stood suddenly.

"Did you come all the way here in those shoes?" she asked slowly, as if remembering something from long ago.

September looked down at her shoes. They were her plain school shoes, and she had to admit they had gotten rather shabby with all the Reveling and dancing in onion forests and tromping through mines and diving through an entire sea. Still, at least this time she had brought both shoes along.

"That must have been just awfully painful. How brave of you," the Marquess said in the same slow voice—but it held no bitterness or cruel jokes. Rather, the Marquess's voice seemed entirely genuine in its pity and sympathy. She shook her head to clear it. The shadow-feathers and shadow-jewels on her hat jingled and quivered.

"You said that to me before," said September curtly.

"I did," the Marquess agreed, but she did not seem happy about it.

"Listen, Mallow, I don't mean to be rude, but whatever game you want to play, I don't know the rules, and I'd really rather sit this round out."

The Marquess's head snapped up. Her thick sausage curls flushed lilac. "Don't call me that," she said, and the old power bloomed in her voice. "It's not my name. I'm Maud. I was Maud."

"Yes, when you lived on your father's farm in Ontario."

Maud started as if she'd been slapped. "I hate my father. I will never go back. You can't make me go back."

"I know," said September, softening a little despite herself. At least back at home, her own mother loved her, and her father did, too, wherever he was.

"I'm sleeping," Maud whispered, her dark shadow eyes large and worried.

"What do you mean? You're wide awake. You oughtn't to be, but you are."

Iago's shadow finally spoke, his rumbly thundering voice rolling over September like a shiver. "She means that she is sleeping, the Marquess up Above, on a bed of tourmaline in the Springtime Parish, where the plum blossoms are always falling. I'm there, too, only I'm not sleeping. Well, really I *am* sleeping a lot of the time. Springtime has a surplus of sunbeams, and I am only feline. But I'm not sleeping in an occupational way, whereas she has been working on a good sleep for a couple of years now, and it'll go on a good while yet. When our shadows got Siphoned down, we woke up— I'd been napping, and don't you dare judge me, it was four in the afternoon, and all cats know four in the afternoon is Twelfthnap, right after Teanap. The trouble is, with her Topside self in such a powerful unnatural sleep, it's addled her a little. Sometimes she thinks she's her old self, sometimes she remembers she's a shadow and doesn't have to be a Marquess anymore."

"I'm a practical girl," the Marquess whispered. Iago licked her cheek fondly.

Suddenly, as quickly as a knife in the ribs, the Marquess put her arms around September and buried her face in her neck.

"I'm sorry," she whispered. "I only wanted to stay. You had it so easy."

September stood stiff in the Marquess's embrace. This girl had imprisoned her friends and twisted her like a rag doll and ruled Fairyland with the very hands which now held her. But she had been so wounded, too. September had wept for her, once. And this was the shadow of that girl. Had not Saturday and Ell and the Vicereine and Halloween and just everyone told her that shadows were not exactly the same as their owners? Hadn't Halloween done things she herself would never do? Hadn't Saturday?

September did not want to feel for the Marquess. That's how villains get you, she knew. You feel badly for them, and next thing you know, you're tied to train tracks. But her wild, untried heart opened up another bloom inside her, a dark branch heavy with fruit.

Poor September! How much easier, to be hard and bright and heartless. Instead, a very adult thing was happening in that green, new heart. For there are two kinds of forgiveness in the world: the one you practice because everything really is all right, and what went before is mended. The other kind of forgiveness you practice because someone needs desperately to be forgiven, or because you need just as badly to forgive them, for a heart can grab hold of old wounds and go sour as milk over them. You, being sharp and clever, will have noticed that I said "practice." Forgiveness always takes practice to get right, and September was very new at it. She had none of the first sort in her. But the shadow of the Marquess wept so bitterly against her shoulder. All creatures are sometimes wretched, and in need.

Slowly, September put her arms around the Marquess. The two girls stood together in the falling snow for a long moment. The Panther watched them, purring deeply.

"Are you doing something daring and clever now?" asked Maud when they pulled apart. Shadow-tears stood unashamed on her cheeks. "You were always so clever. Like me."

"I am going to wake up the Sleeping Prince," September said before she could think better of it.

A strange, canny look moved across the Marquess's face. "It's not always nice to wake up," she said. "It's better to dream. You don't remember the things you've done in dreams."

"You are not like I remember you."

The Marquess shrugged. "I'm a shadow. I do know I am a shadow, Iago. I know most of the time. It's only when I cannot bear how everyone looks at me down here that I make myself forget it. Shadows are the other side of yourself. I had longings to be good, even then. I was just stronger than my wanting. I'm stronger than anything, really, when I want to be." The Marquess's hair turned white as the snow. "Do you know, we're right underneath Springtime Parish? This place is the opposite of springtime. Everything past prime, boarded up for the season. Just above us, the light shines golden on daffodils full of rainwine and heartgrass and a terrible, wicked, sad girl I can't get back to. I don't even know if I want to. Do I want to be her again? Or do I want to be free? I come here to think about that. To be near her and consider it. I think I shall never be free. I think I traded my freedom for a better story. It *was* a better story, even if the ending needed work."

The shadow of the Marquess ran her fingers along the Panther's back—once, she would have come up with something marvelous, a plate of Fairy food or a pair of magic shoes or a bow and a quiver of arrows wound around with icy leaves. But her hand rose up with nothing. She just petted him absently. "I don't have my magic down here," she said mournfully. "My beautiful, muscular, brute magic. I feel it there, like I've got it in my pocket, but when I reach for it I find only myself. I'm just Maud. Just a tomato farmer's daughter. The shadow of Maud, not even Maud proper. But that's really what you ought to call me."

"What's in a name?" rumbled Iago. "People will call you whatever they want. New owner, new name. If it bothers you, you oughtn't come when you're called. They'll learn eventually. I rarely come trotting when someone hollers for me. That's all a name's for, in the end."

"You seem very much the same, Iago, though you're Iago's shadow and not the Panther himself," observed September with some concern, for if Iago was the same, the Marquess might be the same, and Saturday, and Ell.

Iago yawned so wide his eyes bulged and his white teeth showed sharp. He licked his dark muzzle. "Cats don't have dark sides. That's all a shadow is—and though you might be prejudiced against the dark, you ought to remember that that's where stars live, and the moon and raccoons and owls and fireflies and mushrooms and cats and enchantments and rather a lot of good, necessary things. Thieving, too, and conspiracies, sneaking, secrets, and desire so strong you might faint dead away with the punch of it. But your light side isn't a perfectly pretty picture, either, I promise you. You couldn't dream without the dark. You couldn't rest. You couldn't even meet a lover on a balcony by moonlight. And what would the world be worth without that? You need your dark side, because without it, you're half gone. Cats, on the other hand, have a more sensible setup. We just have the one side, and it's mostly the sneaking and sleeping side anyway. So the other Iago and I feel very companionable toward each other. Whereas I expect my drowsy mistress Above would loathe this version of herself, who is kind and quiet and lonely and rather dear, all the things the original is not. My love stands for both. This one pets me more; that one let me pounce on anything I wanted."

"I *am* nice," Maud said softly. "I can be nice, September. I can help you and pet you and give you lovely presents. I can be a faithful guide."

"But not for nothing," said September. She felt as if she were in a dream, repeating the words she had said so long ago. As if she were a shadow of her old self, as if being here now, speaking with the Marquess, were a shadow of every other time she had spoken with the Marquess. "Never for nothing," she finished.

"Not for nothing. Take me with you. I am not really wicked at all. I can be so terribly kind, September. I feel very warmly toward you, and I only want to protect you, as I wish someone had protected me." Maud shook her head again. She covered her face in her hands for a moment, and then dropped them again. "Take me with you. Where is your Wyvern? Your Marid? You need someone. I should know—a Knight always needs a companion."

"I'm not a Knight. I'm a Bishop. Or at least I am trying to be. And traveling with you is the most slantwise, backward thing I can possibly think of, which in this place probably means it's the right thing to do."

Iago crouched down low so that the girls could climb up on his back. Perhaps the most astonishing thing to happen in that lonely courtyard was this: The Marquess demurred the seat of honor and let September ride in front of her. She put her arms around September's waist and did not once reach for the Rivet Gun or slide an arrow up into her heart. September took a deep, nervous breath.

"Up till now I've found a door everywhere I've gone. But there are a hundred doors here. I wish I had Belinda Cabbage's Barometer! But I haven't, so I will have to choose, and hope I have chosen right. Perhaps it doesn't matter, and just passing through a door is enough to keep following the tunnel in Avogadra's book. Perhaps we shall go through a door and find only a pastry shop. I suppose I could use my last ration card, but the last one didn't do me *much* good, and there may be a long ways to go yet. I shall try to be . . . practical. As you said, Maud."

Maud said nothing. She held September a little tighter and rested her head against her back.

"That one has a sign over it, and it talks about 'Anything Important,' so I'll cast my lot with it."

Iago padded over to the sagging door frame. It had a glass revolving door set into it. A few of the panes had gotten shattered in some long ago robbery or escape. As they approached, it creaked, screeched, and began to turn.

CHAPTER XVII

A HOLE IN THE WORLD

*In Which September Loses Her Temper,
Nearly Boxes a Minotaur, Accomplishes Some Magic,
and Sees Her Mother Through a Hole in a
Very Strange Wall*

Darkness.

The revolving door spun shut behind them and vanished. Satiny, perfect blackness greeted them, blacker than the Panther of Rough Storms in the midst of the most livid thundercloud, blacker than the ink-sodden page in Avogadra's book. September's eyes ached with trying to see through the crowblack air. Iago, being a cat, had a somewhat better time of it. He stepped forward carefully, his paws landing quietly as footsteps in snow.

Someone lit a candle.

The orange flame snapped into life, its sudden brightness causing both September and the Marquess to shield their eyes. One, two, three candles lit up, and then three more, the crown of a cast-iron candelabra. The firelight rippled over the round base of the candlestick, where an engraving read: *Beware of Dog*. Slowly, as the candles settled, the place they had found themselves in came into focus. First the candelabra, then the vast, ancient desk it rested upon, polished teak with an ink pot the size of a pumpkin in one corner, with a long peacock feather dipped into it. Then the walls, also scrubbed, gleaming wood, and hung with artifacts like the study of a big-game hunter. Six long, spangled spears hung in a neat row over a dormant, cold fireplace. Seven Greek bronze helmets stared out through empty eyeholes along with seven wide bronze necklaces that covered the chest like breastplates (September knew the helmets were Greek because in one of her books a fellow named Perseus had worn one). A portrait of a beautiful girl wearing a dress of every color and holding a spindle full of thread hung under an arch of three leather shields.

The hand that lit the candle belonged to a well-dressed and bespectacled Minotaur.

The Minotaur rested in a luxurious chocolate-colored chair, like those one might find in a lawyer's or principal's office. September had got quite used to thinking of Minotaurs as boys in her reading, for they always seemed to be—but this one was most certainly a lady. Enormous, curving dark horns crowned her head. She had a very wide nose with a light covering of nearly invisible fur, save that the candlelight made her scant pelt ripple with fire when she moved. She wore a thick brass ring in her nose, and her ears were furry and long like a cow's, but beyond that her face was quite human, with big, liquid brown eyes behind her librarian's glasses, and full, dark lips. Her hands folded gracefully in front of her. Under the desk, strong, hard hooves peeked out from under a plain brown schoolmarm skirt.

"This can't be right," said September, climbing down from Iago's broad back. The Marquess's shadow followed her, but hung back, close to the Panther's glossy flank. "A Minotaur lives in the center of the labyrinth, and I haven't set foot inside one! I think I would know a maze if I had already solved it!" She peered over the desk at the Minotaur, who might have been a statue, she sat so still.

Slowly, the Minotaur laid her head to one side. "What did you think you were doing, then, when you went up through one door and down through another, turning this way and that, through the pages of a book and a deep mine and an entire ocean and the hideout of a wise woman? My dear, labyrinths ensnare and entangle; they draw one inexorably inward—but it would not be much of a labyrinth if you waited in line with a ticket to get in and the door was clearly marked, like some country-harvest hay maze. All underworlds are labyrinths, in the end. Perhaps all the sunlit lands, too. A labyrinth, when it is big enough, is just the world."

"Is Prince Myrrh here, then? Do you have his unopenable box in your collection?"

"No. *I* am here. I am the dark anchor at the bottom of the world. And I will decide whether to let you go further down."

September knew she ought to be asking important, urgent things of the lady Minotaur. But a statement jumped the line and leapt out of her ahead of all those questions. "I thought only bulls had horns."

The Minotaur's thick eyebrow quirked. "And I thought all human girls wore dresses. Yet I am sure you have worn trousers in your life. Do you never prefer to wear boy's clothes when they are more suitable, and more sensible?"

"I suppose so, when I have hard work to do."

"Ah, my dear girl! I always have hard work to do." She stood up. The Minotaur towered over all of them, her shoulders muscled, her legs powerful—that was easy enough to see,

277

even with the plain skirt to cover them. She crossed to a home-hewn rocking chair near the hearth and settled herself into it, taking up a scrap of knitting from a basket, the ball of translucent yarn looking very much like the spindle in the painting above her. She gestured absentmindedly at the black logs with one knitting needle. They burst into eager flame. Her fingers wrapped the yarn deftly as she talked.

"Minotaurs are all descended from the same poor, sorry fellow. You have probably heard of him—Grandfather is quite famous. The Queen of a distant land fell in love with a bull. Nevermind how odd that sounds! The ancient world was an appalling place. Even if it were not, love may unclose itself between any number of seemingly upside-down and turned-around folk. Especially if one is a Fairy Bull who can talk and write poems and have tea and discourse on natural philosophy. In any event, a Queen and a bull are not mixable elements, and so she called on a Fairy Inventor to help her. I believe you met his great-granddaughter. In those days one could transit between worlds as easily as one takes a trolley now. The Inventor came on a pair of wax wings he had invented himself and made a heifer out of ivory and leather and mirrors for the Queen to live inside, so that the royal wedding could take place. When their first child came, he was, as might have been predicted, half bull and half human, huge and monstrous and frightening. His own mother hid behind the bureau when he cried for milk. So the Inventor built a labyrinth to hide the child, so that his mother would not have to look at him, yes, but also so that no one in the country would try to stab him or vanquish him in some way to prove their strength. Every once in a while, they would try to send that first Minotaur friends to play with, but a Minotaur's play is rough, and some did not survive. Others must have. Eventually, the Fairy Bull died in battle with a certain Babylonian scoundrel and his hairy giant of a brother. The Queen found a nice young man who did not inquire into her previous marriage and had a perfectly lovely daughter with him—that's her there, my Auntie." The Minotaur gestured at the portrait above her head. "And all the while, down in the labyrinth, a whole village had grown up in the dark. Grandfather lived quite well with the youths and maidens who had gone down, not very eagerly, to make nice with the monster. They built houses together in the maze, traded grain and oil, had country dances and learned to make cheese and beer. The youths and maidens grew up and found it pleasant that no one bothered them about things like taxes and foreign wars. They stayed in the labyrinth-town to have children or open up a nice carpentry service. The Minotaur wasn't so bad, once you got to know him, and if you were nimble enough to avoid the horns. And it must have been possible to love Grandfather if you were not his mother, for some brave girl made him her husband, and the rest of us owe our lives to that noble maid. We are all Tauruses, naturally. We are good, wholesome monsters. I am named Left, for generally speaking, if one keeps turning left, one finds one's way out of a maze, no matter how tangled."

"Miss Cabbage said I was born under the sign of the Bull," ventured September, hoping to make a beginning of friendship.

"Well, perhaps you have a little Minotaur in you, child. Of course, the town didn't end well. Some years later, a ruffian broke into the place and bashed Grandfather's head in, just to impress his daddy with how big and strong he was. Still, we all remember, somewhere deep and untouchable, that town, those dark corridors. Something in our monstrous blood still seeks the underground, still wants to be wrapped up cozy in a maze, wants to draw youths and maidens to us and judge them, wants to guard, wants to hide. You cannot escape where you come from, September. Some part of it remains inside you always, like the slender white heart in the center of the thickest onion."

"I'm a monster," said the shadow of the Marquess suddenly. "Everyone says so."

The Minotaur glanced up at her. "So are we all, dear,"

said the Minotaur kindly. "The thing to decide is what kind of monster to be. The kind who builds towns or the kind who breaks them."

Iago yawned, showing his generous shadowy pink tongue. "There's something to be said for breaking things. They make a satisfying sound when they crunch."

"I break everything," whispered Maud. Her hair hung deep blue around her shadowy face.

"Hush," purred Iago. "All that's done now."

"I need to get to the Prince," said September, resting her hand on the great desk.

The Minotaur did not look up from her knitting. "I am aware."

"Well . . . are you going to show me the way or not?" September asked.

The Minotaur laughed. "You're terribly impatient! And a bit ill-tempered, I must say. Is there some reason you're in such a damnable hurry?"

"The Alleyman takes more shadows every day, and the magic in Fairyland-Above is leaking out. Soon there will be nothing left."

"Oh? Is that all? Well, perhaps they could do with a bit less magic up there. You saw what this one did with it." The shadow of the Marquess narrowed her eyes in disdain, the old fire sparking in them. "Well, certainly, let's get on with things!" The Minotaur put her knitting aside and stood up. She slipped her long fingers over the mantel of her fireplace, feeling for some hidden thing. "Of course," she mused, "if that's all the danger you've discovered on your journeys, perhaps you aren't the right beast for this sort of thing at all. A more curious child would have arrived at the end with all the knowledge she needed."

"I *am* curious!" said September indignantly. "If there's some other awful thing afoot, you should just tell me, instead of teasing me. It's not very nice."

"We've already discussed the fact that I am a monster, and that I play rough. I'll tell you what. Give me that fine gun of yours, and I'll let you pass."

September put her hand on the grip of the Rivet Gun. She'd only just gotten it, and she'd promised to take copious notes for Belinda Cabbage, which probably did not mean handing it over to the first person who asked and taking notes on what she got for it. But more than that, she wanted it with her. It had chosen her. She felt safer with it, even though she knew it was probably quite dangerous.

"No," she said finally. "I can't. What if I need it?"

"Good girl," said the Minotaur. "A warrior never gives up her weapon."

"I'm not a warrior."

"No?"

Something boiled up in September's heart, hot and furious. The moment she started to raise her voice, Maud put a charcoal hand on her shoulder. This only made the boiling thing spill over. "*Stop it!* I am tired and hurt and all my friends have abandoned me except the one girl I never wanted to see again. I don't even know where I am, and I don't know how to get out. Either help me or fight me or say I'm not what's wanted and a disappointment to the Minotaur Nation, but speak plain and let me keep moving. I want to keep moving! *Now.*"

A wisp of green smoke puffed up from the pocket of the wine-colored coat, smelling sharply of sunny grasses and warm winds. "Oh, no!" September cried, fishing out the smoking, charred magic ration book. It had no more cards, and, in a moment, had crumbled entirely to green ash. "But I didn't ask it to do any magic! I was saving it!"

But the Minotaur had already found the latch on her mantel and turned it. The fire in the hearth went out, and a pearly, waxen light appeared deep in the fireplace, which yawned up and in, becoming a long tunnel.

"You have your shadow with you," said the Minotaur. "Right at your back, holding on tight. I admit, I feel a little silly—I had meant to hold out on you. But you do Want things so terribly hard. Magic gets what it wants. I'm only one monster."

"She's *not* my shadow!"

Maud took September's slightly scorched hand. "We are alike, I said. I said that before. I did say it, I'm sure of it. I am *her* shadow, but I can stand behind you, too." She paused for a moment, as if digging something up from the bottom of her heart. "It would break your heart, September, how alike we are."

"You Wanted it—that was like kindling. That shadow was a spark, and the ration card caught flame. Now, if you're going to snap at me, you might follow me when I am so good as to hold the door open for you." The Minotaur wrinkled her velvety nose.

September yanked her hand away from the Marquess. She did not for a moment want to hear how alike they were. Once had been enough. She stepped over the charred logs and into the tunnel, which seemed to be made of a very nice mud brick, like the basement of some ancient pyramid.

September fell out of a patch in the sky. Iago floated down, and the Minotaur, even larger in this place than her study, simply lifted her skirts and stepped out into a wild, tumbling expanse of moorland, gray and purple and black with mist. Heather and gorse and long curlicued vines of rampion and icy hard peas grew everywhere.

A high wall greeted them, the only object for miles. It did not look like the little wall September had tripped over when she entered Fairyland. It looked infinitely older, of a stone that probably remembered when the moon was just a baby. Weather and abuse had lashed the rocks and left them crumbling here, impenetrable there. As with any wall that has the gall to stand in the middle of nowhere with nobody guarding it, folk had written things on it, painted and chiseled their names or some little message, a thousand years of graffiti. Some were little more than signs and sigils, as old as writing itself. Some September could read, even if she didn't understand most of them.

Philadelphia 9 Million Miles That-a-Way. Beware of Dog. Abandon All Hope, Ye Who Enter Here. No Trespassing—This Means You. I Miss My Mother. Theseus Was Here. I Told You Not to Turn Around—You Never Listened to Me. No Parking Any Time. Never Let 'Em Take Your Necklace.

September ran her hands across the letters.

"Look here," the Minotaur said imperiously, and September did not argue. In the midst of the wall she saw a hole, a crack in the stone. It looked as though someone had put their fist through the wall—its edges sheared off broken and ugly, covered in pale moss, sharp and ragged. Up above it someone had written in childlike handwriting, *"Why Did the Chicken Cross Fairyland?"*

"Is that the way to the Prince?" she asked. "Will I look through and see him?"

The Minotaur said nothing, only continued to point. When September still hesitated, the beast put her hand on the girl's neck, hard and unignorable, rough and hot. She pushed her down before the hole in the wall. September stumbled to her knees and peered through it. This is what she saw: A field of warm, rich grain, still tinged with green, a May field, and a sweet little house at one end of it—why, it was her own house! And the lights were on! And there! Could those be the shadows of her mother and her dog moving behind the distant curtains? It looked like early evening, only a few minutes after she'd left. September laughed and tried to wave to her mother through the hole in the world. The Minotaur stayed her hand.

"No one can see or hear you—yet. There is no wall on the other side of the wall. Only a world. You will not believe me, but that is a part of Fairyland-Above, in the far, far west of the land."

"But that's my house! I can see it! There, in the yard, that's my bicycle with the basket! There's the milkman's empty bottles!"

"It is what Fairyland-Above is becoming, without her shadows, without her magic," said Left softly. "More and more ordinary, more and more usual, more and more like your world, where you cannot plant poems or turn into a Wyvern or build cities out of bread. Very soon now Fairyland will be little more than another part of your world. Maybe a pretty one, but it will have lost all that made it different. You might say it will have lost its Queerness. Belinda Cabbage would say so. Without the shadows and their sorceries and their wildness, the borders are disappearing, and soon enough this wall itself will just fade away into nothing but a nice May field full of waving grass."

September tried to imagine Fairyland stuck into her world like a pushpin. A place that would seem like it had always been there, wedged between Kansas and Colorado, perhaps. Another one of the Dakotas. A magicless new prairie stretching on forever.

The Minotaur went on. "And the people of Fairyland, well—perhaps *you* will remember that the tall, skinny farmer is really a Spriggan, or the short, fat fish-seller was once a Goblin girl, or that the bicycle leaning against your house used to ride wild with her brothers on the high plain. But no one else will know." Left paused, her hand softening. She stroked September's hair instead of pressing her cheek against the stone. She looked back over her immense shoulder at the shadow of the Marquess and played her trump card. "*Her* desires will come to pass, in an odd and slantwise way—no child will go between earth and Fairyland, because there will no longer be any Fairyland to go to."

September shook her head. "I would never let this happen—I mean, Halloween wouldn't. She's still *me*. I'm part of her, I *am* her. She'd never want a thing like this, because I'd never want it!"

The Minotaur sighed. "She is so full of Want and Need that the magic of it fills her up like a jar packed with fireflies. She is your shadow, after all. She is you, if you had never learned that sometimes you don't get what you want. If you had never learned about consequences. Halloween thinks Fairyland-Below will be safe. She thinks if she can pull enough shadows down, we'll stay put down here while the rest floats off. We'll anchor ourselves, the sheer weight of all of us. She doesn't care a bit for the rest, only for her people—an admirable trait in a Queen, really. Not all have it. Oh, and perhaps we will stay, for a little while. But Fairyland-Above is so terribly heavy. Eventually it will drag us through, too. We'll become beetles and worms and moles, moving in the dark under the mundane world."

The shadow of the Marquess looked troubled, blue storms moving across her face. Iago nudged her with his broad dark head. "No more fairies making mischief, spoiling beer and cream, stealing children, eating souls. No more humans meddling with Fairyland, mucking up its politics and tracking mud all over the floor." Grief quivered in her voice, real grief. "Why does that hurt me so? It made me feel so happy once. So safe and warm."

"I thought you would come to me knowing this," said Left. "I thought we would battle, as a Minotaur likes to do. Then you would show yourself worthy (perhaps I would even let you win a little), and I would have given you a helmet to wear, to show my favor."

September threw off the Minotaur's hand. Her eyes blazed. The hot and furious thing sizzled in her once more. Why did everyone keep assuming she couldn't do anything for herself? "If you want to fight, I will fight you. I am not strong or tall, and it would be completely unfair, but nothing is fair, ever, and I have already wrestled a Marid nearly to death, so I'll take you if that's how I keep this from happening."

The Rivet Gun stirred at her hip. Its pneumatic tube snaked around her waist and snuffled like a little puppy, searching for something. It crawled up her chest and found the Järlhopp's Clutch. The end of the tube smacked gleefully and widened like a serpent's mouth to engulf the pendant. September drew the gun. Her hand barely shook at all as she aimed it at the Minotaur—but she could not aim for her heart as she thought she probably ought to. At the last moment, her own heart quailed: *We could talk it out! This will only make her angry! You can't just shoot people—that's not fair fighting!* But September had already pulled the trigger. If she was to fight, the hard, strange, new part of her meant to win.

A bubbling boom erupted from the mouth of the Rivet Gun. A creamy orange cannonball made of all the things that had ever happened to September exploded into the Minotaur's muscled thigh.

The Minotaur studied her for a long while. Blood streamed down her leg, but she didn't seem to notice it. "Good girl," she said finally.

September shook a little with the force of having had to do such a thing when she didn't really want to fight anyone at all. She made fists with her hands, and then let go, covering her face with them instead. All that she had done to keep Fairyland whole, to keep it connected to her own world—and now her shadow would finish the job.

The hole in the Minotaur's leg stopped bleeding. The creamy orange light of September's memories spread all around her great leg. The wound grew wider and wider and taller and taller until the Minotaur had vanished, and all that was left was the hole the Rivet Gun had made, rimmed in creamy orange fire.

On the other side, September could see nothing at all.

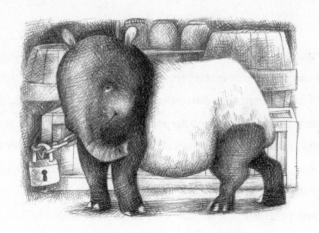

CHAPTER XVIII
Everyone's House

In Which an Unopenable Box Is Opened, an Unbreakable Bier Is Broken, a Tapir Gloats Rather More Than Is Polite, and a Thing Lost Is Found

When September stepped through the fiery wound, she squeezed her eyes shut, bracing herself for something to leap out and fight her for real and true.

Nothing happened. She opened her eyes. Still nothing.

Maud and Iago still stood near her, just behind, as a shadow will, which September did not like in the least. The Minotaur had gone. The rushing wind and the smell of hardy, tangly moor-flowers had gone, too. Instead, all around them stood a silent, dark house. Shadows—the usual, flat, soft kind that can't talk—hung everywhere. September reached blindly and found the bannister to a flight of stairs which she seemed to be coming down. She stepped out into the front room of the house, where a big, threadbare couch sat invitingly. A tall, walnut-wood radio stood quiet and dark in the corner.

"Why, it's my house!" September cried. Her voice sounded very loud in the empty place. "There's our old radio—and look! The sink is still full of pink-and-yellow teacups!"

"No," whispered the shadow of the Marquess. "It's *my* house. There's Father's broken rocking chair, and his liquor cabinet still full up, and tomato soup still on the stove."

September looked where the shadow pointed, but she did not see any rocking chair, nor any liquor cabinet, nor any pot of soup.

"But look, here's Mother's umbrella in the stand, and still wet! And my own books on the table. I'm sure the sunflowers I planted will be just coming up outside the window, you'll see—"

But when September went to the window she didn't see her baby sunflowers peeking up their little heads. She saw a yawning, endless cavern full of glittering stalactites, such a profound red that they might have been black, but for a strange torchlight that showed the bloody color within. A narrow, milky river rippled through a colossal cavern, spilling down in waterfalls where rocks had sheared off or worn away. Gnarled, leafless trees bent and groaned over its current, bearing pomegranates so big you could hardly put your arms around them if you tried.

September gasped, and ran to the kitchen window— there, there she would see her own long prairie, the one she'd stared at so often in the evenings that she knew every furry head of wheat. Where the Green Wind had come for her, and asked her if she wanted to go to Fairyland. But outside that window roared a black and shoreless sea, its waves thundering so tall that should they ever break, September had no doubt the whole world would drown. But they never did break, only rolled on forever.

September dashed upstairs to her own bedroom, where her own bed lay neatly made and her own clothes hung in the closet. Outside the window was nothing but a field of stars dropping down into nothing, no land, no moon, no sun, just stars flaming on as far as any eye could see.

"You're both wrong," Iago said behind her. The pair had followed her up into her room, just as hushed as air. The Marquess looked as though she might cry. She held her arms tight to her chest. "It's my old house in Nephelo, where I was a kitten before I took up with the Red Wind and became a more cosmopolitan cat. There's my cloud-bed with all the nice little cumulus pillows I loved, and my mist-mirror where I groomed myself to be so handsome, and I don't know how either of you can have missed the lightning-hearth downstairs, with a nice fat cloud-roast turning over it."

"Father will be home," the Marquess said, and she sounded so small and afraid September could not believe this was the same girl who had ruled Fairyland with her gloved fists.

But September thought she had the puzzle licked. "If you see your own room, and I see mine, and Iago sees his, perhaps we are not really at home, any of us. There's lizards in Africa that can change color whenever they like, to hide or to make other lizards like them better. Maybe this house is trying to get us to like it—or hiding from us what it really looks like. Maybe . . . maybe we've got here at last, and at the bottom of the world there's a place that looks like everyone's house all at once, because the world has got to have a house just like a person. And the house the world lives in would have to have every other house inside it! And outside . . ." September refused to look at the dizzying plain of stars again. "Outside all the bits of Fairyland-Below crowd in on top of it, because we're under everything. Or maybe they're not even Fairyland-Below, but other underworlds, like A-Through-L said. Underworlds all the way down."

But the shadow of the Marquess was not listening to her. She looked out the bedroom door toward the stairs they'd come up, and before September had finished being very clever if she said so herself, Maud had started down the steps again. The Marquess said nothing, just went down the stairs and around the bannister and through the kitchen to the cellar door. September hurried after her, shivering with an eerie sort of familiarness. Even if she believed all the things she'd thought about the place, it *was* her house. She'd put up pickles with her mother in that cellar last fall. She'd left that pan soaking in the sink, and that teakettle ready for a nice pot. But it stood so empty and awfully dark, with no one inside and no sound, not even of the little dog scrabbling about looking for treats.

The Marquess put her hand on the doorknob. The radio crackled to life, and all of them jumped, startled, their hearts beating wildly. A voice crackled and popped from within.

". . . missing in France after hostilities erupted outside Strasbourg. Early casualty reports are grim—"

September snapped it off. She barely heard the words, the blood in her face beat so hard and hot. *No one said this was a bad place,* she told herself. *No one said the bottom of the world was somewhere terrible. It's only dark, and dark's not so frightening. Everything's dark in Fairyland-Below. That doesn't mean it's wicked.*

The Marquess—Maud—started down the cellar stairs. The old wood creaked loudly under her feet, and louder still under Iago's paws as he padded after her. September wanted to just let the Marquess go. If she was going to be rude and wander off when any fool could see they ought to stick together, well, what did she expect from a girl like that? But the cellar, even back at home, with a good lantern and her mother at her side, still scared her a bit. So terribly dark and full of dust and spiders! And they were not at home, no matter how home-like it looked. And so September went down into the blackness, because she could not let another girl go alone.

This is what comes of having a heart, even a very small and young one. It causes no end of trouble, and that's the truth.

The cellar of the house at the bottom of the world looked like any cellar you have ever seen. Full of old, forgotten things or else things put away for a cold, needful day. Jars of pickles and bottles of liquor and jams, each neatly labeled: *Idun's Apple Butter*, *Bacchus's Best Blackberry Wine*, *Eve's Blue Ribbon Fig Jelly*, *Kali's Red-Hot Pickled Peppers*. Stacks of old newspapers moldered away, their headlines growing dark moss. A hurricane lamp resting on a great sack of *Coyote's Extra-Fine Cornmeal Flour* flickered, guttered, and flared up again, showing Brobdingnagian cobwebs and crowded shelves and the Marquess and her Panther—and a large, long steamer trunk in the middle of the floor. It sat up on wooden pallets, to keep it off the earthen floor in rains and snows. Brass studs stubbled all over it; a brass lock bigger than a hog's head kept it locked tight.

"An unopenable box on an unbreakable bier," September said softly. It just felt right, to whisper in such a cellar. "Though it doesn't look very unbreakable to me, I must say."

The Marquess stared at it. "I thought I heard something," she said. "Something rustling down here. Something . . . *chewing*. But there's no one here. Surely, we can't get any lower than this. It's the bottom of the bottom of the world."

And then September heard it, too: a strange little mumbling chewing sound in the dark. Like a mouse gnawing at something far too big for it. Iago growled deep in his throat and wiggled down on his haunches, his eyes flashing. He crept forward on his belly, sniffing at a barrel labeled *Ratatosk's High-Yield World-Tree Seeds*. His whiskers twitched; his tail snapped from side to side.

"Oh, lay off it," came a low, chuckling voice from behind the barrel. "Call off your cat and I'll come out. Don't you growl at me that way, young Sir. I'll have your ears."

Iago stood up and returned to his mistress, flowing around

her and arching his back to rub against her shoulder. When he'd settled beside her, a large tapir emerged from behind the seed-store.

September, having grown up in farm country, could not be expected to know what a tapir was. The Marquess knew, as she knew all the creatures she had once ruled, though she thought of it by its proper name. For it was not only a tapir, which would be unusual enough, but a Baku. September thought it looked like a cross between a pig and an anteater. It had a long, velvety, double-barreled snout like a miniature elephant's trunk, bright little eyes, dark purple fur with wild red stripes down its back, and round mousy ears.

"You interrupted my supper," it complained. "Such a lovely one, too. He was dreaming of his mother. Those are always juicy meals, with all the fixings."

"You eat dreams?" September said, and not without some wonder.

"Naturally," said the tapir, licking its snout. "Everyone does."

"I don't!"

The tapir rubbed its cheek on the steamer trunk. "'Course you do. If you didn't sleep and dream, you'd get sick and eventually you'd die. Dreams keep the heart alive, just like your boring old suppers keep your body alive. Just because you're ignorant of how your own self works, doesn't mean you ought to get snooty about how I make my way."

"I never remember my dreams," said the shadow of the Marquess quietly.

"You must have rich, tasty ones then. When you can't remember a dream, it's because a Baku ate it. We leave plenty for you to keep your health up, don't worry. We're very careful, just like a good farmer is careful how many cows he slaughters for meat and how many he keeps for milk. But people all look like cows to a Baku, just bursting with sweet cream."

September thought she ought to introduce herself and the Marquess and the Panther, but when she began to do it, the tapir snorted. A little cloud of dirt puffed up from the earth below that powerful snort.

"Oh, I know who you are! He dreams about you all the time. Not the cat, but then, I never paid much mind to cats. They don't dream, so they're of no interest to me. My name is Nod, if it matters."

"Do you mean Prince Myrrh?" September asked.

"Who else?"

"How could he possibly dream about us?"

The tapir shrugged. "That's what magical objects do. They dream of the day when heroes will come and claim them."

"But he's not an object at all, he's a boy, even if he *is* a boy in a box."

Nod jostled the trunk with his round flank. It rocked a little. "Nope. He's an object. Never comes out, never wakes up, could be picked up, put into a wagon, and moved like luggage."

"Don't you think it's a bit awful, you hiding down here and . . . well, eating him, bit by bit?"

The purple tapir widened his eyes. "Oh, no, you misunderstand. It's not like that at all."

September flushed. "Well, I do misunderstand sometimes, when folk are slow about explaining."

Nod chuckled, a watery, snorty, pleasant sort of sound. "I *guard* him. Surely someone told you that all magical objects have guardians. It's good work when you can get it—times being what they are. When I was a calf, I just wandered from town to town, munching on an innkeeper's nightmare about an endless hall of empty rooms with his lost loves' names on the doors, or a wizard's worried dream of retaking the same examination over and over again. Occasionally, I would find others like me, and we'd go in a pack for a while. We'd head down to Baku-Town in Pandemonium and rollick about, go to a dream café and sample something really exotic, maybe a Pooka in her real, original shape lost in a forest of all the faces she's ever worn—maybe a changeling child dreaming of home. But I wasn't a serious fellow. I didn't have a calling and I didn't have a care." September's heart leaned in to listen, for she had hardly yet heard of someone in Fairyland without a calling, who didn't know exactly who they were. "But one night, I had too much vintage leprechaun gold-fever to drink and fell asleep in a twisty old alleyway. I dreamed that I was a zebra instead of a tapir. A lion asked me to dance, and I did, the way you do inadvisable things in dreams. But, lo, what do you know? All of the sudden someone was eating one of *my* dreams, which I did not approve of *at all.* The lion turned into a fellow Baku, a big, green female with a golden rump. I squirmed under the press of her snout on my dream, but I could not shake her. So I bit back—and discovered that she was the guardian of the Widow's Polearm, a weapon that once belonged to Myrmo the Striped. Some witch somewhere says it cannot be wielded again until the end of the world. The Baku had gotten quite fat on the dreams of the Polearm, which were interesting and quite unlike the dreams of creatures who walk and talk and fight on their own steam. I suppose it would be like you were the first person in the world to ever taste caviar. It's a bit funny, but you could really get to like it, if you hold on tight and take it slow. So when I woke up, I joined the union, Local Number 333—Guardians,

Sibyls, Junkyard Dogs, and Scarecrows. That was ages ago now."

The Marquess paid no attention to Nod. She walked slowly around the box as he spoke, prodding the wooden pallets with the toes of her black boots. Suddenly, she knelt and slipped her fingers into the lock. The gap where a key might fit yawned quite big enough to fit her hand. But though it was a good idea to pick that monstrous lock with her own deft fingers—one does not get to rule much of anything without good ideas—nothing happened.

"Not so fast, young lady," snapped the Baku.

"I am not young," shot back the Marquess.

"And not a lady, either, I expect. But I can't let you do that."

September frowned at him. "We have to get the box open, and the Prince waking, and I don't mind telling you that sometimes I do manage to get my way, and when I do, I leave a big mess behind, as often as not."

"I'm a guardian, girl. It's my whole job to make sure no one harms or bothers the lad. I eat his dreams, yes, but he's been down here a good long while, and I have to keep living so I can keep guarding. You wouldn't have me eat what's in these jars would you? What if the folks who put up all this rot came back and expected a nice mature bottle? I'd be stomped on, you can bet on it. And I keep him company, in his dreams. I dance with him, when he wants to dance. I shoot dream-pheasants with him, when he wants to see something beautiful fall apart. We talk about our troubles, and I tell him about the world. He's my friend, even though he's never once opened his eyes. You don't even know him at all."

"There has to be a key," September said, ignoring the argument of the Baku.

"Don't you have ears? It's an unopenable box. The whole idea is you can't open it." Nod sneered.

September grinned. "It's a riddle then! I mean, it must be. Everyone keeps saying *unopenable*—they never say *locked* or *closed* or *shut*. I shall figure it out, presently. I must only think slantwise and backward, as a proper Bishop should. How do you get something out of a box without opening it?"

"You frighten it until it gets out of the box on its own if it knows what's good for it," purred Iago.

"You outlaw all closed boxes," said the Marquess.

September looked around the cellar. She felt sure that she had all the pieces of the puzzle, if only she could think of the solution. When she'd stood in the terrible, wonderful room full of clocks with the other Marquess, the real one, as she could not help but think of that cruel queen, everything she'd needed to defeat her had been lying around her. She'd only needed to think hard enough, and want it enough. Her eyes fell on more jars, more sacks, old, broken wagon wheels and spools and butter churns. Nothing useful, nothing that even looked like a key or a wedge or a hammer. *Anansi's No-Weight Silk Yarn. Erishkegal's Black Label Whiskey.*

And then her eyes fell to the earthen floor, illuminated by the ashen light of the hurricane lamp.

The steamer trunk cast a long, deep, dark shadow.

"Oh!" said September. "Oh. Marq . . . Maud, come here. You must come here." She could still hardly call the shadow-girl in her shadow-petticoats by her poor, small human name. Nevertheless, the Marquess came. Her black hat jingled softly. September pointed at the shadow on the floor. "Don't you see? You've got to open the shadow! It's not opening the box at all. Whatever a thing does, its shadow does; but perhaps, here in the undermost of the underneath and the furthest down of the Upside-Down, it could work the other way, too, and whatever a shadow does, its thing must do, too."

"Why can't you open the shadow?" said Maud. She seemed suddenly reluctant, as though something in the box might hurt her, though only a moment ago she had had her hand inside the lock.

"You understand I don't *know* how anything works. I only *think* it might be that this isn't a shadow like you're a shadow. It's not alive. So a shadow has to touch it and move it, because no *person* can move a shadow, only a shadow can even touch another one. If this is to happen, it must happen all in shadow, or it would count as opening the box. But I've gotten very good at thinking these things out! I've got you to thank for that in a slantwise way. I wonder if thinking can become muscular, like your magic, if you train it up enough. My thinking has become muscular, like your magic used to be."

Nod furrowed his brow. The scarlet stripes on his neck bunched together as he frowned deeper than any tapir has ever frowned.

"It's not openable," he said firmly. "Not any way under the sun. I was told. I was *assured*. This won't work." But his voice trembled, and when Maud, never taking her eyes from September, touched the lid of the box's shadow, the dream-eating tapir bit her wrist to yank it away.

The Marquess screamed. All this time, she had been small and cowering, nothing like herself, a shadow of a shadow. But when Nod sunk his squarish teeth into her dark skin, she screamed and hissed—and then suddenly stood. She stared at the creature clamping down on her wrist. He shook his muzzle to get a better grip on her. Her spine straightened, and September saw her face settle into its old self, a face used to power, to getting her way, and never balking at any single thing.

"How *dare* you," the Marquess snarled. "How dare you put your teeth on me?" She clamped her hand down on his snout and tore him free of her flesh. Shadow-blood welled up and fell. The tip of his elephant-like nose stretched far longer than September would have thought possible. It sought and found her wound as she held him fast. She threw him aside like a doll; his weight shattered a crate stamped with *Pluto's Fancy Mushrooms*. Dark soil spilled out. The Marquess reached down and opened the shadow of the box, her eyes blazing. She opened it as herself, as the Marquess in all her fury and beauty and terror. And for a moment, nothing happened.

Then a clicking and grinding and groaning belched forth from the huge lock. It crumbled as it came open, turning to rusty dust. The lid sprang back—and September looked down on a handsome young man asleep in the steamer trunk, his hands folded over his belly. He wore fine black clothes and a healthy red color in his cheeks. He had brown hair the color of winter branches and a pair of small, furry wolf's ears just like those September had seen on a certain cartographer long ago.

"I thought he would wake up," September said. "I thought opening the box would be enough."

The Marquess put her hands over her mouth. Her eyes slid shut and she shook her head, as if she wanted it all to go away. The fire drained out of her and she was Maud again.

"It can't be," she whispered. "It can't be. How can it be?"

"Of course it can," said Nod, shaking Pluto's Fancy Mushrooms off of his pelt. "I've known since I first set eyes on you. I expect you couldn't have opened the box otherwise—a damnable loophole I'll be speaking with management about."

"I don't understand," said September.

"Neither do I," answered the Marquess, shadowy tears spilling out of her eyes.

The dream-eating tapir took her hand in his mouth—gentler this time. He drew her down onto the ground beside him; she sank to her knees. "Listen," he said, his voice full of rough kindness, the sort an old carouser gives to a young one, or one soldier to another. "Did you ever hear a story where a lady and her fellow desperately wanted a child, but couldn't have one? And they wanted it so much day in and day out that one morning a peach floated down the river, or a bamboo tree grew near their house, or a clay vessel washed up on the shore, and there was a magical child inside? Those children always do marvelous things—they conquer Ogre Island or marry the moon or bring down a wicked emperor. But those little babies inside the peaches and bamboo and clay have to come from somewhere, you know. And mostly, mostly they come from someone who meant to stay in Fairyland, who meant to be a mother and a knight there, or at least a smashing wizard, but the season turned or a banishing storm struck her ship or . . . or her clock simply ran out. Ladies with child who fell back into their own worlds and their own child's bodies, opening their eyes not a moment after they left. The children they were carrying in Fairyland fall down through the earth, and eventually they come to rest down here until some farmer and his wife want a child so terribly much that a peach comes sailing by to claim them. Only this one had all sorts of magic, on account of his parents. His box did not go to some nice tailor or miller. He used the Map Magic in his blood to burrow down as low as any object can go. The burning Wanting Magic he was heir to he used to wait, to wait ages upon ages, and let the peaches and bamboo pass him by. He became an object, one whose dreams touched the roots of everything that grew in Fairyland-Below, until everyone knew who he was, because they'd been eating his beets and onions and drinking his wine, because he slept at the bottom of the world, and his dreams became the water that every root drank. All this time, sleeping and dreaming with me, just waiting. Waiting for his mother to come and wake him up."

"That's why he's a Prince," September said, and almost laughed at the strangeness of it. "He's Queen Mallow's son. He's asleep because he's never been born."

"But he still grows, slowly, terribly slowly," the Baku agreed. "And we've got to know each other quite well, in his dreaming."

September took the Marquess's hand. "Come on," she said. "I know what to do."

After all, in fairy tales, there was only one thing to do. In every story with a long sleep and a waking in it. An easy thing, a pretty thing. Standard currency.

September and Maud bent over the box, over the boy and his shadow. And gently, sweetly, September kissed the Prince. The Marquess, dark, swirling tears flowing down her face, kissed her child's shadow.

His eyes opened.

A pain like the hands of a great clock ticking together burst in September's chest, and the world went out like a candle.

SILVER, BLACK, AND RED

*In Which Prince Myrrh Receives Some Career Advice,
September Receives a Silver Bullet, and the Alleyman Is Unmasked*

The darkness that swallowed September up snapped back just as quickly. She did not feel dizzy or ill at all—but her head still spun and she stumbled a little under the force of sudden noise and light.

Everyone was yelling very loudly and all at once.

Prince Myrrh, quite awake and red with passion, shouted out in pain. Iago snarled and hissed at a red hat with two feathers in it floating in the air. The Alleyman had his Woeful

Wimble out and was screwing it into the shadow of Prince Myrrh, while a lovely lady all in silver hurled loathing at the shadow of the Marquess. A big, burly man in a broad, black fisherman's hat and rain slicker cried out for September to snap to, do something, and another lady, this one in a flaming red gown and red scarves and a red war helmet, leapt at the red hat, which bobbed and dodged nimbly.

September looked down. The pale Goblin's brooch had gone dark. She had lost an hour, and in that hour, somehow, everything had changed. They all stood on the roof of the Trefoil, with the glittering lights of Tain spreading out below them and winds howling all around. The silver lady sat astride a great tiger, and the black-jacketed man rode a striped and hungry-looking lynx of enormous size. *Winds,* September's heart knew before her head had quite caught up.

The Red Wind feinted and lunged for the invisible Alleyman, catching him with a loud crunch of bodies. Prince Myrrh, finding himself suddenly free, rushed to hide behind his mother. The shadow of the Marquess stepped aside in dismay. He reached out for her, wordless and sorrowful. "I can't protect you," the Marquess said desperately. "I have no magic. You should have waited for her. Your real mother, who looks like you and could break them all with a word."

The Red Wind and the Alleyman suddenly disappeared

over the edge of the roof, and all the shouting stopped.

"What's happening?" September cried. "A moment ago we were in my house, or her house—"

"You followed me, child," said the Silver Wind. "As you've been following me all the while. I am weak and small under the world, for there is no open air to whip me into my full power. But I could be a silver thread for you, flashing on in the dark. It is one of my specialties. The Green Wind loves to spirit away the discontent. I love to pull lost things out of the dark. You followed me across your own cornfield with the Black Wind in my boat. You saw me in the Upside-Down, in the onion-field, and in the cellar at the bottom of the world, a little silver sigh on the stairs when you did not know how to get out. You followed me again, back through the doors until you caught me, and I brought you here, just as fast as wind. The Alleyman was waiting for us," the Silver Wind added darkly. "You rode on Cymbeline here, the Tiger of Wild Flurries, and you said your name was Glasswort, which I thought very strange, and that you very much enjoyed being a heroine and might look into it as a new career."

September had to laugh, even in the midst of the chaos on the roof. *I hope you did enjoy it,* she thought. *Because I do not enjoy at all not knowing what happened to me between the bottom of the world and the top. And to miss riding a tiger!*

Prince Myrrh looked startled at the sound of her laugh. He stared at her with big, dark, wounded eyes.

"Hullo, Myrrh," September said.

"H . . . Hullo," he said softly.

But though he might have said more, the Red Wind swirled up behind him, her scarves flying. The Black Wind drew a crossbow covered in burls and blackberries and shot just beneath the red hat, which seemed now to be in the Red Wind's grip, now to be gripping her. The arrow winged too far to the left and missed. He fired once more, and this one connected, driving home beneath the hat, but too far beneath and off center to be a fatal shot. Still, the cap crumpled to the roof, and the Red Wind stood over it, her face blazing.

Where the Alleyman fell, a stone knocked loose. Beneath it, a little plaque gleamed. September and the Winds crowded close around to read it.

RULES OF FAIRYLAND-BELOW

BEWARE OF DOG

ANYTHING IMPORTANT COMES IN THREES AND SIXES

DO NOT STEAL QUEENS

A GIRL IN THE WILD IS WORTH TWO IN CHAINS

NECESSITY IS THE MOTHER OF TEMPTATION

Everything Must Be Paid for Sooner or Later
What Goes Down Must Come Up

"But I know those words!" September cried. "I've been seeing them everywhere!"

The Black Wind nodded. "The Rules are older and deeper than groundwater. They are always in motion, always making themselves understood and obeyed. They are always following, always a part of the very land. They are Physicks—not Queer nor Quiet nor Questing, but pure Law. Halloween destroyed all the postings, but she couldn't destroy the Rules. And here in Tain, the center of everything, she couldn't even smash all the words themselves. This one, loyal public service board stayed whole. And haven't you been following them, even if you didn't know it? Haven't you paid and paid, haven't you found things in threes, haven't you been tempted in your need?"

September had—and she was about to say so when the Red Wind yawned, bored stiff.

"Oh, bother that, brother Black! Let's talk about something interesting! I haven't had a brawl like that since the Cloud War!" The Red Wind exulted. She shook her dark red hair and pulled a pair of carved crimson pistols from her belt, tossing them into the air, catching them by the barrels, and offering them handle-first to Prince Myrrh. "If you mean to be King," she said, "you might as well start by ridding your kingdom of a villain."

Prince Myrrh stood up and gazed steadily at the Red Wind. He did look regal, for all his wolf ears twitched and his lip trembled. "I don't mean to be King at all," he said. "I have had a great long while to think about it, and I don't want to. You can't make me. I just got here. Anyway, being King is a fool's game. You'll only get toppled eventually, and in the meantime, all Kings seem to do is hatch schemes and plot. I'm a practical boy—I don't see a need to scheme when I could just live my life and read books and learn magic and sit out in the evenings, perhaps make a friend who is not too interested in history. I just want to be a boy. I want to experience things like eating and jumping and running and dancing."

"A King may dance," said the Black Wind, whose voice was deep and beautiful as a full well.

"But not whenever he likes," countered Prince Myrrh. "He may only dance when it benefits others, or when someone important wants to dance with him, or when dancing might accomplish some royal goal. I want to dance because I feel like it, because the water tasted sweet or the sun was shining—oh, how I would like to see the sun shine!"

"You should go up to the other world," said the Marquess. "We can go up together if it would make you happy. We can find her, if you wanted to. I just want to lie down on the earth again—let the other me worry over her child and Fairyland and be stared at by everyone. She was always stronger."

"Well, someone has to end this! End the Alleyman and Halloween and keep the worlds separate, or else we shall all have to get jobs in advertising, and I for one would rather blow out completely!" snapped the Silver Wind. "You are the Rightful King!"

"What does that mean?" cried Myrrh. "Rightful how? Anyone can be King if they're bloody-minded enough, or unfortunate enough, or want it enough. Or even if they're just born with the right parents, in the right order. That doesn't mean anything at all. Why should I be King and a poor changeling child should not? I don't know a thing about Kinging, and I daresay I'd be just as good at juggling if you forced me to. But no one calls me the Rightful Juggler! They used to fish for Kings in a lake, did you know that? Nod told me all about it. Doesn't sound like anyone cares about Rightful until they want to kick someone else out of the chair. So thank you very much, but I want my *mother*. I want to be alive for half a second before I'm meant to shoot somebody!"

"Then who?" said the Black Wind, throwing up his hands. "If the magical object won't do his work, what are we to do?"

"It's been me all along," said September slowly. "Me who gave up my shadow, me who went down into Fairyland-Below and Fairyland-Lower-Than-That to wake up the Prince. Me who shot the poor Minotaur. You oughtn't just hand the whole business over the moment a Prince comes on the scene. I've got to see it through, don't you see? The Hollow Queen is hollow because she's missing the part of her that's me. We've got to come together again. And he can't do a thing about that."

"Very well." The Red Wind shrugged, turning the pistol handles toward her. It didn't matter a whit to the Wind who did the deed, as long as it was done. She seemed to look at September fully for the first time. "You know, I do believe that's my coat," she mused. "And that is most certainly my cat."

Iago roared—a roar of love and remembering and recognition and regret. He did not leave the Marquess's side, but the roar said that he was sorry about it.

"I've never been able to bring myself to find another, since you left me." The Red Wind sighed.

The wine-colored coat wriggled with pleasure. "You may keep it," said the Red Wind expansively. "I gave it up, after all, when I had to go Below a century ago to battle with a young upstart ogre-maid who wanted to take my place. I thrashed her soundly, of course. Don't get to be a Wind if you're faint of anything."

September took the wine-colored coat off anyhow, and gave it back to its mistress, who it clearly sorely missed. She could stand now, in her Watchful Dress, and not feel ashamed of her finery or herself. Nor did September take the pistols.

"She has her own, Red," the Silver Wind said admonishingly. She dismounted from her Tiger, whose eyes fairly glowed in the night. The crystal moon showed a bold 11 on its smooth face. The Black Wind left his Lynx as well, and both held out their hands to September.

In one was a silver rivet, in the other a black one. The Red Wind sighed and reholstered her guns, joining her sibling Winds. She held a crimson rivet out on her palm.

"Take one," said the Silver Wind. "Take one and bolt yourself to your shadow once more. The Alleyman is blooded. We can hold him—or kill him as you like. We don't mind. Winds are cold in that way—after all, storms have no hearts."

"I wish my Green Wind were here!"

"The Green Wind and the Blue Wind are Topside breezes," said the Black Wind. "They deal in fresh, growing things. Only we venture Below."

"What if I choose wrong? Are they very different?"

"We can only offer you ourselves. The Red Wind is a War Wind. The Silver Wind is a Following Wind, to fill up your heart and blow it along. The Black Wind, and Banquo, the Lynx of Gentle Showers, is a Fierce Wind, to blow one off course. We do not know which you need."

September considered that she had been following the Silver Wind for so long, and it had brought her so far. She took the silver rivet and tucked it into the Rivet Gun's tube, where the gun chortled and took it up. But she did not go down into the Trefoil—she could not yet.

September marched over to the Alleyman, and the Rivet Gun rejoiced, for it felt sure it was going to be Used most delightfully. September stood over the red cap as it lay on the roof with nobody beneath it. What a wretched, horrid creature! How hideous he must be, to hide himself with whatever magic made him invisible! She hated him, with all her galloping young heart. Her face flushed with anger, and September reached down and snatched the two vicious, horn-like feathers from his hat, throwing them to the ground.

The Alleyman shimmered and between two blinks, September could see him as clear as anything, bleeding from his shoulder, his dark face gone ashen.

It was her father's shadow.

CHAPTER XX

LET ME LIVE

In Which All Is Revealed

*S*eptember bore the weight of her father's shadow as they descended the steps into the Trefoil, leaving the Prince and his mother and the Winds above. Besides the wound in his shoulder, his leg seemed twisted and weak.

"Papa, why? How can you be here? Why would you hurt all those people? I don't understand, I just can't understand!"

But he could not speak. Shadow-blood seeped from the Black Wind's arrow. When she pushed open a great dark door and let her father collapse against a column, a sharp, sudden cry cut off her questions.

"Papa!" Halloween cried, and leapt up from her throne, a bright thing made all of pumpkin rinds and green gems. It rested beneath a chandelier hanging down into the chamber like a false sun, its curling bone arms holding bowls hollowed out of gourds and squashes and pumpkins and great huge eggs, all filled with liquid fire. Saturday's and Ell's shadows lounged nearby on their own plush cushions (rather a lot of cushions in Ell's case). Aubergine stood a ways away, looking miserable, holding silent. "Who's done this to you?"

The Hollow Queen put her hands on his wound and shut her eyes. The arrow snapped and the blood vanished. The Alleyman smiled weakly and brushed back Halloween's shadowy hair. Then he saw September and groaned.

"Did I do it?" he whispered. "Am I home?"

"What are you talking about?" said September, horrified.

"Don't you talk to him," snapped Halloween. "He's *my* father, *I* brought him here, you haven't got any right!"

"What do you mean you *brought* him here?"

Halloween grinned. Her dark face glowed with triumph. "Government has its privileges. I'm sure that silly cow showed you her precious wall—well, a hole opened up in Tain long before it got all the way down there. Right in the current of the Gingerfog River. You could see all the way through. I figured it out—much faster than you! I started pushing—here, there—to see where I could get through, to see if I could . . ." September's shadow broke off, throwing her arms around her father. "I just wanted everyone to be together and happy and to see how marvelous my kingdom is. I wanted him to be proud of me. I wanted him to see Saturday and my Wyverary and how grown-up and good I could be. You want it, too. You just tell yourself to be patient and everything will be all right. Well, I knew it wouldn't be all right! I saw him through the water. He was fighting, and his leg had broken—just like ours did, do you remember? I took a deep breath and I grabbed him. I just reached through the hole in the river and I grabbed his shadow and pulled him through. At first he was so confused, he kept shouting, *'Les Allemands viennent! Les Allesmands viennent!'* Half the city heard it. They started calling him the Alleyman, because he said it so often. For weeks, he didn't even know where he was."

"Les Allemands viennent," whispered September's father weakly. "The Germans are coming."

"Hush, Papa, it's all right now. You're safe. He didn't even know where he was at first, September. I nursed him back to health. All by myself."

"I know where I am," said September's father, his voice a

little stronger, a little more like his old self. "I'd been reading the books we found in an old woman's house near Strasbourg. All fairy stories and old tales. One was about a Lutin—an invisible spirit who wore a red hat with two feathers. A house-spirit, who protected a home and made it safe. When she pulled me through, I was still thinking about how nice it would be to be invisible, to be able to pass through the lines without being seen. Then all of a sudden, I *was* invisible, and I had a red hat. Everything had changed. And my daughter was here, as if by magic—at least, something like my daughter. A shadow, like I am a shadow. Like we are all shadows down here. But at least I could hold her, and talk to her. She said it happened because I wanted it so much my wanting turned into magic, only when she said *want* the word seemed so much bigger than I imagined it could be. And she told me to take everyone's shadows. I thought she was mad, and so cruel—how could I have raised such a cruel girl as that? But she said if I took all the shadows, everything would come rushing together, this world and Nebraska. And I thought, *Maybe then I could go home.* I could go home to my real daughter and my wife. And no one would be hurt, they'd only live in a different place, and it's beautiful back home. It really is." He swooned against the pillar; his shadowy eyes slid shut.

"Stop that, Papa," Halloween said. "*I'm* your daughter. I told you." The Hollow Queen kissed his cheek and stood up. "Everything is nearly perfect now," she said. "I've got my family, and I've got more magic than anyone's ever had. It'll keep us here while the ungrateful Topsiders float away. The shadows will have their country, and we will all be together. Soon I'll be able to pull Mother's shadow through, too, and then I won't need anything else. I'll have everyone and everything I could want—Saturday and Ell and Mother and Father. I don't have to choose like you do." Halloween grinned sweetly. "Saturday and Ell were always my dear ones and not yours, September. I mean, really. I told them to go with you and play along as long as they could bear it. I told Ell to go wait for you at the bottom of the stairs. I told the whole country to crouch down in the dark just to leap up and surprise you. But you must see that they're shadows—they could never help you bind them into nothingness again. They want to live. I want to live."

"We're sorry, September," said Saturday miserably. "We do love you, but you want us to go back. We can't go back. If only you'd just forgotten like you ought to have we could have lived together so happily."

"It won't work," September said. "You'll float away, too. And we'll all be home, only Fairyland will be gone forever, and we'll be in Nebraska and that will be that. You'll just be shadow and light again."

"You're lying," Halloween scoffed.

"I'm not. And anyway, it doesn't matter. You and I are taking Father home, right now."

"Come now." Halloween laughed. "You can't do a thing to me. I have everything and you have nothing. And the Revel will be starting again soon. You can hear the trumpets and the harps sounding." Indeed, from far below, a sweet, wild music picked up.

"Take my hand, shadow," she said.

"No, girl," Halloween whispered.

September leveled the Rivet Gun at her.

Saturday and Ell cried out desperately.

"Please, September!" Ell wept, his great heart heaving with the strain of being torn between two girls he did love so terribly. "Leave us alone," he whispered. "We just want to live our own lives. We just want to keep on being alive."

"Where did you get that gun?" Halloween said fearfully.

"Belinda Cabbage gave it to me."

Halloween's face trembled. It was September's own face, and it broke apart, tears trickling down and her voice shaking. "You can't do this to me. I'm you. I'm your sister. I have been with you all your life," she said. "I have only done what you've done—tried to think slantwise and be brave and ill-tempered and irascible, tried to make my family happy, tried to have an adventure and grab hold of magic when it came near me. Please, September. Please. Let me live. You get to live—no matter what happens, you get to live. Why is it so terrible that I want to live, too?"

September did not shy away. She pressed forward, reaching for her shadow's hand to bind them together, but Halloween slipped away. She fled into Saturday's and Ell's arms, and the three of them cowered from her, terrified—they had never had to be afraid for themselves, only afraid when their sunlit selves were afraid. It undid them. They buried their faces in each other and braced for some awful pain. Halloween kissed Saturday and then Ell, tried to smile for them, held them close.

But Aubergine did not quaver. She stood very still. So very still, as still as only a Quiet Physickist can. And instead of fading from view, a cold, thin light flashed from her violet feathers, landing upon the tableau of the Queen and her friends, freezing them where they stood.

"I didn't know what they meant to do, September." Aubergine whispered a whisper so light and gentle it could hardly be called sound. "You must believe I didn't. You see? I've held them fast for you, because you are my friend. And I did it, I really did it. I controlled it. The Quiet came from me and did what I told it to." The Night-Dodo could not help puffing her breast-feathers a little.

"I do believe you, Aubergine, I do," September answered softly.

September looked at her frozen shadow, her frozen Marid, her frozen Wyverary. They were helpless now. She could use the Rivet Gun to socket them together and Halloween couldn't do a thing to stop it. She could do whatever she liked. Yet somehow, she could not. She could not be pitiless and cold with her father lying behind her. She could not—because that was the power of the Marquess and of Halloween, too. To simply not care and do what you wanted.

She had pitied the Marquess, but not enough to hesitate when she had to hurt her. Yet her raw, young heart beat boldly now, and as it looked on the shadows of the folk she loved best, it broke open. She could not call them wicked, could not see them only as selfish and savage as villains must be seen if they are to be fought without pulling punches. Halloween was *her*. A little girl had gone after her father, breaking the worlds in two just to get him back. Wouldn't September herself have done the same? But then again, perhaps she would not have even thought of a thing so daring and slanted and strange. That dark, still girl holding her friends close had done a hundred things September had not. She was a sister—she was not September herself.

September lowered the Rivet Gun. She would not do it. Even though the weapon ached to perform its Use, the thing it had been made for, everything in its little mechanical heart yearning for this day—she would not. She would do something else. Something slantwise.

"Aubergine," September said. "Come and hug me and say hello. I've missed you."

"If I move, they'll move too!" warned the Night-Dodo.

"It's all right. Don't worry."

Aubergine fluffed her feathers and crossed the throne room in a few short strides. She pressed her soft head against September's and flushed silver with relief.

Halloween stirred. Saturday and Ell gasped as they came to with a jolt and a shudder.

"Come here, Halloween," September said. "Come here. Don't cry."

Halloween stood, her face plainly saying she thought she still faced her executioner. A moment's stillness couldn't change that.

September held out her arms to her shadow.

"Surely, we can think of some other way."

Halloween hung back.

"Surely we are clever enough, the two of us," September whispered. "There *are* two of us, after all."

And the shadow-girl, with her need and her love and her terrible Want all held before her, flowed into September's arms. They held each other. After a while, Saturday and Ell touched the girls' shoulders, and hugged them, too, Ell's tail snaking around them. At last, Aubergine nestled down beside them. September was completely covered in shadows.

She smiled in the dark.

The door of the throne room burst open. A creature came screaming into the room, greenish-silver, looking like a printing press with claws and teeth. It galloped around the room, startling the shadows apart. A woman stormed in after it, cursing and scolding.

It was Belinda Cabbage.

"Blasted thing! Slow down!" the Fairy hollered.

"What are you doing here?" demanded Halloween, adjusting her crown and wiping her eyes.

"The Sameness Engine bolted off in the night, horrid beast. It's caught the scent of a Use and there's no stopping it. Heel, Engine!" The Sameness Engine whined and bonked into a dark wall. "I don't suppose you need the marauding old fool for something?"

The Sameness Engine whirled around and charged toward September. It clacked its claws at her and its moveable types spun. It bounded once, twice, and with a stroke had sliced off a hank of her hair in its teeth. It clicked and crunched and thrummed.

A moment later, a green, misty shadow spooled out of the face of the Sameness Engine, falling gently at September's feet. A wisp touched her heel and a tiny warm crackling spark went up inside her, a fire beginning like the one she had never gotten to make in the glass forest. The fire flowed into her, a small ember of wildness and of boldness, of beastliness and magic. The hard, strange voice inside her twisted up together with the dark flowers blooming in her heart, and September at last knew what to do.

CHAPTER XXI

ALL AT ONCE

*In Which September Sees the Sun Again,
Along with a Great Many Other Things*

September climbed into the basket of the Alleyman's truck. She held the hand of her father's shadow, who looked unsure and faraway still—and faint, his knees buckling from time to time. The basket rose and rose.

Halloween flew up beside her. Behind her came shadow upon shadow upon shadow, hundreds and thousands of them, a long black train. They spiraled around the basket, up, up, up. They passed the crystal moon. A bold I glowed darkly there.

"What if you're wrong?" said Halloween.

September smiled, and such wild, giddy hope was in that smile that Halloween smiled, too.

"What goes down must come up," she said, and squeezed her shadow tight.

When the basket reached the ceiling of the world, September put her hand up to the earthen sky. It was warm. She could feel the sunlight on the other side. There was nothing for it—this was no time to worry about making a mess. September clawed at the earth, digging up and out, roots and worms and clay and dust spilling out over her head. She held her breath, stretching for the sun she knew was there. Every so often, she reached down to pull her father's shadow up behind her, only to find Halloween helping him, pushing him upward and onward.

The work hurt her. Her fingernails ripped, and her arms ached. But on she dug, on and on. One finger broke up into the light, into a long field of green and waving grass, dotted with puffy nimbleflowers. Then a second. Then one arm, and the other. But September could not pull herself up, quite. She was so tired. She had been in the dark for so long.

It so happened that two stout crows with unusual names were flying over a bright field just then, on their way back from a most satisfying day by the sea. They saw something flash in the grass and darted toward it, for anything that flashes seems wonderful to a crow. A girl's arms! With a brooch on one shoulder that sparkled like a star! The two crows clapped hold of her hands with their talons and tugged. They did not know what had gone wrong to get this poor child caught in the earth like that, but they'd get her out—they were strong, after all. Strong enough to leap into another world and feed themselves mightily there.

"Come on, girl!" Wit cawed.

"Just a little further now!" cawed Study.

And September came loose, her legs scrambling out, kicking dirt free, her skin streaked with mud, the Watchful Dress torn. Her hair lost its black and colored stripes as quickly as soap washing out, her curls fading into their own familiar chocolatey brown once more. The crows lifted her up into the air for a moment, but their strength was not quite up to Fairy standards yet. They set her down more or less gently and winged off to pursue their own corvid adventures.

"Good-bye, girl!" cawed Study.

"Be more careful next time!" cawed Wit.

Out of the hole in the earth, a fountain of shadows flowed up and into the sunlit air, where September stood blinking in the blaze of it all. All the shadows of Fairyland, fluttering darkly and singing and laughing, singing so loud that the folk they belonged to could not help but hear. They sang and sang, a song of beckoning, of like calling to like, of family calling their loved ones home.

At first, only a Gnome or two peeked up from over the hill and ran down to meet their shadows. But then a centaur trotted up, and more, Dryads and Wairwulfs and Goblins and Trolls. As each one found his shadow, they hopped and whirled together and shot fire or snow or light from their fingertips, magic spilling out of them without so much as a spell or a chant. The folk came thick and fast, and the song grew stronger. All of Fairyland moved toward that little dell where its shadows waited.

One shadow, wearing a very fine hat, rode astride a Panther's shadow. They shot off from the crowd, soaring northward, to a place where it is always Spring. Before her on the great cat a little boy nestled in, smiling in his mother's arms.

"You see?" said September to her own shadow as an Ouphe made lightning cat's cradles in his shadow's fingers. "It's working. It is, it really is."

And that would have been enough. September would have been happy, just to see Fairyland coming back together and magic flowing back into the sunlit world. We could leave her here, and she would not be angry with us, for she had done well, and when we have done well, we can be content, even if all is not perfect. But we will not leave her yet—not just yet—for one more surprise awaits.

Over the hill a blue boy came walking. Beside him, a great red creature with no forepaws lumbered down a long grassy hill on his scarlet three-toed feet. The sun folded them up in gold. Their colors gleamed bright and bold.

September cried out in joy and ran to them, her own dear Saturday and A-Through-L, who had not pushed her into the sea or stolen a kiss, just her dear Marid and her Wyverary, after all this while. She leapt into their arms—hooting, crowing Wyvern joy shook the clouds. Saturday blushed in her embrace.

"I missed you so much," he whispered bashfully. "Where have you been?"

"You're Back!" hooted Ell. "All the B's in the world are not enough for how Back you are!"

"Oh, Ell! I shall tell you everything, I promise! It will take days and days to say it all, but we shall have time now! Oh, Ell, so much has happened!" The Wyverary *haroomed* and nuzzled her with his warm red cheek.

Saturday stood very close to her, his eyes shining.

"I have missed you so much I could kiss you," he whispered.

September's face fell. "Oh, but Saturday! I've had my

First Kiss and I didn't mean to, I didn't want to, but your shadow is very rude and impulsive, and he took it before I could say two words! And I've had my second and third and maybe fifth, too. Come to think of it, this has all involved rather a lot of kissing."

Saturday furrowed his brow. "Why should I care about your First Kiss?" he said. "You can kiss anyone you like. But if you sometimes wanted to kiss me, that would be all right, too." His blush was so deep September could feel the heat of it.

She leaned in, and kissed her Marid gently, sweetly. She tried to kiss him the way she'd always thought kisses would be. His lips tasted like the sea.

The evening wore on and the vale filled up with souls. As such magical folk will do when more than three are gathered, someone struck up a drum; someone else a pipe. A great music filled the night, and Fairyland began to dance. Each person danced with their shadow, spinning fast and fleet, magic sparking between them.

September held out her hand to Halloween; the Hollow Queen took it. The girl and her shadow danced together, slowly, under the real and true moon.

"It doesn't have to be one or the other," September said as they twirled together over the meadow. "Shadows or Topsiders,

Queen or farm girl. You can be everything, all at once. Go and be Queen in Fairyland-Below. Prince Myrrh doesn't want to, but you do! I'll visit you sometimes. And once a year or twice—or more if you like—bring the shadows up to meet their brothers and sisters and fill Fairyland with wildness again. Maybe some will want to stay. Maybe some of the others will want to use Miss Cabbage's Engine to make new shadows for themselves that are only a trick of light and not a real alive girl. But you can come and go, and keep Fairyland whole, and keep on living just as you want. Only keep the worlds together. Keep the roads open. *This* is the Revel, Halloween, the biggest Revel you could ever imagine."

As the moon got high, the dancing grew faster. Saturday and his shadow bowed to each other and waltzed, two beautiful blue wisps of air. The shadow led and the boy followed, turning perfect circles in the grass. Ell and his shadow hooked tails and whirled around one another, whooping and stamping. Aubergine squawked, loud and long, as though she had been holding it in all her life. She danced in a ring with a green flamingo and several very large, very Quiet, and very solemn quails.

And finally, over the hill, a man in a green smoking jacket, and green jodhpurs, and green snowshoes came riding down on a roaring Leopard.

"My darling daisy, my pumpkin-dear, light of my moony-sky!" the Green Wind cried. "Dance with me, my autumnal apple of my springtime eye!" He swept her up into his arms, swinging her into a wild jig that soared up into the air with every turn. September laughed while the air filled up with the scent of green growing things.

Halloween laughed, too, and offered the Green Wind's shadow her arm.

Only their father's shadow stood alone, leaning on his good leg, watching the dance and unable to take part. September, a blush high in her cheeks, left the Green Wind to the Silver Wind's attentions. He kept time on a green mandolin he summoned up out of the Leopard's fur.

September took her father's hand.

"We did it," she said. "We're almost home."

At that moment, somewhere far off and elsewise, the last trickle of sand fell out of a tall hourglass, and September winked out like a firefly at first light.

CHAPTER XXII

You Can Never Forget What You Do in a War

In Which September Returns Home

Morning was coming on bright gold and pink over the prairie. September found herself in the tall wheat, just where she'd gone rushing after the Black Wind and the Silver Wind in their rowboat. She was in her birthday dress again, and fiercely hungry for breakfast. *I wonder what did happen to Prince Myrrh, if he found the Marquess—what if he should wake her up? I wonder if I shall ever know where the Fairies have gone? And why Dodo eggs are so special? When I go back, I shall find out, for surely nothing else can go so awfully wrong this time while I am gone! Ell and Saturday and I will have a real adventure, with no sadness or dark places.*

September rubbed her eyes, which ached from so much sunlight after walking in the gloom. Everything was so bright she might almost have thought Fairyland-Below was all a dream—except that in her hand she held a scrap of blackness that might have been a flag caught in the wind, but September knew was not.

It was her father's shadow. She still held his hand.

Across the wheatfield, her familiar house waited, cozy and warm.

"Is that home?" her father's shadow said. "Is it really home?"

"Yes, Papa. It's home. Mother's there, and good coffee, and our old dog by the fire. I've brought you all the way home." She did so want him to be proud of her.

"It was worth it, then. All the things I've done."

"Don't think about that, Papa."

Her father's shadow looked sadly down at her. "You can never forget what you do in a war, September my love. No one can. You won't forget your war either."

They began to walk toward the house, though September

dragged her feet. She wanted to savor this last moment with her father, for of course this was only a shadow. Her father's body was still fighting in France, and once they got to the house she'd be fatherless again.

Finally she stopped, and the shadow stopped with her. September fought her tears. She held up her arms as she'd done when she was just a little thing, to be held, to be safe and warm.

"I miss you so much," she whispered. "Sometimes I dream that you've died, and I shall never see you again."

September's father turned back. He picked her up and held her as he had done long ago, his black eyes squeezed shut, his big, dark hand on her curly head. She buried her face in his shadowy shoulder and held on. If she let go, he'd just vanish, she knew it.

A light came on in the house. September saw it—and more, she saw *two* people moving and talking in the light. Her breath caught.

Could it be? Could it be true?

September scrambled down and took off running through the wheat, pulling her father's shadow behind her. It couldn't be. It just couldn't.

By the time she reached the stoop where the milkman had left his bottles, the shadow had dwindled to a scrap of dark hardly bigger than a blanket. September squeezed it to her chest and hoped as hard as she could, Wanted with all her might.

Her mother stood in the hall near the tall walnut-wood radio. Her face was streaked and puffy with tears as she held September's father close, her real father, not a shadow but a man, in a soldier's brown uniform and a hat with golden things on it. He leaned a little on a dark crutch, for his leg had a white cast on it.

When September's mother saw her daughter coming in with the milk from the stoop, she smiled like the sun coming up and opened her arms to invite her little girl into their embrace. September's father looked tired—but he smiled his old crooked smile and said her name. He could not pick her up in his arms as he would have liked to. But he held his daughter tight all the same, and the small, amiable dog leapt and jumped and yipped around the three of them.

September gently pressed the black cloth to her father's side as he put his good arm around her. His shadow flowed into place, relieved, exhausted. She did not need a Rivet Gun in this world to keep them together. The shadow longed to be whole again. It would never speak of what happened, except with the shadow of his wife while their bodies slept. But shadows keep secrets better than anyone.

The three of them held each other for a long time.

When the tears and hugging and what shall we have for breakfasts were done and the cheerful, impossible, wonderful day was getting on with its business, September's mother finally saw a strange thing. She did not say anything—who would, when her family was together again and there was so much to think about? But she could be almost certain that her daughter's shadow had gone a deep, profound shade of green—just the color of the smoking jacket of a man she'd known long ago, when she was just a small girl.